Also by GREG BEAR

TAKE BACK THE SKY

TAKE BACK THE SKY

GREG BEAR

www.orbitbooks.net

Orbit
Hachette Book Group
1290 Avenue of the Americas
New York, NY 10104
orbitbooks.net

First Edition: December 2016

Orbit is an imprint of Hachette Book Group.
The Orbit name and logo are trademarks of Little, Brown Book Group Limited.

The publisher is not responsible for websites (or their content) that are not owned by the publisher.

The Hachette Speakers Bureau provides a wide range of authors for speaking events. To find out more, go to www.hachettespeakersbureau.com or call (866) 376-6591.

ISBNs: 978-0-316-22397-3 (hardcover), 978-0-316-22396-6 (ebook)

Printed in the United States of America

LSC-C

10 9 8 7 6 5 4 3 2 1

*For those in my family who traveled far in company
of service members, and those who waited at
home in times of war:*

*Florence Bear
Earl Bear
Irene Garrett
George Garrett
Lorraine Garrett
Lynn Garrett
Dan Garrett
Kathleen Garrett
Colleen Garrett
Devin Garrett
Barbara Julian
Wilma Bear*

TAKE BACK THE SKY

PART ONE

DANCING ON CLOUDS

I hate transitions, and this is the worst.

In the control cabin of our Oscar, a gigantic centipede made to swim and fight in Titan's freezing saline sea, a dozen klicks below the scummy, icy crust—

Pinched and stabbed and wired through and through by the suits we thought were meant to protect us—

I've never been more afraid and lost and in pain. We're exhausted—no surprise, after our passage through the ice station's freeze-dried carnage. Seeds deposited from the stores of our orbiting Spook fused with the station's walls, chewed them up, and converted them into five Oscars—ours and the four others flanking us before the labyrinth of the bug archive.

Our former enemies are hiding in that maze. Our former allies are creeping up from behind to destroy us all.

Lieutenant Colonel Joe Sanchez, Captain Naveen Jacobi, Sergeant Chihiro Ishida—our Winter Soldier, half of her body replaced by metal—First Sergeant Tak Fujimori, Starshina

Irina Ulyanova, and me, Master Sergeant Michael Venn, are in this Oscar. The second carries Commander Frances Borden, Corporal Dan Johnson—DJ—Sergeant Kiyuko Ishikawa, Polkovnik Litvinov (I've never learned his first name), and our mysterious Wait Staff reps, the former servants and right-hand men of the Gurus, Aram Kumar and Krishna Mushran. The rest of the Russians occupy the last three.

On my recommendation—and on threat of ice torpedoes closing in from all sides—we've stopped trying to defend ourselves and have surrendered to the birdlike creatures we've fought for years on Mars and elsewhere. We call them Antagonists, Ants or Antags for short.

Starshina Ulyanova frantically resisted that surrender and had to be subdued by Tak and Jacobi. She lies quiet now in her sling behind Jacobi. Her rank is roughly equal to DJ's, corporal, but edging over into sergeant. She's still having a rough time. Her cheeks and forehead are beaded with sweat, and she stares into the upper shadows of the cabin, lips pressed tight. Her instinct is to continue the fight, even if it means self-destruction—either resisting the Antags, who are presumably here to save us, or trying to destroy our own people. I don't really blame her. She's surrounded by leaders and soldiers who haven't had time to explain the fundamentals we're all facing. Besides, we don't speak Russian, and her English is rudimentary.

Even so, there's something odd about her, as if she's listening to voices none of the rest can hear—except me. Why do I think that's possible? That she's being subjected to an experience similar to my own, maybe to DJ's...

Maybe not so much to DJ. Maybe just to me.

No evidence for any of these hunches, really, but that by

itself doesn't mean she's crazy. Hearing voices is why I was returned to Mars, then hustled out with DJ to Titan.

On Mars, inside the first Drifter, DJ and Kazak and I all got dosed with a powder produced by deep-buried fragments of ancient crystal brought to Mars billions of years before on pieces of exploded ice moon. We called the powder Ice Moon Tea, and my sensitivity to its messages was what convinced Commander Borden to rescue me from Madigan Hospital, where I was scheduled for execution. I'm one of the special ones. Glory be. So is DJ. Kazak—Sergeant Temur Nabiyev, our favorite Mongolian—was also one of the special ones, but he died on Mars before I returned.

In our heads, ancient history bumps up against the captured and stored memories of fallen comrades. Sometimes it's like dancing on a cloud—impossible, but if you don't believe, you fall.

I can't shake the strangely lovely image of Captain Coyle settling into her peculiar death. On Mars, when she tried to blow up the first Drifter, under orders from the Gurus on Earth, she and her teammates turned into shiny black glass. We thought those who turned glass were dead. But some came back to haunt us. Absorbing and co-opting enemies is one way the ancient archives preserve themselves. That's what the Drifter's crystals contained—a gateway to records kept billions of years ago by our earliest progenitors—inhabitants of the outer ice moons of the ancient solar system.

Giant, intelligent bugs.

Coyle first came to visit me after I returned to Earth and was locked up at Madigan. In those early hours, her presence was confused, less an actual voice and more like word balloons in a comic—empty word balloons. But soon enough they filled in, and what was left of Coyle did her brusque best to take me step by step through the courtesies and techniques of the bug archives. She introduced me to the semiautomated steward who parcels out that memory, if you're qualified, if you know how to ask the right sort of questions.

The bugs are long gone, but their voices still echo. At Madigan, and on the way back to Mars, I relived bits and pieces of bug history, watched those ancient ancestors of both humans and Antags burrow up through the icy shells of their moons and discover the stars. Life had first evolved on those moons, long before Earth turned green, in deep oceans warmed by residual radiation and the constant tug of tidal energy from their gas-giant planets. I learned that this wasn't the first time creatures like the Gurus had entered our solar system and provoked wars. I learned that the bugs had fought one another long, long ago—class against class, changing the shape and disposition of the outer solar system.

Dropping big chunks of moon down to Mars, including the Drifters.

Helping seed life on Earth.

Then Coyle warned me that she was about to *really* die. Her final act was to introduce me to the Antag female who's now my direct liaison, who's waiting across the midnight ocean to save us from our own forces.

Coyle's voice went silent and all that was left of her, the absorbed data of her life and her body, spread out before my inner eye like a beautiful crystal tapestry. The captain was no longer capable of talking, acting, or learning, but she was still full of instruction.

How like Coyle.

YOU CAN GO IN NOW, BUT PLEASE DON'T

My grandfather was a colonel in the Rangers. My grandmother was a fine Army wife and very smart. One of the things she taught me is that God can do anything except change a man's mind. "That's why there are wars," she said, and knew the subject well. In two wars she had lost a husband, two sons, and a daughter, leaving her with just my mother, who was thirty when her sister died. "Men are so goddamned stubborn they will insult, curse, and shout until they can't back down, and then decide it's time to send our children out to die. The fellows who order up wars almost never go themselves, they're too old. But they're still cowards. If you're a leader and you screw up a war, or maybe if you just *start* a war, you should blow your brains out right in front of all the Gold Star mothers, sitting on bleachers in their Sunday best—and that's what *I* say, but don't quote me, okay? This kind of talk upsets your mother."

Until I was eight and my mother and father divorced, we lived on or around military bases. I bounced through five or six concrete blockhouse schools and hated every minute of it. My mother believed in the goodness of the human race. As if in spite, the human race tried with all its might to prove her wrong. After her divorce, she jonesed for handsome, crazy men and usually ended up with cashiered ex-Army or bank robbers. I thought I had to protect her. Or at least I remember thinking that; maybe it just turned out that way. None of that stopped me from enlisting to become a Skyrine, but now it haunts me.

FISH MARKET DREAMS

In the front slings of our Oscar, Joe and Jacobi try to maintain communication.

"Minnows are quiet," Jacobi says. "Maybe they're being jammed."

All the rest of us can do for now is listen to the sounds gathered by the far-flung sensors, clear and sharp and mysterious in the deep cold, and wait for the Antags to make up their minds. We're mostly silent, lying slack in our harnesses like aging beef.

Our minnows, silvery drones the size of fingers, act like cat whiskers. They flow smoothly back and forth between us and the Antags, tracking their ships behind the great, dark ridges of the old Titanian archives.

The hovering flocks of Antag ice torpedoes haven't moved in. We still have hope, I guess. But we've surrendered. What does it matter?

When we abandoned the station, other ships were entering Titan's orbit—human-crewed ships. One of them was the big

Box, newer and far more heavily armed than the Spook that brought us here. On our way out to Saturn, leaving Mars's orbit, the Spook managed to count a little coup against Box, trimming some of its sectional field lines before it was fully prepared—but that won't happen again.

I wonder what Mushran and Kumar are thinking. They arranged for all this, and for years benefited from their connections with the Gurus. I suppose knowing is better than ignorance, but we're still screwed. As wars go, this one is a complete fraud. But then, aren't most? Killers of the brave, the loyal, the committed—killers of our best.

Somehow, I don't believe that describes me. I'm not one of the best. Joe, maybe, or Tak or Kazak. Not being one of the best may mean I'll live. But that's bullshit. Wars don't discriminate. Wars are blind and violent and nasty, lacking all morality. If they last long enough, they'll do their best to destroy all hopes and dreams.

Wars try to kill *everybody*.

But until now, they've never actually succeeded.

What's become very obvious is that the cavalry descending behind us in Titan's cold sea, other machines carrying other humans, is no longer our friend. It may not know it, but it's chasing us down in order to cut off human access to bug history—the archives on Titan and maybe elsewhere in our system. Our joint sponsors, the Gurus, do not want any of us, human or Antag, to learn about our bug origins or the ancient wars the Gurus encouraged. If we're killed here on Titan, and if Titan is finally destroyed, this cancer won't spread.

Our duty now is to survive, even if we have to join up with our enemies.

COLD TRENCHES

Something's changing overhead. We hear the echoing, drawn-out groans of deep pack ice, like an idiot playing a pipe organ in an empty cathedral. This profoundly scary and stupid noise is punctuated by the softly ratcheting clicks of Antag machines keeping station out in the darkness. Why don't they just suck us up? They're hiding in the cells and cubicles of the ancient archive—what I'm starting to call Bug Karnak because for some reason it reminds me of ancient temples in Egypt. Bug Karnak, after billions of years, is still transmitting bug history to those who react to Ice Moon Tea. I could tune in if I want, but it's much clearer if I coordinate with my liaison, and she seems to be distracted. Maybe she's waiting for her fellows to make up their minds about our usefulness—thumbs up or thumbs down. Do they have thumbs? Maybe the Antags think we're decoys. Maybe this sort of thing has happened to them before—recently. Deception and betrayal. They're being extra cautious.

I wonder if she has a hard time hearing me, too. Yeah,

we're related, but that's hardly a guarantee of compatibility. To add to the suspense, our replacement pressure suits continue to work us over, slicing through flesh and bone with wires and blades to integrate and control—presumably to make us quicker and more responsive.

What was left of the ice station is probably gone. After our seeds were done shitting out Oscars, and while we were leaving, more seeds must have dropped from Box and finished the job. Seeds save a lot of weight when transporting weapons upsun to places where raw materials are abundant—places like Titan, covered in methane, ethane, and silenes, and spotted with deposits of naturally generated waxes and oils and plastics. But even with an abundance of raw materials, when time is short, efficiency rules. The station was preprocessed. The seeds from Box likely dug in like hungry mastiffs. I wonder what happened to the corpses. Maybe they're now part of brand-new weapons. How is it possible to stay human in all this? Facing these examples of a fucking hellish ingenuity?

"Antag movement up front," Jacobi says.

There's Russian chatter from the third and fourth vessels—unhappy, strident. Litvinov opens up to his troops in the dissident transports. "We do not act!" he shouts in Russian, then in English. "We are here. We have no more decisions to make. If we return, our people will kill us."

I watch Jacobi's crescent-lit face, just visible around the rim of her helm, then expand my gaze over to Joe, slung beside her. Our suits creak in the slings. Six of us. How many Russians were crammed into the last two Oscars? Not full complements. Not six, maybe only three, not enough to form true teams, share the stress, subdue panic. Since we didn't fight together and didn't have long to socialize, they never made much of an impression, except for Litvinov, of course, and those who died out on the Red…and Ulyanova, softly singing to herself opposite.

Long moments pass. On the second Oscar, Borden reports scattered soft targets—organic. "Looks like a shoal of big fish," she says. "Native?"

No one confirms. No one can answer one way or the other. We close our plates to access displays and pay attention to the forces directly in front. I don't see the soft targets or anything that answers to what she means by organic—squishy and alive—but more machines rise into view, twelve of them, longer and thicker than Oscars, escorted by scouts like nothing we've seen before—robot falcons flexing ten-meter serrated wings, slung with bolt weapons and pods filled with cutting tools. Butcher-birds, I think.

"Oscar's about to be cracked like a lobster," DJ says from Litvinov's ship.

"Shut the fuck up!" Ishida says, half shell herself.

The fourth vessel's debate has turned to what sounds like fighting. The fifth joins in. The Russians are falling apart. Litvinov's not with them. His influence isn't nearly enough.

It's painful to listen to.

Ulyanova, under her breath, still sings. But then she opens her eyes and looks right at me.

She smiles.

Something inside me smiles back. Goddamn.

Joe taps his helm and looks around his sling at me, eyes flicking, examining. Can he tell? I work to recover.

Ulyanova's turned away again.

"I'm not sure our fellow warriors are going along," Joe says. I do not want to fall into another instauration, another

Guru moment—not here and not now. But how could the *starshina* be connected with all that?

As we watch the serrated falcons maneuver in the deep ice-pudding, banking fore and aft to block any escape, the best scenario I can imagine is that the Antags are being really, really cautious. No surprise given our history and the strangeness of this new relationship. They're doing everything they can to discourage us from responding defensively or mounting our own assault. With twelve big Antag ships against our five, how can we put on any sort of offense? By acting like we've surrendered, perhaps—catching them with their guard down. Who knows what happened on Titan before the stand-down and reboot? Traps and stratagems aplenty, no doubt.

"What the fuck are they waiting for?" Jacobi cries out. My concern exactly. We're not resisting. How will they carry us out of here, take care of us? Wasn't that the deal? How long can any of us afford to stick around?

What do they think about the fresh human ships dropping from the surface, no doubt to wreak total destruction?

I finally detect a jumble of thoughts from my Antag opposite. Their ships in orbit are under attack. Just like on Mars, all of us are being targeted. Those who support the Gurus want to find and obliterate us—fellow humans included. On Mars, we saw ample evidence that the Antags were similarly divided.

Inquire.

Again the voice of bug steward. It usually pops up when decision points are reached. However, I'm not sure I can formulate any relevant questions, and bug memory isn't about current situations or possible outcomes. Or is it? There's a kind of urgency in the voice. Maybe it knows something, or has been tapping deep into my thoughts and has enough of its own smarts to guess.

Inquire.

About what? I pick something out of my own jumble of questions. If we lose Titan—

"Are there other archives like this one?" I ask, and feel DJ's approval.

Unknown. Accessing what you know, it is probable that massive force will soon be deployed to destroy this entire moon.

Inquire.

"Do we already know enough to survive on our own?"

Unknown.

"Where are the archives you know about?"

Nothing is certain. Some could remain out on cold moons in the dusty reaches, or on larger worlds far from the sun, completed by our engineers before our own wars nearly destroyed us.

Aha, I think. "The Antag female gave us a glimpse of something she called 'Sun-Planet.' Is that what you're talking about?"

Possibly. It may have been the last world where our kind lived before we passed into extinction. Many hundreds of millions of solar cycles have gone by, but that world may have preserved its own archives. Still, the connections are broken or at best incomplete. There could be much that is new and different. And it is possible the ones you call Gurus have found and destroyed them already.

A long answer. We have no idea what's being planned for us. No way to survive if we stay where we are. We'll soon be overwhelmed, or caught in one amazing shit-storm of high-tech combat.

And to add to the tension, my liaison may be what she says she is, a sympathetic presence arguing for our survival, but she's still grieving for her dead. She still hates our guts, as do her fellow warriors. Most of us feel the same about Antags. They don't trust any of us and we won't trust them even if they give us a chance, even if the tea and bug memory say we should.

In a communication colored by apprehension, she informs me that the process is moving slowly. Not every Antag in her force believes human captives can be of use. She's in a minority, and there's a bitter argument under way. She's defending the present plan—defending our survival. If the opposing faction on those waiting ships wins the debate, we could all be gathered up and rescued only to be dumped naked into the frozen sea—or worse, tortured and summarily executed.

Just a heads-up, she assures me. She's working hard to convince the others they're wrong, arguing on the basis of Antag honor and loyalty to the ancient ones, whose inheritance runs through all our veins.

The bugs.

Antag *honor*?

Christ, what have I gotten us into? What if it's all a sham? How could we expect any better?

In the round cabin, Starshina Ulyanova is shouting in Russian, trying to get Litvinov to order us to fight, to do something!

From many klicks behind our vessels and the Antag ships comes a deep, visceral *thump*. Heavy overpressure passes, making the Oscar squeal at its joints. Then the pressure fades, leaving us all with headaches—caught with our helms open. We close and seal and immerse in the display.

"There they go!" Joe says. The fourth and fifth transports, with their Russian crews, have had enough. They're trying to turn and head back to what they seem to hope is salvation—the human forces descending behind us.

The Antag falcons have passed over and beneath us and stand between the fleeing vessels and the deep night of Titan's inner sea. The transports try to respond with weapons—

But Joe has locked firepower to our own centipede. The others can't fight unless we do.

Suddenly, the wayward vessels are wrapped in a brilliant balls of glowing vapor, followed by another slam and more overpressure. Our hull is struck by whirling bits of debris, like a hard, hard rain.

"Who the hell did that?" Litvinov shouts. "Sanchez! Unlock weapons!"

"It wasn't Antags," Joe says. He sounds sick, as if none of this is worth it, life has passed way beyond what can be borne. I have to agree. We're down by two. How many seconds before we all sizzle?

"We're seeing long-range bolts from one of Box's machines," Borden says, and Ishida confirms. "They're getting closer."

Friendly fire, as the shitheads say.

No time left, I tell my Antag female.

From beyond the walls of the stony labyrinth, bolts pass around us, almost brushing the centipede, into the shadows behind—Antags returning fire. Something far back there lights up, refracting through a cloud of slushy ice like fiery diamonds and throwing a weird sunrise glow across the solid gray ceiling.

The wide-winged falcons swarm our remaining Oscars, pods thrusting forward and fanning out tools. Here it comes.

"Antags moving in to recover," Borden says, her voice strangely calm. Is this what we're all hoping for? Is this our only chance?

A cutting blade spins into our cabin space, narrowly missing Ishida. Our helms suck down hard at the loss of cabin pressure. My fellow Skyrines cry out like kittens at the roaring flood of subzero liquid. But our suits keep us alive.

Once the cutting is done, with banshee screams, torches provoke scarlet bouquets of superheated steam that bleb around inside the cabin until the cold sucks them back. From superchill to steam heat and back again in seconds—and still, our suits maintain.

In my display, I see more and bigger bolts rise from behind the walls of Bug Karnak, penetrate electrical gradients, make the entire frigid sea around us fluoresce brilliant green— followed by more sunrises behind. Strangely, I feel justified. Wanted. The Antags are defending us. But they're also killing humans. My guts twist.

From the first rank of falcons, steely gray clamps fan out and jam in through the wedge made by the cutting blades and torches. The Oscar's head is pried opened by main force. Spiked tentacles shoot from the nearest falcon and insert into the ruined carapace, where they cut through our straps and shuck us like peas from a pod. We're jerked up and over, bouncing from the edges, dragged through darkness punctuated by more blinding, blue-white flares to an even bigger machine rising over the walls like a monstrous catfish, its head dozens of meters wide. A dark mouth swallows us whole.

Three minutes of tumbling, blind darkness. The seawater around us swirls and drains. We're in the catfish's belly.

A little light flicks on below, then left and right, and the tentacles suck down around our limbs, grab us up again, then drop us through an oval door into a narrow tank filled with cold, silty liquid. Soon we're joined by other plunging, squirming shapes—the crews from the other Oscars. Most of the outside lights switch off. It's too dark in the tank to recognize one another, but I'm pretty sure one of the suited shapes is DJ. Another might be Jacobi, another, Tak. Then Borden. I hope I'm right that they're both here. Another, slightly smaller, could be Kumar or maybe Mushran. I try to count but we keep getting swirled around. Rude.

Where's Joe? Where's Ishida, Ishikawa, Litvinov, Ulyanova? Then the tank's sloshing subsides and we drift to a gritty, murky bottom, settling in stunned piles like sardines waiting to be canned.

A dim glow filters through the tank's walls—translucent, frosted. Sudden quiet. Very little sloshing. My sense of integral motion might be telling me we're rising, retreating, but I can't be sure. Nobody's making a sound.

Why are we here, being treated like this? Haven't we been told to become partners, to solve a larger riddle? How did we end up so thoroughly screwed, and what did Joe do to get us here? Joe has gotten me into and out of more scrapes than I can number. But our first encounter, I was the one causing real trouble—or reacting the only way I could. Now we're both here, and I'm not sure what Joe means to me, to us, anymore.

Has he sold us out? Is he even alive?

Thinking you've fit all the pieces into a puzzle, then

having it picked up, shaken, and dumped—being forced to start all over again—they can't teach you how to react to that in boot camp or OCS or the war colleges. That's a challenge you have to learn from experience. And mostly at this level of confusion and weirdness, you don't learn. You just die.

Bumping and bobbing along the bottom of the tank, listening to my suit creak and click, listening to the distant twang of wires working through my flesh—a never-ending process—I try to keep it together, try to remind myself that the Antags may be connected to the wisdom of bug memory but still have every reason to hate us.

Judging from the contortions and soft moans, the suits are still causing everyone pain. If you don't move they hurt less. But still, they keep us warm.

There's ten or twelve left. Way down from our contingent on Spook. Were some dumped? Did the Antags select us out like breeders on a puppy farm?

After a time, everything in the shadows becomes part of a sharp, awful relaxation. I can still think, mostly, but want to slide into old, safe memories, then dreams. Dreams of better days and nights. Of places where there *are* days and nights. I don't think or feel that I'm about to die, but how can I be sure? When you die, you become a child again. I've seen it, felt it through the return of Captain Coyle. She introduced me to a little girl's bedroom and her comic books. But I don't feel like a child just yet, though young memories, memories acquired when I was younger, even bad memories, are more and more desirable, if only to block out the pain. I can't just give up. Not after all the shit I've put others through.

Then, despite my focused concentration, I experience my own moment of panic. I start to scream and thrash. Everything in this fucking tank is entirely too fuzzy and I'm not ready to accept whatever dark nullity is on the menu because I really want to see what's next, I want to *be there*, *be out there*, I want to learn more about what our enemies are up to and who they really are, which ones are our enemies, I mean—learn more about how the Earth was screwed over by the Gurus. When you die, you stop learning, stop playing the game. Is that true? I'm not sure it's always true. It may not have been strictly true for Captain Coyle. But she turned glass. Maybe that's a different sort of death, like becoming a book that others can read but not you. And now I don't hear her in my head because her settling in has finished, the ink in her book is dry and she's part of the memory banks of our ancient ancestors.

Is that any different from real death?

I just want to keep on making a difference.

To that end, and because my throat really hurts and thrashing around is pointless, I stop. I keep bumping into the others and I don't want to hurt them.

And I'm worn-out.

I roll left and try to see through gummy eyes. Through the murk and foggy walls, I make out blurred outlines of Antags flapping their wings like penguins or seabirds, swimming or flying by the tank. Checking on us. Are they actually flying, or are they in liquid like us? I grasp at this problem like a sailor grabbing at a life preserver. I say to myself, out loud, like I'm a professor back in school, "Their ships may be filled with oxygen-bearing fluid, like Freon—which allows a different relationship to the pressures outside. Maybe we're being subjected to the same dousing. Or maybe it's just warmer water, seawater. Maybe they come from an ocean world. I don't *know*. I have no fucking idea what's what, I'm just making shit up."

So much for the professor.

I try once more to retreat into better times, better history, but I can't find my way back to the sunset beach at Del Mar, to wearing shorts and T-shirts and flip-flops, to hitchhiking and walking with Joe before we ever enlisted, hoping we could pick up girls or girls would pick us up. I was fifteen and Joe was sixteen and given the age of the girls who might have been driving those cars that flared their lights and rumbled or hummed by in the night, that wasn't likely.

But I can't reach back to good times. I keep snagging on the first time I needed Joe, the first time we met, before we became friends.

THE TROUBLE WITH HARRY

A warm, dry California night. I was dragging a rug filled with my mother's dead boyfriend down a concrete culvert, trying to find a patch of brush, a ditch, any place where I could hide what I had been forced to do just an hour before. I looked up and stopped blubbering long enough to see a tall, skinny kid rise up at the opposite end of the culvert. Bare-chested, he was wearing cutoffs, carrying a long stick, and smoking a pipe. The bowl of the pipe lit up his face when he puffed.

"Hey there," he said.

"Hey," I said, and wet my pants. Why I hadn't done that earlier I didn't know.

"Who's that?" he asked, pointing the pipe at the rug.

"My mom's boyfriend," I said.

"Dead?"

"What do you think?"

"What'd he do?"

"Tried to kill us."

"For real?"

I was crying so hard I could not answer.

"Okay," said the shirtless boy with the pipe, and ran off into the dark. I thought he was going to tell the cops and so I resumed dragging the body in earnest farther down the culvert. Then the shirtless boy returned minus pipe and with a camping shovel. He unfolded the shovel and pointed into the eucalyptus woods. "I'm Joe," he said.

"Hey," I said.

"There's fill dirt about twenty yards north. Soft digging. What's his name?"

"Harry."

"Anybody going to miss him?"

I said I did not know. Maybe not.

Joe took one corner of the rug. "How did it happen?" he asked as we dragged the body between the trees, over the dry leaves.

"He broke down the door to my mom's room."

"What'd she do?"

"She didn't wake up. She's stoned."

"And?"

"When he saw me, he swung a big hunting knife. He said he was going to gut my mom, then me. I had one of his pistols."

"Just as a precaution?" Joe asked.

"I guess. He'd beaten her before. He taught me to shoot." That seemed unnecessary, but it was true.

"Then?"

"I threw a glass at him, to get him out of her bedroom. He followed me down the hall and I shot him three times."

"Shit! Suicide by kid. Anybody hear the shots?"

"I don't think so. He fell on an old rug. I rolled him up and dragged him here."

"Convenient."

No more questions, for the time being. We dragged the body together and in an hour or so had dug a not-so-shallow grave and rolled him into it, down beyond the reach of coyotes.

Then we filled it in and spread a layer of topsoil and dry brown eucalyptus leaves over the patch.

"I'm Joe," he said again.

"I remember. I'm Michael," I said, and we shook hands. "No one's going to know about this, right?"

"Right," Joe said. "Our secret."

I was thirteen. Joe was fourteen. Hell of a way to meet up. But Joe had judged me and I had judged him. In the next few months, he blocked my downhill run to drugs and crime. He even talked to my mom and got her into a program, for a while. He seemed to know a lot about human beings. But for all that, he wasn't any sort of angel. He always managed to get us into new and improved trouble—upgrades, he called them, like that time on the railroad bridge, or in Chihuahua when we found the mummy and brought it home.

Matter-of-factly, over the next year, Joe assured me that he and I were a team. By being associated with him, with his crazy self-assurance, even his tendency to vanish for weeks, then pop up with plans for another outlandish adventure, I began to feel I was special, too—a capable survivor. As we crisscrossed Southern California and Mexico, hitchhiking or getting our older friends to drive, we kept nearly getting killed, but more than once he saved me from other sorts of grisly death—and together, we helped each other grow up.

The police never did find my mom's crazy boyfriend. He might still be out there in those woods. And my mother never asked about him, never mentioned him again. She was probably just as glad he wasn't around to beat on her. Good riddance to one miserably screwed-up bastard.

Most of that shit isn't worth going back to. My whole life has been a parade of crazy hopes. Hardly any rest. Joe was part of it from that time on. And now we're stuck here, waiting to be canned. Sardines waiting to be packed in oil.

Then why am I still thinking, still trying to solve problems? Thinking. Sinking. I really *am* sinking. Before I go to sleep, in my head, all by myself, I spout maxims and rules of thumb like a drunk DI at his fucking retirement party. I'm an old man in a young man's body. That's what Joe told me years back when we stood in line to recruit. "You're an old soul," he said. "And that ain't necessarily a good thing."

It's even more true now. That's what battle does to you. That's what…

Shit. I'm forgetting the best stuff. Really clever stuff. It was all so clear just a moment ago.

Someone grabs my helm and shoves another helm in close. Through the visors I see Jacobi. She looks angry. Her lips form words: "I don't think they like us!"

No shit. So sleepy. I can't hear much. All comm has been jammed or cut and the suits are too insulated, too heavy. Jacobi's hands let me go. She's checking other helms. Poking, looking, poking again—taking a count. Then she half-walks, half-swims through the silty fluid and returns to me. Again she's trying to say something, but she points emphatically at the wall. Hey! There's an Antag peering in, checking to see if we're still alive. Fucking ugly bird with useless wings, except they seem to be able to swim. Or maybe they're weightless and that's the only place those useless wings work—in zero g.

Jacobi slams her helm hard against mine, twists my head left, and I see what's beside the Antag. It's a big, shadowy mass, slowly morphing or rotating, can't tell which, but it has long, sinuous arms. For a moment, it looks like a catamaran viewed head-on—two bodies linked by a thick bridge. Each body sports two very large eyes. Arms emerge from the tips of the bodies, below the eyes—slow, lazy arms.

I have no trouble reading Jacobi's lips through her visor. I'm thinking the same thing: *What the fuck is that?*

That's not all that's new. I see smaller forms that superficially resemble Antags, crawling by the tank on their knees or feet, wings folded, like bats. Never saw either the squid or the little bats on Mars.

Then the silhouettes move off and the tank goes dark. Hours pass, maybe days. How much in the way of sips and gasps do our heavy suits carry? We finally get organized enough to sit up and form a long oval in the murk at the bottom. We could be in a twelve-step program. At Jacobi's prodding, some of us stand and try to walk, but there's nowhere to go.

I get lost all over again in trying to remember Camp Pendleton, Hawthorne, Socotra off the coast of Yemen, Skybase Lewis-McChord. Madigan. Why can't an *instauration* come along, one of those preprogrammed moments that make me think I'm somewhere else? Compared to this, that would be a vacation. But there's no such relief.

I can almost imagine those far-off places are still around, and might return to my life—that I'm here but they're still out there, still real, and some of the memories carry so such detail—

But the damned suit keeps pinching, cutting, insinuating, and that blocks me from losing myself in any memory, any setting, any world I want so badly to re-create. Worse, it keeps diverting me to the pain of my first year as a teenager. Listening to my mom get beat up. Sitting with Harry, her boyfriend, on the couch as he drank beer and smoked and made me watch grisly YouTube videos with him. Accidents, corpses, history shit. Kept him from beating on Mom, but I hated those videos. Made life seem frail and nasty. Poor fucked-up Harry. Maybe he never had a chance.

I don't want to remember any more about Harry.

TIME IS NOT ON MY SIDE, AND NEVER WAS

More days, or maybe just hours. Couldn't be days, right? The lights brighten. Antags swim or prance by the walls, peer in, make gestures with their mid-joint wing-fingers. They do have thumbs!

I see no more catamaran squid with their sinuous arms. Could be robots or machines or weapons, but they looked alive to me.

Then the top of the tank opens and those damned spiky metal tentacles reach in and pluck one of us out by an arm and a leg. I think it's Litvinov, the Russian colonel. The opening closes. We move around, frantically bumping, trying to stay away from the opening.

Can it get any worse?

The tentacles poke back down and explore, roiling the tank's rippling, foaming surface. In a few minutes, four more suits have been plucked up and out. And now it's my turn. The cold saline drains from around my suit and a warmer something surrounds me. My joints ache and lungs labor.

Pressure has changed. Maybe there's air outside the tank. Could also mean my suit has sprung a pressure leak.

Then the tentacles relax and release. I'm lying on something but I can't see what—a table, a rolling cart? I'm moved along a narrow, cramped tunnel that curves sharply off to the left, and then I'm dumped on a slab. The slab is in a small cylindrical room. Two Antags strut around me, then the room quickly fills with the smaller bat creatures, all carrying wicked-looking tools. They climb up and lean over me, over my suit. I can't move.

But then something sparks in my head—a little communication from the Antag female. She's making it clear to me and probably to DJ that we're still not where we want to be. We're on a small transport ship, in orbit around Titan, and the first thing the Antags are going to do is cut us out of our suits, in case we have secret weapons, in case we can still cause damage, wearing them. The big Antags back off and let the smaller creatures do their work. They surround me, heads bobbing, tools dancing, and make low grunting noises.

I hope they kill me quick.

A scratchy voice, sound not mental, through a translator, says, "Helpers will remove your armor. It will hurt."

Together, the bats start cutting. Their torch-saws make quick work of the outer shell, which is roughly pulled away, revealing underwear and then naked flesh, with wires stretched taut like guitar strings—

And I'm the frets.

I scream.

The bats work quickly, pulling and extracting and clipping while grunting and whistling, and I bleed all over the table before a bigger Antag sprays on a kind of floury powder that stanches the blood.

When I'm too weak to scream, two big Antags lift me from the table with those damned wing-fingers, shrouded in elastic gloves, and wrap me in gray blankets that fit snug to my body. Where the blankets touch, the pain goes away.

I'd rather die than go through that again.

A big Antag leans over me as I'm carried into another, much smaller room. Expressive damned eyes—two outside, two inside, near the beak. Then I know. This one is the female, my liaison, my connection—those vibrations. Again she does not rely on our private circuit, but uses a translator to tell me in hashy English that the others will also have their suits removed, for her crew's security but also for our own good.

"They are designed to control you," the scratchy voice says. "The Keepers are afraid of you."

"Who're they?" I croak.

She wipes my mouth with a cloth. "If you join us, you can fight to kill them."

"Yeah. Sure. When can I speak to my friends?" I ask.

"On a bigger ship, we will find a place for all of you to live together."

"What about Bug Karnak?" Somehow, through our connection, she knows what I'm talking about.

"It will stay here," she says.

"But someone's going to try to destroy it, right?"

The Antag female leans over me, four eyes glittering in the dim light of the cell, beak open to show a raspy tongue. "You will sleep. We are moving to bigger ship."

She thinks there's something unusual about this particular bigger ship—I can feel it in the overtones. Something powerful, dangerous, and puzzling.

"Where to after that?"

"Far away," she adds. "Long journey. Many days."

"You travel between the stars?"

"We go home," she says. "If we live."

Lots of ifs. "Where are you from?"

Through the overtones, I'm left with an impression of something like a big basketball on a billiard table, slowly rolling across gravity-dimpled felt and scattering smaller balls every which way. Makes no sense to me.

Then I realize this might be Sun-Planet.

"You don't come from another star system?"

No answer to that and pretty soon I'm numb, sleepy all over again—

Asleep.

This time I dream of walking across the dry, brushy hills between the close-packed, apartment-strewn suburbs of San Diego. My mother is walking with me and one of her boyfriends, it's Harry, goddammit, and he's packing a Colt pistol in a fast-draw holster slung on his hip. Harry's about to teach me the basics of high-powered weapons.

Christ. Why can't I dream something pleasant, something wonderful?

SORRY, CHARLIE

My eyes are open, though I'm still in darkness. I'm wearing a loose kind of pajama bottom. I fall against a wall and back my way around a circle. I'm in a small, cylindrical room. A can. Tuna, not sardines. If I spread my arms, I can touch both sides. I have no idea how much time has passed. I'm comfortable enough, though my body still throbs and aches. It's dark in here. Dark and close.

"Joe? Jacobi? Commander?"

No answer. Where are we?

Have we left Titan?

I feel the peculiar vibration that tells me the female Antag isn't far away. I pick up a jumble of her deep thoughts, then more overtones, and no doubt she can feel some of mine. Images and emotions. She's hard at work—maybe she's in the control room, but I can't see what that looks like. My vision and hers still don't sync.

But her fellows are ragging her. Some hate her for getting close to humans and not killing us. Our being here puts a

tremendous strain on their command structure, their cama-
raderie. So many want us dead.

Even putting that aside, I don't think she has a lot of respect
for me, for us. After all, they were able to capture us alive—
and even though that was what the bug steward wanted and
she had told her superiors that was what should happen and
everyone in her crew signed on to that course of action—

Even though we surrendered reluctantly, and two of our
Oscars tried to break and run...we didn't *really* put up a
fight. We chose the coward's way, right?

How old is Antag culture? That kind of shit thinking
usually passes after a really bad war or a few thousand years
of scouring the countryside and raping and killing peasants.
After a while, that kind of thinking gets stale.

But they're in charge.

The female delivers another sip of precious knowledge.
We're on the move; our cans (we're all in ventilated cylinders
like this one) are going to be packed into a transport, awaiting an opportunity to rendezvous with a much larger ship,
that dangerous puzzle ship, even now swooping down from
behind other moons. Antags do like to hide behind moons.
But she insists this is not one of their ships. Makes no sense.
She shows me that leaving Titan was less difficult than leaving Mars. Duh. That's why we hardly felt it.

Will my air last that long? That *really* pushes a button. I
remember being told back in basic that you'd be flunked out
if you got iffy in tight situations. No claustrophobes allowed.
Skyrine training leads you into lots of trials that involve con-
finement, being closed in, squeezed tight, sometimes for days
or weeks. But usually while asleep or waiting to be dropped,

when adrenaline and our favorite drug, never given a name but we called it *enthusiasm*, kept you up and prepped.

But that's a long time ago. We've been through a lot since then and this fucking can is too much. It's tough to quit a panic once engaged. All I manage is to stand flat against the wall and shiver all over. For the first time in my life, I'm asking God to just kill me. Get it over with now. I've lost all interest in whatever will come next, because I'm *IN A FUCKING CAN* and *can't get out*.

Then another kind of panic grips me. If I survive, I think, I'll never be what I was before—whatever and whoever I was before. Shithead before, but at least I was a semifunctional Skyrine and a faithful member of the Corps. What will I be in a few hours?

Just when I'm about to lose the last of my dignity, my discipline, I am bathed in a kind of autumnal light. A kind of opening is revealed through which I see something, through which I can experience the outside and try to control my fear—

It's in the overtones. It's my connection with the Antag female—Bird Girl.

I try to remember where I've heard that name, *Bird Girl*. My mother read me books all the time. I was five or six when she started us on bigger novels, usually from the base library, but sometimes from bargain bookstores. I try to recall the titles—something to distract me, and it helps by bringing another round of memories, this time so sharp and sweet I can almost forget the can.

I feel myself wrapped in a blanket, nestling up against my mother's warmth and hearing her voice as she reads. Crickets chirp outside, a breeze puffs the curtains through the window screen—the last dry heat of day fading into Fresno night. We haven't moved to San Diego yet. My mother and father haven't gotten their divorce. These are good times, cozy times. I feel secure and happy.

Bird Girl. This may be where I first heard that strange name. Mom read me Vance and Le Guin, Martin and Tolkien, of course, but there was also this book set in South America that told about a girl in a big green jungle. It takes me hours to remember the name, then it just pops up. *Green Mansions.* Rima was the bird girl's name. I feel so clever, I want to tell Joe and DJ, but I doubt they've ever heard of the book.

Mom's reading to me continued even after my father left us and my behavior went downhill, exasperating her, but when she read to me, we could imagine better times and places. She moved us down to San Diego. Started dating the string of crazy dudes. But she still found time to read to me. I think now, digging deep, that the love of reading I picked up from her—that, and Joe's influence—is what kept me from becoming a narcissistic monster. As she read she mused, talked about our life, tried to explain what she was feeling—I didn't always want to know about that. Embarrassed the hell out of me sometimes. She drew out lessons and revealed a kind of wisdom she rarely applied to her own life, but passed to me nevertheless, along with those stories—a kind of mother's milk full of immunization against the insanity that all too often surrounded us.

When she found a new man, of course, all that was put on pause for a few weeks, so I didn't actually like any of her men, and she knew it and that added to our strain.

But for right now—

Listening to the overtones coming from the liaison—

"Hey, *Bird Girl*," I whisper in the darkness, in the can. "Read me a story. Give me something. We're partners, right?"

My words must come wrapped in their own overtones, a haze of comfort and the sound of crickets, the heat of a Southern California summer—and so many strange words. Maybe Bird Girl knows about Tolkien and the others. Maybe she was told to study us as a culture. Maybe she's a scholar of humanity.

Yeah. Right.

There's a pause, a kind of mental question mark, and then I get another round of overtones. I desperately reach for them, like grabbing flowers out of a falling bouquet, so sweet because they're not in the can with me. Most of it turns out to be bug memory, a constant flow of old history and planetary geology. Bug steward is still there, acting between Bird Girl and me, coordinating this ancient flow—and maybe trying to give me some relief.

But there's also a young memory and it has to be from Bird Girl, because nothing about bug steward is young—

Very sharp—

A tangled ball of wings and grasping hands. Momma Antag has just hatched five babies, and they pile up against one another in a soft bowl, mewing and thrashing and waiting for something to be deposited in their barely open beaks. A tube drops down. Momma doesn't regurgitate—maybe it's not Momma—

It's not. This is a place where they make soldiers.

The infant soldiers eat. It's pea soup and salt and anchovies, by the taste, or at least the smell. Ecstasy. Not in the least cozy from my human perspective, but it's one of Bird Girl's favorite early memories.

Fair exchange.

The overtones fade. For a long, long time, I resonate again between panic and trying to reach out in our weird, four-part thought space—DJ, Bird Girl, the steward, and me in four hypothetical corners—and get relief, plus answers...

DJ is barely there. I think he's actually asleep. I don't want to dig into DJ's subconscious, which is mostly old movies and memories of porn, so I avoid that part.

And then—

I feel a pressure down my centerline, pooling around my feet like I'm in an elevator cab. We're definitely on the move. I can stand, but it's easier to squat and press my back against the cylinder wall. The pressure grows on my butt and feet. I focus on that pressure, that sensation. Something's going to change.

After a while, I stop squeaking like a mouse and rise from the bottom, then float up inside the cylinder until I bump my head. Somehow that's better than just sitting. We're still in orbit, I guess, but no joy on getting the can open. We're waiting for that big powerful ship, but it's not here yet.

The ship we're all stuffed into at the moment is little more than a light transport, the last of those that once delivered weapons and reinforcements to Antags on Titan. The Antags retrieved their survivors and the few remaining catamaran squid. I get a kind of doubled picture/impression of these remarkable creatures swimming in Titan's deep icy slush, the supercold, super-saline fluids, and wonder how that makes sense, how they survived—

But I know now that the squid are not native to Titan. They belong with the Antags! And how many Antags remain? Not many. They've dumped the falcons and the smaller weapons that faced us across the walls of the archive—Bug Karnak. Those are all gone.

The big ship that's supposedly out there is not one of the ships that deliver Antags to Mars. Those are much smaller, less powerful, and slower. This one is bigger than big and stranger than strange, and for some reason no Antag is really at all sure it will allow us inside, or how the Antags will take control and fly it, but if everything works out right—if we acquire or earn infinite amounts of luck—we will meet with it soon and be transferred over.

So Bird Girl informs us, DJ and me, reluctant to reveal even this much. She's doing it only because she's also scared, and that resonates with our fear. Still, bug steward approves of the resonance. We're truly related, the steward observes. Proof of some ancient concept, some ancient—

I lose the rest of that overtone, which seems to come out of nowhere specific—the depths of the saline sea, Bug Karnak, maybe—

Or the squid? Did I just touch the mind of one of those? Or something even stranger…

The *starshina*.

I shudder.

This new and strange ship, if our luck holds, will take us very far away, very swiftly, because of a *haze of branching green minds*…whatever the hell that means.

Ulyanova again—just briefly. Like tiptoeing over razor blades. I want that to stop, really I do. I try to blink in the darkness. How do I know when my eyes are closed?

Fascinating stuff, no?

But I'm still in a fucking can.

DELIVERED

I have a moment through the awfulness to wonder how the others are doing, if they're also still in cans. Maybe we'll all end up drooling basket cases, no use to anybody, and the Antag commanders will just dump us out in space like old garbage. Antags should have no idea how to fix us—only how to kill us. We'll become part of Saturn's rings, supercooled packets of meat caught in the grind of orbiting ice and rock boulders, forgotten by everybody...

Bug steward seems to be keeping its presence, its interference, low-key, to encourage the connection with Bird Girl. And I feel Bird Girl more intensely than ever. She's exploring me in detail, overcoming an inherent reluctance, listening closely to *my* overtones, but so far, it's strictly a one-way exchange. Perversely, that makes me both happy and even more queasy.

Then, as if in payment for her intrusion, she provides another blurry impression of our transport working to join up with the big ship. No idea where that is. Maybe it's still orbiting Titan. If so, why hasn't Box attacked it?

For a time, I feel like I'm floating in space, no body, just a pair of eyes—vision doubled, so it's a quartet of eyes—but very low rez. I can barely make out the stars. Then my perspective shifts and I think I see Saturn's rings, lightly sketched and again doubled, giving me a weird ache in my eye muscles. There are little flashing symbols on the different rings, the shepherd moons—then the view goes back to that goddamned ship. I have to guess through Bird Girl's eyes, or maybe what someone is telling her—because she can't see it directly, can she?—how big it really is.

The vessel we're closing on is maybe nine or ten klicks long and has a short, blunt tail. Forward of the tail swells a gray bulb maybe two or three klicks in diameter. Full of fuel to get home? There's a cylindrical midsection about four klicks long and a klick in diameter, and at the prow or nose, a long, skinny tube like the needle of a hypodermic. Big and ugly. Forward of the bulb, just back from the nose, five long containers are arranged in pentagonal frames around the middle cylinder like bullets in a revolver. Not all that different from the Spook, actually, but maybe ten or fifteen times bigger. I can't see what drives it. I'm given the impression the big ship has been hidden away for years—kept in reserve, but by whom, and why?

Why can't Bird Girl view it directly? Is it invisible?

What's obvious is that no Antag has never seen or experienced anything remotely like it. The transport's crew is approaching cautiously, critically, in no hurry, because they're ignorant of what could happen, but also, Bird Girl is their only connection to someone or something crucial to activating the ship. Maybe two somethings.

One appears to be an Antag, a ragged, poorly treated

creature with a sad, shabby demeanor. In Bird Girl's eyes, this bedraggled Antag is a monster, a traitor, a true atrocity, but essential to the success of this mission.

And there's something else, something she won't tell me about or allow me to see. Not an Antag, but a Keeper, fallen so far from grace, after flying so high, that the crew simply wants to kill it. But Bird Girl won't let them.

And this Keeper, whatever it may be, is afraid of *me*? Of humans? More afraid of those who are connected to the archives, I'm guessing. That makes my brain itch. The enemy of my enemy is my enemy's former friend?

For some reason, I don't draw the obvious connection. I'm not at my best in this situation. As far as we are concerned, her fellows don't trust Bird Girl not just because of that weirdness, but because she has a connection with humans, and will force us all to meet and interact. In their eyes, she's tainted all around.

Great. I try to screw down on our link, to see these complications more clearly, or at least begin to understand them—but now a debate, maybe even a fight, has broken out around Bird Girl, not for the first time, and she's totally absorbed trying to defuse the tensions and get along with her fellows. There aren't that many of them left, maybe thirty. Hard to count.

The last Antag warriors are convinced that this journey, this maneuver or feint, will be the last thing they'll ever do.

Ice Moon Tea has connected us, the steward of bug memory has connected us, but Bird Girl will be very, very glad when our sharing ends and she can revert to her lone fighter self. She feels *violated* by having to deal with DJ and me and the mysterious Keeper. She feels she's been sacrificed, her honor discarded.

GARDEN OF ODIN

When her troubles have eased, Bird Girl passes along a tidbit of information, and it's a wrencher—that the crew believes, or has been informed by their commanders, that there's something about the big ship that's frightening and forbidden—taboo.

It's not an Antag ship. Got that. And it's not human, either. Something huge, invisible, alien, unknown. A lost artifact filled with angry gods or creatures of light? Cosmic zombies or vampires? I try not to let my subconscious get out of control.

Then our link fades. I'm back in the dark. I sniff, sniff again, feel the coolness of the container wall—smooth and dry. If I don't stretch out my arms and press, I float. The air actually feels fresh, though I can't tell where it's coming from. That's a plus, an offer of hope that we're not just being executed by slow suffocation. But I'm still thirsty and hungry. Should I be grateful we haven't eaten since being peeled out of our lobster suits? I haven't had to fill the can with unseemly stink.

More motion—sideways, swaying, followed by creaks and pops I feel in my ears. Possibly the cans are being sealed off, and the swaying may mean we're being transferred.

As much as Bird Girl has no interest in keeping us fully informed, I get occasional glimpses of this and that—of two transports entering an opening in empty space, of cans being winched in clusters out of one transport. I try to chuckle at a memory of beach parties on Socotra, beer cans slopping in plastic-strapped six-packs. The chuckle fades into a gurgle.

This is all she sees, all Bird Girl can know. She's not a pilot, has no connection to the pilots, if this strange, taboo ship can have real pilots. But from what she does convey, it's obvious the ship is vastly more powerful than either of us has managed to use or create. We've both been contained, coached and prepped to go at each other on almost equal footing. How much does equality of tech and knowledge equal a longer, more entertaining war? Who's been dealt the stronger hand?

Who's favored?

Bug steward seems irritated by my density. *Whoever most pleases the masters of this ancient game.*

Gurus? Keepers are the same as Gurus! Bird Girl has been telling me that *Antags have Gurus*, just like humans—showrunners for their side of our war. Bird Girl's commanders, her people, have been told that humans want to kill all Keepers—all Gurus—and all Antags and dominate the solar system, while Keepers, like Antags, just want to live in peace. Same story we've been fed, but in reverse.

The air in the can becomes close. I can't simply stop breathing. I need to get out. There's that damned squeaking again—it's me, I'm freaking.

Then the can opens like a lunchbox. The lights come up to

unbearable brightness and three of the small, bat-wing critters rustle close, wings folded tight, to peer at me. Their four
reddish-purple eyes blink. Big Antags are at least four times
larger—if the small ones are even Antags and not lackeys or
servants. Nobody wants to touch me. I rise from the can and
nearly float out, then grip the edge, casual as can be, except
that I'm laughing like a maniac. I try with all my willpower
to stop. Don't want to lose it. Not after having survived all
that crap—not when there's finally hope.

I stuff my hand in my mouth and look around.

The cans have been tied down with rubbery gray cords on
a brightly illuminated platform. We're in zero g, surrounded
by a space that shades off to warm darkness. Four more of
us are released and cling to the edges of the cans or the cords
themselves: Borden, DJ, Kumar, Joe. Our sounds echo—
retching, crying out, calling names.

Bats pull the rest of the cans up against the first five, tying
them to the others with more cords. They're opened next.
Here's Tak, Ishida, Ishikawa—Jacobi. We're all in pajama
bottoms and nothing more. Jacobi looks cool and collected,
but vomit spatters her chest and arms.

Litvinov emerges with a gaunt, haunted look on his lean
face. Ulyanova rises from her can with arms crossed. I see
Kumar, also covered in vomit. I don't see Mushran.

Most of the Russians must have died back in the Battle of
the Titanian Sea. The two that are still with us, besides Litvinov and Ulyanova, I barely know—a couple of *efreitors*: one
male named Bilyk, the other a female named Yagodovskaya, a
few years older than Ulyanova.

Christ almighty. Fourteen, barely a squad. Six are still
spewing thin vomit that makes the bat critters shuffle and

flap. For some reason, that insane comedy makes me want to cry. But at least I've stopped laughing.

Physically I'm okay, but DJ is taking this poorly, as are Ishikawa and Borden. We've been through too many changes.

Five of the big Antags watch from the side of the platform. I recognize Bird Girl at the center—same orange and blue colors around the eyes, same blue, raspy tongue. I fix details of Antag appearance in memory—wingspans of about three meters, outer tips sprouting small fingers, more substantial gripping digits on each wing elbow or middle joint—basically two upper sets of hands. The bats seem to have similar arrangements. Beneath a thick tunic, the thorax presents a central breastbone like a turkey's. Under clinging pantaloons, the lower limbs are short, thick, and tightly muscled, with hands on knees and prehensile feet, mostly covered now in buttoned pockets and flexible booties. Bird Girl would make a great juggler.

The bats gather around Bird Girl like dogs at a hunt. She moves her wing-fingers and issues light, sweet whistles, to which the bats respond by helping mop up the vomit. Everything is hidden in shadow. Antags, bats, us, a couple of transports maybe thirty meters away—surrounded by gloom. No more overtones, no more clues. Bird Girl is no longer broadcasting on our private wavelength. DJ looks pale and serious. At least he's stopped spewing.

Kumar hangs on to my arm, pushing his face close. "Where are we?" he asks, eyes darting. I hope I'm not surrounded by total loons. Most of the others have been far more isolated than me. Ulyanova stares off into the shadows and doesn't once look my way.

The bats pry us apart, space us out, then hand us more ropes. After they've persuaded us to hang on, they tug and guide us out of the shaded chamber and along a curved tube. The walls of the tube are equipped every few meters with rungs that both big and small Antags use to navigate. The rungs do not seem designed for them but they're making do. Bird Girl is behind us. This phase of our journey takes about ten minutes. The tube veers sharp left, and we're pulled through the crimp with hard knocks.

The bats and one of the Antags then tug and shove us into a cubic space like a giant racquetball court, its corners also lost in shadow. All we can see clearly, in the center of the court, is a spherical cage about thirty meters in diameter, made of thick wire mesh and cabled to the side walls.

Some of the bats nicker and whistle, then poke out wing-fingers in sequence. They seem to be counting, maybe counting us. They can count to forty-eight on their fingers, should they be so inclined.

Four Antags enter the court. Bird Girl is again number three in their lineup. Two wear tunics, including Bird Girl. The others are equipped with what could be light armor, covering the breastbone and forming protective collars over the wing-shoulders.

Bird Girl surveys our pitifully reduced group. Her purple-rimmed eyes light on me, and she approaches with evident reluctance, no doubt disgusted by everything about me—certainly by my appearance and smell. Man, have we been primed to be enemies.

I look left down our rope line. We're all scarred in pink lines and scabs from the removal of the lobster suits but appear to be healing. Ishida's metal parts are lightly scored but seem intact. I wonder how they knew which parts were hers and which the suit's.

We half-bob, half-float, hanging on to the rope and to one another. Bird Girl informs us through the translator that all our cuts and bruises were due to the activities of our suits and were not deliberately inflicted by Antag healers—by which she means the bats, not just technical rates but general-duty helpers. She also confirms that we're going to be kept for the time being in the spherical cage. Her voice through the translator is edged with something like electronic bird sounds—grating, hashy, not at all soothing. But then she adds that these quarters will be temporary. The Antags are presently exploring, hoping to find better living spaces deeper in the ship.

To DJ and me she relays directly that there's something complicated about that process—something that scares her. Keepers are involved, and there's one major, nasty, foul impediment, accompanied by mental expletives of sharp bones in the throat and patches of fresh guano, applied to the only way forward, and to a gate that is also a trap—a *puzzle* gate. If we solve the puzzle, we might be able to get the hell out of here, wherever we are.

And if we don't, the obscenity will kill us.

I was under the apparently false impression that we left Titan's orbit as soon as we could, to avoid being obliterated by Box and the others sent after us—but Bird Girl seems to think we're still close to the big orange moon.

No questions allowed. Not that DJ or I try…She's worried and tired. The cage is it for us for the time being, but it could be worse—has been worse. Inside the sphere we can be fed, looked after, kept clean…and closely watched. Mats will be provided. Maybe we can wrap ourselves up and bounce around like Ping-Pong balls in a church raffle. I suppose to keep us clean they'll hose us down, right? No comment. We can exercise, Bird Girl suggests. Get stronger. She isn't sure how we'll do that, but her commanders want us strong and healthy. I get the impression the commanders are the ones wearing armor. Her relation to them is less clear—she's not exactly inferior in either station or rank. Civilian? Consultant?

Unwilling volunteer?

She makes clear that she wants *one of us* in particular to stay healthy. Again I see a naked Antag, oppressed and unkempt, but I don't recognize the human she shows me, except that it could be one of our females. Maybe a Russian? We all look alike to the Antags.

One by one, we're guided through a hatch into the cage. Ulyanova doesn't put up a fuss. Yagodovskaya, the *efreitor*—Verushka or Vera—seems to have a calming influence. The bats toss mats through the hatch, then swing it shut with a clang and click a double-stranded lock around the latch. Something to jiggle with later, to see if escape is possible.

The lights around the court dim, as if we're in a nighttime zoo. We can no longer see more than a meter beyond the mesh—can't see Antags large or small, though now and then I hear the bats nicker. Maybe most have left, gone to work, getting ready to finally go home—or to fight again. Fight their own kind. If they fail here, I suspect suicide missions are the next option. And they'll take us out to die right beside them.

At least we're not cramped. The big ball could hold dozens more. We take this time to examine one another in more detail. Tak has corpsman training, as does Jacobi. All who came out of the two surviving Oscars are here—all except Mushran. Nobody remembers seeing him after the centipede cabins were split open.

DJ moves closer to me, along with Joe and Jacobi, and we grip hands in a loose star-knot, like a parachute team. Joe pulls in Jacobi and Bilyk. Ishikawa and Tak join next and draw Ishida in. Yagodovskaya—Vera—grabs Ulyanova and they join us. Borden and Kumar and Litvinov cap our formation. We seem to want to cling like monkeys, anticipating more misery.

"We need to show some fight," Joe says, keeping a wary eye on the *starshina*. "We've been through a meat grinder. We need to show them they can't get away with treating us like shit."

"When will they feed us?" Jacobi asks.

HAMSTER LIFE

Our first sleep in the cage is deep.

I come out of my void to see Jacobi marshal her team and lead them in limbering up—another diagnostic, I think, making sure they can still fight, or at least move together in a coordinated fashion. Ishida works the hardest, complains the least. Litvinov gathers up his three Russians and does the same.

Kumar seems content to drift to a far side of the cage, where I imagine he's making plans. That's what Wait Staff do, all they're good for, right? Without Mushran, can he possibly carry on?

Joe rolls and floats up beside me, asks, "I wonder if the Antags will make us join their fight."

"They're doing everything they can to avoid a fight," I say.

DJ flaps by, ineffective at swimming or flying or whatever he's doing, and chimes in. "They're really unhappy. They've spent their whole lives training to push us off Mars and get ready to invade Earth. And now—they're giving up and planning to get the hell out."

"Fuck 'em all," Jacobi says as she bounces along the bottom of the cage.

"Just passing it along," DJ says and slides against the mesh without benefit of a mat. He grips the thick wire with his fingers and hangs on. "Some fucking hamster ball, ain't it?"

I lie back beside him, stretch out my arms, and stare toward the center of the cage. DJ joins Kumar and some of the others in pretending to sleep. Being hooked in by the tea isn't easy on either of us. I hope it doesn't leave mental scars to match the ones from our lobster suits.

There's now a faint suggestion of g-force. We seem to be accelerating. What can this ship do? What kind of maneuvering? How fast, with what kind of power?

I can't drift off. I let go of the mesh. DJ follows. Borden and DJ and I join in another daisy, gripping hands and pulling our heads almost together. Our feet impact softly against the cage.

Jacobi swings by and grabs a hand from Borden.

"What do you know about this ship?" Borden asks DJ and me.

"Not much," I say. "Bird Girl's not very consistent at keeping us informed." I tell them about the apparent connection between our Gurus and their Keepers.

"What the hell are Keepers?"

"Their Gurus," DJ concurs.

"This whole war was arranged and coached on both teams?" Jacobi says.

"We knew that," Borden says.

This sobers them, but in fact nobody seems very surprised. "Awkward communication could be to our advantage," I say.

"As the weak partners in this dance, DJ and I should listen close and hope for more embarrassing revelations."

Borden looks at us with some surprise. "Strategic thinking?" she asks. I smile, showing my teeth.

Now Joe is with us. Not many of us can sleep. "Vinnie always thinks strategically," he says.

"Whatever's out there scares the hell out of the Antags," I say. "They need to take control, but they don't know how. And it all seems to involve Keepers. Gurus. Whatever."

"Wonder if that explains where Mushran is?" Borden asks. That hadn't occurred to me, but the idea gains no traction in ignorance.

"Where are they planning to go?" Jacobi asks.

"No idea," I say.

"There's something they call Sun-Planet," DJ says, and I give him a severe look. He's getting ahead of what I'm comfortable speculating on.

"What the hell is Sun-Planet?" Borden asks.

"Still collating," I say.

"It's way out there," DJ says. "Could be Planet X."

Joe and Borden frown.

"Planet X," he says, about to launch into that story, but they raise their hands and he cuts himself off.

Do I truly understand the import of that basketball-on-felt diagram Bird Girl fed me earlier? She doesn't seem to remember Sun-Planet in any detail. She's got textbook knowledge, nothing sensual or immediate. I wonder if she's ever been there.

"Anything else?" Joe asks.

I hold back a few subliminal impressions because I'm not

sure they make sense. Antag family structure? Something important is missing, but maybe about to arrive. "They're way below strength. Maybe only thirty or forty Antags, not including the bats."

"Got that," Borden says.

"I saw some squids," Joe says. "Did you see them, too?"

"Yeah," Jacobi says. "Haven't seen them since, and I wasn't sure I saw them the first time."

"What about the hunters out here in orbit?" Borden asks. "Ours and theirs—Box and the rest?"

"Doesn't seem to be their biggest worry," I say.

To my relief, the group breaks up to return to exercising.

Every few hours, three or four bats show up with a tank and a hose and let loose a spray of water. The spray cuts a tangent across one side of the sphere. We wash in it, drink from it, or simply avoid it.

More hours. Nature takes its course.

"Dignity in the Corps!" Joe calls out. "We get to crap behind blankets."

Exactly right. Nobody's much embarrassed, but we hold up the mats for individual privacy.

After a couple of hours, the bats lob fist-sized green balls through the hatch. I grab one and bite into it. It's dry and yeasty, slightly salty, slightly sweet. The others see my tacit approval and grab their own.

The lights go down every thirty hours. That leaves those of us who are still not sleepy to cling to the mesh or bump into one another.

ROTATIONS

Jacobi specializes in light martial arts, Borden in building strength. The Russians exercise separately and keep busy trying to catch Litvinov unprepared. Our respect for the colonel grows. *Polkovnik* is equivalent to a colonel in the Skyrines. He must be twice the age of the others, especially Bilyk, a skinny but wiry opponent. Litvinov experiences a lot of bruising, some bleeding, but no broken bones, and sluices every time he gets a chance, urging his soldiers to do the same.

We need distraction and information, and for the time being nobody outside is talking and nobody or nothing within me or DJ is volunteering new facts, which I find both peaceful and like another little death. Can't put up with ignorance much longer, but Joe and Borden and Litvinov and Kumar (I think) are maintaining, and so is DJ, and so will I. But we can't maintain forever.

Still, compared to the cans, this is a real improvement.

One big question—if this isn't an Antag ship, and not a

human ship, why is there pressure, a breathable atmosphere? Who designed the lights? Who's controlling?

And how did the Antags know to dock their vessels in empty space, find that hangar, and get us on board?

Something obvious I'm just missing, and it's pissing me off.

DIVISION FOUR

Jacobi and Ishikawa take Ishida and Tak off to one wall of the cage, where they grip in a four-petal flower and quietly talk. Kumar watches from his curled position across the cage. He's saying little but tracking everything, especially Litvinov's exercises.

Then the flower breaks and Ishida crosses the perimeter of the cage. She adjusts her tack by changing her center of gravity like a circus gymnast. Impressive.

Then she spreads her arms and legs to slow her spin and glides up beside Kumar.

"Tell us about Division Four," she says. The former Wait Staffer turns his head to stare back at her, and blinks. The gouges and scars along her formerly polished body parts, added to the pink lines of withdrawn wires and other scars on her flesh, give her a fierce, tattered look that's more than a little scary.

And maybe a little sexy.

I hope we're not coming apart. I have to admit that before

we landed on Mars, and after, I thought she was kind of awesome, but none of that matters now. I just want all of us to be allowed to keep it together, stay sane, fight again.

Win this time.

Kumar seems to relax and relent. He waves for us to gather around. DJ wakes up, extends an arm, and marches with his hands along the mesh to join the condensing pack. Borden seems to materialize beside Joe. Litvinov and the Russians, including Ulyanova, arrive last.

Kumar's voice is low and hoarse. For the moment, it seems we've got back some of our cohesion—but who knows? It all depends on how much Kumar feels the need to keep us ignorant.

"None of you, possibly excepting Master Sergeant Venn, has ever met a Guru or had much to do with Wait Staff until recently—correct?" Kumar asks.

Litvinov says, "Russians give Wait Staff tours, on Mars. *Starshina* was there."

"Ah," Kumar says. "Perhaps she will contribute?"

Ulyanova doesn't react.

"The commander's hung out with you guys, hasn't she?" Jacobi asks, referring to Borden. Borden keeps her eyes on Kumar but says nothing—possibly waiting for him to reveal something she doesn't know.

"Just me, until she met Mushran," Kumar says. "She was not involved in political decisions on Earth or elsewhere until the last few months. What I am approaching, on a roundabout, is describing to you what it is like to deal with Gurus and their representatives, to carry out their orders without truly understanding their goals." He sounds as if the loss of Mushran has put all this on him and he feels the weight.

"We're listening," Jacobi says.

"Good. Listen critically," Kumar says. "I think it will soon become important."

"What do Gurus look like?" Ishida asks.

Kumar affords her another blink, then a small grin. "Do you believe I have seen them? Seen them as they really are?"

Ishida nods intently.

Borden says, "I know you've seen them."

"I, on the other hand, am not so sure," Kumar says. "The Gurus who interact most with humans are about the size of a large dog. These have four walking legs and four arms, rather like canine caterpillars. Their faces are broad, with small, sensitive ears. Their eyes are large, like a lemur's, possibly because they want us to think they're nocturnal.

"Whatever we thought we saw, it early became apparent to the more discerning Wait Staff that the Gurus are talented at creating illusions. They have shown themselves capable of altering both physical shape and how we see them. How much of what we have witnessed is in fact real, I do not know. I doubt anyone knows."

"Wait Staff fooled?" Ulyanova asks, looking up and shifting her look around the group as if to see how astonishing this might be. "You do not see from inside? Or see outside clear?"

"I am not sure what you mean," Kumar says.

She smiles her strange smile and waves her hand—continue.

"Are they ugly?" Jacobi asks.

"We never saw them so. Usually, as I said, they appear cat- or doglike, with multiple limbs but pleasant faces, evoking a certain domestic familiarity, likely to make us feel a positive connection—to establish affection."

"They look like pets," Ishikawa says.

Kumar nods. "It is the highest privilege to be in the presence of a Guru," he continues. "They evoke peace of mind, calmness, stability, loyalty. Neither Mushran nor I, nor our closest colleagues in Division Four, spent more than three years working with them. If you serve in the presence of Gurus for longer than three years, betrayal of any sort becomes unthinkable."

"But for you—thinkable?" Tak asks.

Kumar gives a small shrug. "It was Lieutenant Colonel Joe Sanchez who brought back to Earth the first Martian settler exposed to the Drifter's green dust."

"I'm right here," Joe says. Kumar looks past him, past us, like we're living through a bad haunted-house movie and Joe is one of the ghosts. He doesn't trust Joe, I think. That makes me trust Joe more—for now.

"That was five years ago," Kumar says. "The settler was smuggled past all security in ways about which I have not been informed—perhaps because I myself still do not arouse trust."

"No kidding," Jacobi says.

Kumar is unfazed. "It was this settler who first told a select few about the ancient pieces of memory buried deep in the Drifter. At first, none of us believed, it seemed so fantastical, so opposed to the history taught us by the Gurus. There was discord in the divisions, but word slowly leaked to our top leaders, and then, we presume, to the Gurus. The settler was stolen from our care. I learned later he was executed. That was our first shame, but also the first indicator of how desperate the Gurus were to keep this information away from Earth and from our fighters."

"They didn't want us to know about our origins?" I ask.

"That may have been part of their concern. But also...the knowledge that our ancestral forms on the outer moons of the solar system—"

"We call them bugs," DJ says, looking grimly serious. "That's what they were. We get used to it. Mostly." He's forcing the issue.

"That's what you see in your heads?" Borden asks.

"Yeah," DJ says.

"You?" The commander looks at me.

"Yeah," I say.

Ishida and Jacobi make disgusted faces. Ulyanova eyes the cage limits.

"The *bugs* had long ago encountered a species like the Gurus, or the Gurus themselves, and had been led by them to fight many wars."

Litvinov and the Russians jerk as if they've been poked, perhaps realizing something significant. This may be their first hint that the Antags themselves have Gurus.

"The Gurus are that old?" Ishida asks.

"It seems they are. Endless wars, millions of battles, billions of deaths, before our progenitors cleared themselves of that plague."

"It can be done," Joe murmurs.

"The bugs, as you call them, settled through the outer solar system about four and a half billion years ago. They took their wars with them. That is about the time Mars and then Earth were struck by chunks of some of their moons. We think that at that time, they were divided into rigid social classes. The Gurus aggravated these divisions and set them against one another. Very soon, the bugs began to fight to preserve class and racial mixes, to exclusively honor a certain social or family unit—or some representative philosophy. Wars over philosophy, or within families, can be the most vicious and long-lasting. Their wars under the tutelage of the Gurus may have lasted a hundred and fifty million years." He looks at me and DJ and tilts his head. "Is any of this incorrect?"

"Not so far," DJ says.

Kumar seems amused that DJ should become an expert.

"Did the bugs' Gurus share technology with them—better weapons, better ships?" Ishida asks.

"Their battles kept them mostly in the outer solar system and the Kuiper belt," Kumar says. "They did not themselves visit Mars or the Earth. But yes, they seem to have been given insights to help them—but only up to a point, a carefully selected *strategic* point. Only enough to maintain a balance between opposing forces, with occasional swings of victory and defeat. The Gurus always try to keep things *interesting*. And the bugs must have fascinated their intended audiences a great deal. We are, perhaps, only a late sequel...an afterthought." Kumar lets this sink in. "After the debriefing of three Antagonist survivors, under cover of gaining tactical knowledge about the battle situation on Mars—"

Joe won't meet my eyes. He's been in on it almost from the beginning. Always coming upon surprises, always ending up in the center of action. And only telling me when I might be useful—or if, conceivably, I might get hurt if I do not know.

"—we combined the knowledge gained from them, with the history outlined by the Muskie colonist who had been successfully exposed to Ice Moon Tea. But that was not all. Even then, we were provided with certain confirming truths by Antagonists who had reached similar conclusions, or had themselves been exposed to the green powder—like the female who speaks her mind to Master Sergeant Sanchez and Corporal Johnson. A number of these brave enemies tried to reach out and warn us. Most died at the hands of our troops—sacrificed as they tried to spread the truth.

"Mushranji sent records of these debriefings to Division One, which promptly buried them—followed by more executions. He managed to keep himself separate from all that, to play as if he were still in the camp of those fanatically devoted to the Gurus. But he carefully enlisted and informed other Wait Staff—making sure that none he approached had spent more than three years in the presence of Gurus. That they had at least a minimal chance of being persuadable.

"And soon, Mushranji had a large enough cadre of the informed and the like-minded that Division Four secretly split from the other divisions, from top politicians and administrators. Soon, we began planning and then directing operations on Mars to confirm the existence of the Drifter, its contents, and its effects on a number of other Martian settlers.

"I fear that because of our tight limits, and our failures, all of you became involved in painful confusion. We were still learning, still trying to understand how we might survive this new and growing base of unwelcome knowledge. Mushranji himself kept me in the dark, ignorant about certain matters, that I might play my part better. I hope he is not lost…"

"*Antagonista* take orders from Gurus, too," Ulyanova murmurs, again with that peculiar expression—an expression of feeling pain in a place one doesn't know one has. Her companion, Vera, sticks by her like a faithful puppy.

Litvinov looks away and says softly to her, "We knew this must be so."

"We are not special!" Ulyanova says. "So many have died to be part of special." Bilyk's glower deepens. Did he want to be special, too, or is he just reacting to the loss of friends, the end of ideals, the loss of any real reason to fight?

Tak echoes his dismay. "This has been going on for millions of years?" he asks. At Kumar's nod, his expression crumples. "What kind of evil shit is that?"

"We do not know the occasions when Gurus broadcast these wars," Kumar says. "There may have been long gaps when old species burned themselves out, like movie stars at the ends of their box-office appeal, and new species found intelligence, only to have the Gurus arrive, or revive, and recruit them."

"We're just entertainment!" Jacobi says, words sharp as flint.

"That is the truth of it, in a nutshell," Kumar says.

Quiet around the group. The big picture, even the nutshell, is more than most of us can immediately process.

"One big, bloody reality show," DJ says with a sniff. He rubs his nose, his far gaze showing the wear he has sustained. In the second Drifter, on Mars, for a time he had been truly happy. Then that, too, had been taken from him and destroyed—by Jacobi and her team. And now we may be about to lose Bug Karnak, the ancient archive, and our steward.

Ishikawa says, "What I want to know is, who's paying the cable bills?"

Nobody feels like laughing. What I feel like is punching my fist into something until it's mush. Finding out over and over again how much of a sucker you've been, what your real place is in this nasty old world, is something Skyrines and other fighters should be used to…

But having my life and death, my relations with friends and enemies, the saving and the loving and the hating and the killing…

Having that spread around and *laughed* at, commented on by Guru audiences, *critiqued* like a TV show—

"Are we sure this is all on the level?" Jacobi asks, looking past the others at Joe. Joe shifts their attention adroitly, with a nod, to me, with the evaluative expression I've always hated. The same expression he used when we first met on that concrete culvert. The same expression he used before we went to take care of Grover Sudbury.

He wants me to answer.

And God damn us both, I do. "It's real," I says. "As real as anything in this fucked-up life."

"Who's seen the broadcast? The cable feed?" Jacobi asks. "Whatever the hell you call it."

"I may have," Kumar says. "It is what finally pushed me into Mushranji's camp in Division Four."

"Where did you see it?" Litvinov asks.

"In a Guru domicile in Washington, D.C.," Kumar says. "A door alarm failed and I entered without being noticed. I saw a room filled with war, and in the center, like an orchestra conductor, a Guru who looked human. It noticed me and quickly changed shape, then tried to wipe my mind of this memory, but apparently that failed as well."

"They're not perfect," Joe says.

"No," Kumar says with regret. "I almost wish they were."

"What was it?" Ishida asks him. "What was the show?"

"Fighting between Oscars and Antagonist weapons on

Titan. Spectacular, fully involving—looking at it, just from the corner of my eye, I was there. It took me days to recover."

This is still sinking in for the others. Loss of illusions is a long, hard process, and Kumar has not been the man we've trusted the most.

"They're actually *broadcasting a show*?" Ishida asks in disbelief. "Broadcasting from where? What kind of antennas— *to* where? How do we even ask the right questions?"

Kumar says, "It is the belief of the people within Division Four, and it is my belief, that the signals begin in your suits and are edited locally, to be delivered by some means—perhaps this ship—to the outer limits of the solar system to be sent on their way. We have yet to confirm any of that, however. I must emphasize, the Antagonists on this ship seem to be part of that group fighting and dying to change things. Analogous to the group of us that Mushranji helped create and organize— and supply."

"Antags still hate our guts," Jacobi says.

"Also true," Kumar says. "But they have sacrificed many in their own civil war, and many more fighting to save us. I hope we will soon learn their final disposition."

"There's a word for what they're doing, the Gurus, living off blood and misery," Tak says. "They're blood-sucking parasites, like mosquitoes."

"Worse," Borden says. "Mosquitoes need to eat. This is war porn. Who is out there, caring not a damn, getting off when we fly to our deaths—paying to see!"

I'm fascinated by the change in her features. This is no longer the disciplined, all-together commander we've come to expect. This is a frightened, angry mother, disgusted by what someone is doing to her children.

"We used to think the aliens would be like angels, or like demons," Kumar says. "I was raised on those fantasies. But Gurus are neither. They are in show business—arranging to get us to kill each other in ingenious and protracted ways to provide entertainment for heartless armchair rats."

"Jee-zuss!" Jacobi exclaims. She's dug her nails into her hands.

DJ says quietly, "We're no angels, either. Snug kids and their mommas and poppas eat dinner in front of the TV and watch us die on the evening news. Leaders push their causes over our mangled corpses. Civilians get off on our dying and blood and salute us in airports. Gurus didn't show up and recruit us until recently, right?"

Kumar doesn't know how or even whether to answer.

"We're perfect for this shit," DJ says, flicking his sharp eyes between us. "Doesn't matter what you call it—it's been going on for thousands of years. I read the *Iliad*." He waves his long fingers, arms still marked with red lines. "Happy little soldiers, paid rich in blood and shit and sometimes even respect." He snaps one of those akimbo civvie salutes. Having finished this tirade, packed with far more eloquence than we are used to from DJ, he folds his arms and looks through the mesh as a couple of bats bring up a hose.

"What do we do when we get out there?" Ishida asks, also tracking the bats.

"If," Tak says.

"Out where the Antags live. Will they let us fight with them, let us help clean this up and put it right?"

There it is. Our team wants to fight some more. I wonder if this was Kumar's plan all along.

"What's it like out there?" Ishikawa asks.

"Venn? What do you get from your connection?" Jacobi asks. I shake my head. DJ seems ready to leap in, but I give him a hard look. Right now, we're in limbo, but judging from what little I've been fed, we're going to have to get used to a whole new scale of weird. And I don't want to add to anyone's confusion, not now.

"What kind of worlds are they from? What do they look like?" Jacobi persists, as if they still might trust me or DJ to know the score.

"It's confused," I say.

"Fuck that!" Jacobi says. "We need to know." But she's barely whispering and her expression has lost focus. Then, as if they've reached their limit, they all break loose and scatter across the cage. Some gather mats and wrap up in them.

The bats look on in confusion. Are they supposed to spray the mats, as well? They nicker and knock on the cage, as if to warn us. We ignore them.

Joe pulls me and Litvinov and Borden together. "We can't keep on like this, on the inside with a view to nowhere. Can you pass that along to the Antags?"

Litvinov looks around at our scattered survivors. "We are not crazy minks in trap," he says. "Tell them *that*."

"I've been trying," I say. "It's not exactly a two-way street."

"What do you get from Bug Karnak?" Joe asks.

I've been wondering about that myself. "Nothing much," I say. The last few hours there's been something peculiar about our circumstances, about this ship, that is either blocking the steward or making it go silent—withhold judgment. Or the signal is simply losing its strength. Maybe we're already too far away.

Or…

What I've been dreading—the destruction of the archives—may be well under way.

"What about DJ?" Joe asks.

Borden says, "He's been dealing with this since Mars."

Ishikawa passes close on a personal Ping-Pong exercise from one side of the cage to the other. "Heads up," she says. "Twelve beady little eyes."

From a dark corner of the racquetball court, well outside the cage, three larger Antags have joined the confused bats to silently observe. We rotate as best we can off each other, off the cage mesh, an awkward low-g ballet, to face them. I recognize Bird Girl.

Her translator rasps and hisses. "Choose three," she says, focused on me. And then she adds, through our connection, an image of the one she especially wants—a surprise. Or maybe not. "We are leaving Saturn."

"We'd all like to have a look," I call out.

It takes her a few seconds to respond.

Everyone in the cage is at full alert.

"Others see later. Choose three," she repeats, and I feel another something brush the inside of my head, a deeper inquiry—but also a kind of reassurance. Bird Girl believes her fellow Antags are slowly coming to understand the trauma they've caused us and to believe it might be counterproductive.

Litvinov says grimly, "Old debts still need paying. How long?"

Joe says to me in an undertone, "Be careful." I know what he means. The shape we're in, our people may conclude I'm selecting the first three to be dumped into space. I don't like being put in such a position, but I drift and climb around the cage and pick DJ, Borden—and Ulyanova. Borden because equality in our fate seems the right tone. Ulyanova because hers was the face Bird Girl showed me.

When I'm done, the others look relieved—all but Joe, who seems severely pained—then move away from us four and from one another like drops of water on oil to grip the limits of the cage.

Had I not received the *starshina*'s image, I would not have picked her. There's more going on with her, inside her, than I can fathom. I might feel a connection to that weirdness, but without reason or explanation. Or rather—scattered shards of explanation, which do not, unassembled, take any satisfactory shape.

The hatch opens in the mesh cage and the four of us pass through, Ulyanova last. Vera clasps her hand, then reluctantly lets her go.

Bird Girl extends with her wingtip hand another rubbery rope about ten meters long. With a shake, she indicates all of us should take hold. Then she and her companions move out ahead, drafting us out of the racquetball court and into another long, curved hallway.

Being in this ship is like living in a gigantic steel heart—or intestine. That's it. We're literally in the bowels of the ship.

Borden grimaces as she bounces off the tube. Ulyanova continues to look as if we're all being led to the gallows.

"Pretty obvious where this ship will be going," DJ says, gripping the chain and rotating slowly around an axis through his sternum. "What else is out there but Planet X?"

I ignore him for the moment. I'm getting signals again.

Bug steward is sending more tantalizing, brief snippets. Things are changing rapidly down on Titan—nothing good.

"No, really!" DJ insists to nobody's stated objection. This is his chance. "What else? They've been looking for it since the nineteenth century. It was what pushed astronomers to discover Neptune, but Neptune was weird...tilted over and shit. So they looked for Planet X again and found Pluto. But Pluto was too small!"

Borden can't get the rhythm of our movement through the tube. "I'm more concerned about where we're going right now," she says, teeth chattering.

"But that's the big kahuna! The Antags call it Sun-Planet."

Borden looks to me as the rope torques us about. We bounce and correct. "You've heard that?"

"Yeah."

"Their Sun-Planet is Planet X?"

"Of course it is!" DJ says. "It swoops down every few hundreds of thousands of years and scatters moons and stuff like billiard balls."

Borden drills me with her eyes. "You did not mention any of this!"

"None of it's confirmed," I say.

"If *she* tells you something, shows you something, give it to me and Kumar!"

"Sure," I say, and she's right. DJ also looks apologetic. Knowing when to divulge and what to divulge is a real art form in this situation and around this crew.

And there's worse to come. I just can't put the fragments together, not yet. But I'm keeping my eye on Ulyanova because Bird Girl chose her, and because I sense she's at the center of everything about to happen. I just can't figure out why.

The tube widens and the Antags have more freedom to keep us from bumping and bouncing. Our trip goes on for more long minutes, time enough for me to get bored.

I remember the nighttime lectures under the amazing skies of Socotra that seemed to dwarf both the ocean and the island. The DIs had brought in a crew of professors and they were trying to convert a bunch of grunts into stargazers. Pleasant memory, actually. That's when DJ became fascinated with the idea of Planet X. Maybe he's always been the prescient one.

Ulyanova crawls up the chain and grips my arm. "I feel someone!" she says. "Is not right, is strange!"

"Yeah," DJ says. "You don't know it yet, but you're one of us."

Borden looks back at him, lip curled. More stuff not reported?

"How?" the *starshina* asks.

"Were you ever exposed to the green dust inside the Drifters?" DJ asks.

She frowns. "Possible," she says. "Help pick up bodies."

"Welcome to the club," he says. "See things?"

Ulyanova frowns again, shakes her head. She's lying. But how, and why?

And why does Bird Girl care?

We reach the open end of one tube and emerge on one side of an aggressively amazing space. It takes a few confused seconds to process what we're seeing.

Big ship indeed.

A wide curved landscape stretches beneath us, rising on

two axes to a central shaft maybe half a klick away, itself a hundred meters thick. The curved surface butts up against the shaft and then smoothly spirals around it, like the surface of a screw or the inside of a shell. No way of knowing how many turns the spiral makes, or how long the shaft is, but what we can see, upper surface and lower, is coated with a carpet of bushy green, red, and brown vegetation. Enclosing this giant spiral is a blank, almost featureless outer wall. The way the lighting concentrates on the screw itself is mysterious—no obvious source and very little scatter against that surrounding wall.

Ulyanova makes a growling sound and taps her head, as if to knock some wiring back in place.

"Oxygen processing?" Borden asks.

"Or a big salad bowl," I say.

"What do Antags eat?" Borden asks, as if we'd know.

DJ just squints as if thinking hurts.

Our escorts tug on the rubbery rope and pull us up close, then point their wingtips at a rail running around the outer edge of the screw. From around the long curve comes an open car, empty, automated. It stops right beside us.

Bird Girl suggests we all climb in and hang on to the straps. We do that. Then, without a jerk, just smooth acceleration, the car whisks us around the long spiral of the screw's edge—forward, I think, toward the prow of this monstrous ship. Our progress is leisurely. These cars may be made for bringing in the crops or carrying farmers—not for mass transit.

"We're being kept in the back of the bus," Borden says. "Aft of sewage treatment or whatever this is."

Bird Girl turns, her four eyes glittering, and says, "Not

shit. Not food." Through our link, she's trying to convey something about this ship, but to me it's a muddle, and I doubt DJ has a clue.

Here it is again—the difficulty of meshing the ways our brains work. We may be relatives, but we haven't been connected socially or biologically for ever so long—maybe for as long as there's been complex life on Earth. There's another conflict as well, an invisible fight to receive and act on information while we're losing one of our most important sources.

Bug Karnak is shrinking. Our links are fading, dying.

I look at the endless acres of whatever sort of growth or crop rises along the spiraling curve.

"Are they trying to speak something?" Ulyanova asks. "I do not feel it right."

Beats us all. None of us feels it right.

OUTER OF OUTERS

In fifteen or twenty minutes—no helms, no timekeepers of any sort, how are we supposed to know how long things take?—the transport has wound us fourteen times around the screw and never a difference, never a change—reddish, brownish, greenish broccoli-like bushes. Not food. Not for air. Not to suck up shit and process it.

Like DJ and Borden, and maybe Ulyanova, who has this puzzled look all the time now, watching the inner shaft and the acre after acre of broccoli…we're getting hypnotized.

Then we slow. The rail frees itself from the screw's edge and lofts over the brushy surface, and for the first time I notice there's no new upper surface; we're nearing the end of this particular line and we're still nearly weightless. If the ship is moving somewhere, it's accelerating at no more than a few percent g.

At the end of the screw is an inverted dome, also featureless—gray and smooth. The Antags do not get out of the transport, so we hang on while it rolls for a couple of hundred more meters. The center shaft of the screw gardens passes up and maybe through that dome, but before the shaft and dome join, there's a hole in the shaft's side—no hatch, just a hole. We enter that hole and with a sigh and a jerk, as if hitting a bumper, the transport comes to a halt in darkness.

The Antags—visible to us now only as shadows—swing away and tug on our cord. More cords and cables have been stretched from the darkness above to a few meters below the transport, and we are encouraged by gestures and Bird Girl's brief screechy words to climb into a deeper darkness. Antags seem to love darkness. Maybe that's why they have four eyes. They're used to darkness and night, or dark ocean.

Ulyanova stays close to me. Borden stays close to DJ. Three of us with some sort of connection, but one deaf and almost completely blind to the greater messaging of Ice Moon Tea. Borden's wondering why she's been allowed to come this far with us, the *special* ones. Why Bird Girl chose her. Really, it's because *I* chose her. There's something about her we need right now, a steadfastness and stability, perhaps a lack of imagination. Because things are about to get really strange.

I have to ask myself if Borden knew even at Madigan, even before I came back from Mars, that Ice Moon Tea was important, that some of us were going to be crucial and had to be saved. Well, there's one more of us now. One down, Kazak—and one up, maybe. Ulyanova. Balance of forces. Not for the first time do I wish that Coyle was still around, still explaining, still bitching. Bird Girl can't seem to explain the most important things in ways I understand, and we're both tangential to the information contained in Bug Karnak…

Which is melting away like a sand castle at high tide. "Inquire" indeed. After being hidden from the Gurus for so many eons, maybe it'll just wash out with the roaring tsunami of human and Antag forces down on Titan—and leave us literally dumb.

And what's about to be revealed is frankly horrifying. It may save us, but at what cost? Assembling the same fragments in his own head, DJ's starting to look faintly unhinged, even more lost and puzzled than Ulyanova.

Ahead lies a great circle of seven circular openings, each maybe thirty meters across. The Antags pull us through the closest and then draft us another hundred meters—until the gloom brightens. I think we've been corkscrewed around the outer diameter of this part of the ship, but how they knew which opening to choose, and why, is still a mystery.

Sunlight glimmers through transparent slits that rise for several dozen meters along the outer wall, showing us that here the ship's hull is exposed to space. The Antags jerk hard and our cables curl into loops, then grow taut again, as we pass into another large chamber, this one stranger than the last. It contains a series of great, dark soccer balls, wrapped in a conical net…

We're pulled sharply outboard into a long, cathedral-like side chamber with dark gray tiers but no seats—a big, bizarre medical theater. For all its size, only three other Antags occupy the tiers, spaced out, separate, as if they bought different tickets or don't like one another. They watch us closely with glittering gray- and green-rimmed eyes.

My attention turns to the apparent reason we're here. Bird Girl is fulfilling her promise. Behind us as we entered, but quickly dominating, this weird theater opens wide to a direct portal at least sixty meters high. Beyond the portal slowly moves the orange and tobacco-colored ball of Titan. This confirms what we already did not doubt, that we're in orbit and maybe about to shove off.

Titan at great leisure slides clockwise out of view. The spaceship is rotating. Beautiful, but I've seen it before. I look back at the tiers. The Antags, all but Bird Girl, are wearing light armor. I sense the three in the gallery are not happy we're here. Not happy about any of this. I get from Bird Girl that these are important individuals, the equivalent of commanders or generals—one might even be a commander in chief of this particular combat theater. And the reason they're here is that Bird Girl is being put on a kind of trial. They're judging her. They're judging *us*.

But she has power over them. How?

We hear far-off booming noises, liquid noises, and then a kind of buzz-saw thrumming whine that sets my teeth on edge—hard to imagine in a ship so large. We've rotated far enough that we can see a broad curve of Saturn's rings, then Saturn itself—too large to fit inside even this theater's broad view.

Another round of liquid noises and again the distant buzzing. The important, silent Antags reveal neither surprise nor appreciation, hardly any indication they're alive. Tight discipline. I doubt they've ever spent more than a few minutes in the presence of humans, and that in quick, nasty combat.

But right now I don't give a shit about protocol or Antag feelings. I'm impressed all over again by what lies beyond the window. I've seen it before but never presented this way, and I'm still capable of awe. The rings and the immense yellow and gold gas giant cradled within are mesmerizing. The light on the rings, intersected by the planet's shadow, reminds me of the shine off old vinyl records. Even though the rings are hundreds of thousands of klicks away, I can make out the braids formed by tiny moonlets navigating between the larger rings. Skips in the record—God's favorite songs, played over and over.

Across its visible surface, Saturn shows incredible, subtle detail—faded pastel yellow bands, storms big and small revealing brown depths, an overall softening haze that seems to end abruptly against the blackness of space. Beyond the curve of night, thunderstorms light up the murk. Some flashes are bright enough to compete in daylight. I wonder that anything could ever survive down there. Maybe it hasn't—ever or now. The ocean moons make even more sense as the origin of life.

Bird Girl sticks out a wing and draws our attention away from Saturn, away from the gallery, and with a little flourish, toward her. The longest, claw-tipped finger at the wingtip moves along her beak, almost to her eyes, and she has our full attention—but why? What's she up to?

Borden tracks our former enemies like a rabbit watching a circling hawk.

Slowly, like a magician, with the inboard hand of her opposite limb Bird Girl raises a long object like a cheerleader's baton. First she touches and then twists a round knob, four eyes shifting. She points again to her eyes, then to my eyes, then to Ulyanova's, then back to hers.

"Four, two," the translator rasps.

Bird Girl draws an X in the air. The knob lights up and projects doubled ghosts. Our eyes aren't easy targets for Antag displays—four into two. She then covers half of the knob with stretchy tape.

Finally, she lifts her left wingtip finger, shapes an oval in the air, and into that oval the knob projects a map of the outer solar system—Uranus and Neptune beyond Saturn, then, beyond Neptune, a long void, followed by a brief, grazing flyby of Pluto and its moons, then outward farther still—across a seemingly endless gulf, empty but for unimaginably distant clouds of stars.

The image swirls to show us the receding solar system, the sun alone bright, the rest indicated by arrows and orbits. This display has now taken us too far out to see most of the planets.

We watch, transfixed, as Bird Girl sweeps us all in a long, long arc over what lies beyond the diffuse region of dust and moonlets and comets beyond Pluto—chunks of primordial ice spread thinner than mosquitoes on a winter lake, most of the chunks no bigger than gravel (I think, it's hard to guess and impossible to read) or even a grain of sand, but some are truly massive—great dark spheres hiding in deep space, more than a hundred billion kilometers from the sun; many times the size of Jupiter but not cold and apparently still too small and dark to attract the attention of Earth.

Then the view moves out farther still to circle a black void, a shadow-haunted world scribed by reddish map lines, five times more massive than Jupiter and ten times the diameter, its density far less than water—like a great cosmic balloon. A balloon with a nuclear core. I can almost feel that unborn star pulsing at the heart of this monstrosity, this enigma—this impossible thing.

Planet X.

If that really is the Antag home world, they're not interstellar visitors. They're near neighbors, astronomically speaking. They've apparently been out there all along and we on Earth never noticed.

"That is ours," Bird Girl says. "That is our life. We will not get there without you."

Borden is ignoring the documentary and studying the view, frowning deeply, a common expression for our commander. "Where's our pursuit?" she murmurs.

Good question. We seem to be alone out here, facing no obvious threats, yet all along we've been harassed by both sides, intent on wiping us out with all our knowledge.

"She's trying to tell us—" I begin, but Borden is having none of this. She covers my mouth with her hand.

"Think, goddammit! Why are they taking so long to get the hell out of here? Ask her!" she insists.

The translator works for any of us, but no sense adding to the confusion. "Where are the other ships?" I ask. "Why are we waiting?"

The translation is quick. A bristly outer layer like soft porcupine quills rises around Bird Girl's wing-shoulders and the back of her head. She looks behind us at the distributed trio up in the tiers. The Antag commanders issue melodious commands and then, with all the dignity they can muster, not much in my eyes at least, flap their limbs and depart through a forward, funnel-like exit.

Bird Girl stays with us—banished to our company. "We have no quick danger," she says through the translator. "But we do not control. We cannot leave yet."

"What does that mean?" Borden asks.

"We do not control."

Borden gives me a sharp look, as if this is my fault and I've been deficient all along. "How can they not control their own ship?" she asks.

"Others do not see this ship," Bird Girl says. "No other ship will attack."

"Jesus!" DJ says. "It's been in my head all along! I've been an idiot!"

Sometimes it's difficult to tell Bug Karnak's data dumps from memories of bad dreams, and the steward has not always been helpful in laying down boundaries between the two. But now it's becoming more and more clear—

We've been clued in, through fragments waiting for our need, for our necessity, to join up, to take shape, and the shape they finally assume is a confirmation that this large ship is very old, and tinged with menace and uncertainty—a dire, ancient bug memory that can only be labeled "Guru."

"This is Keeper ship," Bird Girl confirms. "Dark to our forces and yours. We have taken Keepers prisoner and brought them here. One knows *her*." She points a mid-wing digit at Ulyanova. "They were joined on Mars. Together, they can help us guide ship home."

We turn our unwelcome attention to the *starshina*, the stern-faced, serious young woman with hardly a clue to what she really is. But now my own fragments are starting to come together. The instaurations, the meeting at Madigan, something behind the observation mirror implanting and perverting me...

I know at least a little about what could be inside our *starshina*, tormenting *her*.

"You're the one?" DJ asks with comic wonder, like he's discovered the punch line to a joke in a stack of playing cards. "You've been linked to a Guru! Jesus...How can that happen? They used tea on both of you?"

Ulyanova draws her shoulders square and cocks her

head as if listening to a conversation in a distant room. "Did not know…" She's frightened by her own doubt. "Not my choice!"

"Maybe not," DJ says. "But if it's true, it's worth at least a couple of pay grades."

"Venn!" Borden insists. "What the hell are we facing?"

"Bird Girl could be right," I say.

"*Could* be? We were told the Gurus didn't have ships anywhere near this big. And how the hell could Antags find, much less board a Guru ship?" She diverts her anger to Bird Girl, whose quills barely shift. Borden's voice has become shrill, and realizing this, she pulls back and swallows hard. "What in hell have I got us into?"

"I've been asking myself the same question," I say.

Titan rotates back into view, looking like lumpy pastry dough stirred by a huge stick. Massive disturbances are taking shape in the orange and tobacco overcast. The centers of the disturbances open to reveal huge cracks in Titan's surface. Through those cracks rise flashes of blue and orange, impossibly bright, impossibly large. Our diminishing communication with the steward, our shrinking connection with Bug Karnak, makes awful sense.

Bird Girl winks with her outboard pair of eyes, which I assume means, do we feel it, too? The loss?

We do.

Together, our forces and the Antags—those still under Guru influence—are grinding through Titan's icy shell and churning the deep oceans, finishing the destruction of Bug Karnak. In all our heads, the steward DJ and I and had almost come to know, to anticipate and expect, to rely upon, is dying by falling chunks and increasing silences. Subjects are winking out. Untapped potentials are marked as blanks, then simply closing up, going away.

In Fresno, I once watched a library burn and tried to feel the pain of the books, the loss of their stories—the loss of my mom reading those books to me. I couldn't. Now, I do.

It hurts.

Bird Girl's translator addresses Ulyanova. "You must show us how to go through puzzle gate, how to reach ship's control, or all ends."

Ulyanova hasn't had much time to feel the potential of her connection. She and DJ and I are points on a polygon. How many points there are, ultimately, I don't know.

Bird Girl raises a small ridge of soft quills and elegantly ripples her wings a full beat. Then she rises to the funnel-shaped exit and jerks on our rope, which we're gripping like a lifeline.

And away we go.

But not before we get one last broad look at Titan, lightning lancing from cloud to cloud—dust and volcanic plumes of water and ice being swept under by a dense shroud of heated gas.

"Gawd almighty," DJ says, wiping away tears, moving his lips in prayer at the end of what we had never really understood in the first place: the influence of the archives. Our links with the liaisons and the steward. The wisdom of the bugs.

Our reason for being out here.

AFTER KARNAK

Bug Karnak didn't have time to contribute much to our info about this vessel, only that parts of it looked familiar and that the bugs may have encountered similar vessels once upon a time—might know more about them and tell us more about them if we simply observe more, exchange more—help the fragments come together.

As for getting more information from bug steward—

That's no longer possible.

I'm not sure if it's an actual shock or just another bloody brick in a wall of cruelty and confusion, but we've been dragged to another cube-shaped racquetball court and another round cage suspended by cables.

There are people inside this cage. Or rather, they were people once. A sour, stale smell tells us all we need to know about their present condition.

Bird Girl tugs on the rope, making us loop around each other. We swing past the cage. Inside are clumps of tangled mummies, black and brown and gray. As Bird Girl warned us, based on the evidence clumped in this identical trap, we're not the only humans on board, but we may be the only live ones.

Borden absorbs the view with a darkening of her face that could be prelude to a heart attack, but I know it's just more rage—rage pumped up and then barely suppressed by discipline and training. All along, since she sprang me from Madigan, I've had a difficult time figuring the commander. That may be because for Borden it's not so much honor and duty but closeted fury that keeps her going. An urge to vengeance. And not vengeance on our former enemies. There are people and *things* back home she's gunning for.

Borden hates Gurus. I pity them all, despite the strong suspicion that none of us will ever see Earth again.

More important to our fate, if the *starshina* is part Guru, how much longer can she stay human, stay useful to the Antags?

"How many are there?" DJ asks. We try to tally but it's not easy. The bodies are in bad shape, and not just from decay. They appear to have died while engaged in desperate hand-to-hand. Biting. Rending. Ripping. Severed, shriveled limbs drift slowly across the cage, along with blackened scraps. Some of the bodies are still tied in combat knots, limbs embracing torsos, fingers tight around necks, wrestling holds so much like coitus—others, just plain inexplicable. Last-ditch. Chaotic. Most still wear clothes, pants and shirts dark with old blood. Shoes are not in evidence. A few of the scraps have escaped the mesh. We bat at them with instinctive grunts of pity and disgust.

"Seventy or eighty," I guess.

DJ covers his nose and mouth with one hand, keeping his other hand on the knotted rope. Borden is beyond expression but her body is stiff and her jaw waxen.

"Didn't they feed them?" Ulyanova asks, but I doubt they were trying to eat one another. A few, I see, are draped with banners or ribbons covered with symbols I can't read. Maybe they had all been pressed into some sort of competition, strong against weak—and the Gurus handed out prizes.

"No women," Ulyanova says. "Maybe all men."

"How can you tell?" DJ asks. "Not much of the fun parts left."

She gives him a perplexed look.

"Did Antags kill them?" he asks, but we already know better. These poor bastards were put in a cage and left to their own devices until the fighting made them too weak to live. The Gurus could have recorded their combat and their agonies. Makes sense if this is a Guru ship. Plenty of studio space. Plenty of program opportunities.

Wonder who was the last one and what he was thinking, and how long he lasted after he'd won and the fighting was over?

Ulyanova looks startled. "Getting stronger!" she says.

Whatever she's hearing isn't coming from either of us or the steward. Those signals have faded to nothing. Bug Karnak is blown to bits, melted down, buried in ice and Titan's interior magma. What the *starshina*'s hearing seems to be from a source much nearer—but we have no idea how all this works.

Ulyanova swings close. "*Antagonista* are frightened!" she whispers. "No control, no way out…and something wild bad up front."

Borden's darkness has gone pale. Her jaw juts. Our prospects aren't improving. What if Gurus were and are still smarter than bugs? Could they reverse the whole weird, tricky process? Like turning a telescope around.

Are they already looking at *us* through Ulyanova?

A WORLD OF SHIT,
WITH RAZOR BLADES

The three ranking Antags wait for Bird Girl to catch up. We've gathered the looping cable between us and clump about three meters behind her. So far we've managed to avoid bumping into structural elements—columns, beams, bulkheads, all smoothly sculpted, no signs of manufacture or refinement, like surfaces in a computer rendering.

"Big fucking ship," DJ says, belaboring the obvious. "But we're still back in the tail. Maybe we just passed the asshole."

The translator renders this for Bird Girl. A sidewise glance from her two inner eyes is her only response. Blessedly, we're beyond the corpse smell. The air here is smooth and cool.

Slow as always, I mull over another obvious data point: Gurus breathe terrestrial air, at terrestrial pressure, even on their own ship—even way out here. Is this their native atmosphere? At the very least it's what they suck in while they're here, and that makes the ship human and Antag compatible...

But what do Gurus breathe when they're at home?

Do Gurus *have* a home?

And now that the ship is infested by Antags and humans, can it flush out the good air and pipe in the bad, can it fumigate to get rid of us like rats? Or is that too blunt and obvious? After all, how interesting is extermination without conflict, without pitting us against one another? Without cages and corpses and shit?

Fuck the inquiring mind. I do not want to know.

We emerge from another tunnel into a doubly curved chamber, like being inside a big, rope-cinched eggshell. The light here has no obvious source and is orangey-peach in color. At the egg's large end, blocking any obvious path forward, is a round black plate about six meters across, sectioned in thirds through the middle. The most grizzled-looking of the Antag commanders, whom otherwise I can't tell apart—no visible signs of rank on their light armor—folds its wings tightly to its body, lower hands clasping. The others follow this one's lead, including Bird Girl. She's waiting for a decision. After several minutes, one of the Antags musics some words, which the translator picks up and returns with rough overtones as, "This is difficult place. Many reasons not all are brought here. May cause disease."

"Illness," Bird Girl corrects. "We cannot go forward and take control until we pass through a puzzle. The puzzle changes. When we do not look correctly, do not solve, the gate will not let us through. If there is no going through, we stay until we die. No other place to go now."

"All righty!" DJ says, waving his hand and splaying his fingers as if weaving a protective spell. Not much reserve left for DJ and I doubt there's much in either Borden or Ulyanova. How much for me?

An Antag commander approaches the "gate." The others

hang on to its lower hands, as if it might be sucked through. At a slap of a wingtip hand, the gate opens in six parts that withdraw into the bulkhead. At first, through the gate I see only gray uncertainty. Then the gray area acquires a spiky focus. A geometric, weedy growth spirals out around the edges, bulging toward us with thorny fingers.

I think of showering after gym class in high school, in the echoing tile washroom, sitting on a damp aluminum bench, when I tried to simulate druggy experience by pressing an index finger against the sides of my eyeballs. But that was juvenile shit. This is real. This is messing with my brain, maybe with my soul.

The patterns inside the gate become simpler and solid, as if the puzzle has learned who and what we are, how we see, how we think, and has isolated the most effective way to entrance or confuse us.

This pattern leaves perverted afterimages.

And then—

Having found our nature and our weakness, what lies beyond becomes a tortured maze of the nastiest crap I hope to never encounter again, and I've become part of it—trapped, strung out on machines with steel teeth that chew me open and then retreat to allow dancing steel arms with needle and thread to stitch me back together before I bleed out.

I see all of us stuffed into big iron caskets like iron maidens, filled with sharpened spikes—not much worse than the suits we had to wear on Titan, but then...

Yeah, they're worse.

DJ is twitching, neck corded, struggling to look aside, but he can't. Ulyanova I can't see—she's drifting behind me and, caught in more ways than one, I refuse to turn away from the gate. Winding nests of razor-scaled serpents dart forward to grab my head. I'm dying, but I should already be dead. Somehow, even in the middle of my horror, I think: *You crazy bastard, you're pegging at around seven—can't you ramp it up to eleven?*

Never taunt an evil genius, right?

Gurus like it interesting.

The puzzle gets personal. Skyrines and Antags are now personally tearing my flesh. There's Joe, Tak, Ishida—and even Kazak, dead Kazak, teeth buried in my stomach. Pain isn't enough. The gate plays with every human fear great and small: of being broken or isolated or eaten, a great shrieking chaos of *You'll never breathe again, you'll never eat again, you'll never fuck again, you'll be lost and nobody will ever find you, and if they do, you won't care because there's so much pain, and worse, you're crazier than clockwork apeshit and now you're laughing, watching your fellow Skyrines join you in a never-ending hell—*

And if such images can have physical overtones beyond the pain and the shock, here they are: the sense that everything in one's body is about to fail, piece by piece, causing not just pain but deep uncertainty, and maybe it's already happening or has already happened—

Worse than any instauration, because this one stabs in and hooks forward the socially outcast, the living who are worse than dead, who will shit their pants and soil their souls and *embarrass* themselves and all who know them and love them, simply by failing in form and duty.

Combine that with the mincemeat grinders and the hooks and the flaying—

And the overall impression that it will all go away, all be

forgotten, if only *we turn on one another and fight and kill*! I can have everything back, my youth, my innocence, freedom from pain, a young, whole body—if only I fight.

All will be forgiven.

My God, that has real power. That reaches eleven. My hands form claws. Borden has curled up like a pill bug. I hear DJ growling like an angry cat, but Ulyanova keeps quiet. I've rotated enough to see her face, a paleness waiting to be smashed—I reach for her—

Bird Girl jerks hard on our cable. We cannot keep our eyes on the gate. The Antags close the hatch. It's over. They haven't been caught up, not this time, leaving us ignorant humans to bear the brunt. Borden is still tucked up in a tight ball. DJ and I cling to each other.

The nightmare inside the gate was completely convincing to us—but not to the *starshina*. She licks her lips. She's into it. She's ready for a change. What did the gate promise her? Life as a Russian soldier, as a Skyrine, is total misery, and now she's seen her way clear to being special and in control. A fucking awful transformation, but I see it in her eyes. Already she's thinking like a Guru.

"Four of our own have tried to enter this gate," Bird Girl says, and passes us impressions of bloody pieces being returned. "Not just illusion. Death trap. Deadly, killing puzzle." Now she addresses Ulyanova directly. "Tell us what we must do, how we must think, to pass through."

The *starshina* wipes her forehead and inspects her palm, as if she might have mopped more than sweat. She turns to DJ and me. "There are Gurus here—I feel them! They are unhappy and weak. They believe they will die." Her English has improved. What sort of expertise can she access now? She looks up, aside. "They do not mind dying, but are surprised and angry I see into them. They did not expect that—ever.

"And now we must meet, no?"

DJ looks at her in abject wonder, then at me. We're still sweating like worms on a griddle.

Bird Girl tugs us back from the closed gate. "We go to see Keeper," she says, and points her wingtip at Ulyanova.

The *starshina* seems to suddenly spark. Whatever's inside her, whatever has combined with her, is making its first moves. She addresses Bird Girl in Russian. The translator hashes and wheeps back English, then Antag. "To do this, to finish it, I am in charge," she says. "You will show me to *Antagonista* who looks into Gurus. All my comrades will see, and all of you will see, because gate will kill if we do not go through at once. Understood?"

"Understood," Bird Girl says.

The Antags have their own Guru mimic.

More sides to the polygon.

GHOSTS, DEAD PEOPLE, AND THINGS THAT NEVER WERE

Bird Girl and the ranking Antags escort us into another access pipe that extends quite a long ways aft through the ship, opening into a chamber that has the benefit, for us, of not being excessively changeable or excessively large. On one side of the chamber, outboard, maybe not too far from the first racquetball court and our hamster cage, is a makeshift hangar where three smaller vessels have been parked—not the same as the larger transports that brought us here, more like orbital fighter craft, suspended in a web of rubbery cables that keep them from bumping. A few Antags in that hangar are busy winging from ship to ship. And finally, we see a squid. Mostly the same as I remember through the foggy walls of our liquid-filled tank on the first transport up from Titan—squidlike in some aspects, but arranged like a catamaran, two grayish-pink bodies with four or five arms each linked by a kind of bridge—but not in water, not this time, and not floppy like you'd expect from a squid on Earth. This creature slides gracefully into a fighter craft and emerges a few seconds later, arms carrying equipment wrapped in dark fabric or plastic.

Borden ignores the squid and concentrates on what she can understand, what might be more immediately important. "Five ships," she says. "Probably not big enough to take us home, or anywhere far from Saturn."

DJ stares at the squid. "Wouldn't want to tangle with one of those."

The Antags around the corded fighters move into a tunnel. Three emerge a few minutes later with a bundle floating between them, an irregular squirming object wrapped in a flexible bag with a squat brown cylinder attached—some sort of pressurized sack, I'm guessing.

The Antags are going to introduce us to some Gurus. The ones they captured on Mars and apparently kept alive? Maybe not. Maybe we have no idea where their Gurus come from. Wherever, I want to be any fucking place but here. I don't have a home, not really, but I want to go back there, even if it's Virginia Beach turned black glass.

We are in the grip of an unpredictable enemy whose motivations may not add up, who have spent years trying to kill us on Mars and on Titan, and that's bad enough—

But what about meeting something that wants to *watch* us kill one another? Gurus. Keepers.

But no choice. We're either useful or we're dead.

And goddammit, even with all that, even with my brain telling me to shrink up like a penis in a Speedo swimming through a daiquiri, I can't tamp my curiosity back into its Prince Albert can. I have to ask—what have we done with *our* Gurus? Did they return to Earth and get set free in time to visit me at Madigan—one of them, anyway? Did our mutual access to the influence of the tea make me a sitting duck for those implants—the instaurations?

What about Borden? Is Borden a fucking mimic? Joe? Kumar? Mushran? Could we ever know? Shapeshifters just love frozen ice stations, according to the movies. Imagine crossing a cruel fucking movie producer with the Thing from Another World.

That's it for now. Having worked my way back to pop culture, I'm done with curiosity. I don't share any of this with DJ or Ulyanova. Better to keep my poisoned imagination to myself.

Bird Girl makes a wide spread of her wings and the others draft into a smaller side chamber with their bundle, away from the ships. I don't even hear two more Antags come up behind us and take control of the rubbery cable. We could let go and just drift, but Bird Girl turns to look at us and I swear there's something imploring in her four eyes, like she's asking, begging, for help. They want to go home, too, and this is the only way for them—even if it's only a sliver of a chance.

Borden speaks first. "Let's go see," she says.

I wish Joe was here, but she's right. It's time to face reality. Time to stop trying to think things through and find out what's really in store.

Ulyanova hand-overs along the rope. The Antags behind herd us to where the package was taken, tank and all. We're closely watched by six other Antags who have emerged from the ships in the hangar. Several more enter furtively from another angle, I'm not sure where—can't watch all sides at once—and now there are twelve: six smaller, batlike critters having joined the party. They all watch with far too many eyes as we enter the far room.

Bird Girl takes hold of the cable and carefully persuades us into another curving, bean-shaped hollow with its own red-dish glow. The hollow winds on around curvy corners into other hollows, other voids, spaces bean- or kidney-shaped, like we're being scooted through Leviathan's intestine. This place is aft of the important bits. What's forward is protected by the mind-shit gate, the infernal combination lock with agony for tumblers. Until we find our way through, we're stuck in the ship's asshole, as DJ called it—where Gurus store humans they want to torment.

On one side of a kidney void, three Antags have suspended the wrinkled package between them. It's partly inflated, and something kicks at one end like a kitten about to be drowned. One armored Antag has extended its left wingtip hand to a clasp on the side of the bag. At a musical tweep from Bird Girl, the clasp is flipped and the bag splits along a seam, then peels up and around, revealing a grayish, glistening shape, like two or three wet, furry animals glued together, legs folded, single head tucked in…

"Kumar wasn't lying. It *is* like a dog," DJ says.

"A couple of dogs," Borden says.

"I see rabbits," I say. I'm remembering the odd dream-like interlude I experienced on the way down to Titan, when I either imagined or was deceived into believing that I had never left Madigan, when the guy who said he was Wait Staff but was likely a Guru told me all about Joe and how he was central to my being here, being anywhere, and how Joe had—

Fuck that. What's important is that I saw the Wait Staff sort of admit to the deception and convert back into being a Guru, but it didn't look anything like this lumpy, limp bundle.

"We need Kumar," DJ observes.

"They didn't tell him to come," Borden says. She then asks

Bird Girl, straight out, "Is that supposed to be a Guru?" The translator sucks in her words and rasps out more tunes.

"It is Keeper," Bird Girl says.

The damp train of rabbits or dogs unfolds a set of ears—floppy, basset hound ears. Six legs unfold as well, two ending in three-fingered hands. The whole thing is about a meter and a half long and masses in at maybe thirty kilos.

So far, Gurus turn out to be pretty much as Kumar described them. Very little like what I was shown or imagined in my *instauration*. This one, whatever its real shape, looks pitiful, weak—defeated.

Ulyanova trembles and strains against the cable, taking deep, hiccupping breaths. A seizure doesn't seem out of the question. "Not *finished*," she says, and then reverts to Russian. The translators again convert this to both Antag music and English. "Where is the other? We cannot go through the gate with just one."

How does she know this? Presumably because she's channeling this poor damp creature, plugging into the way it thinks.

Ulyanova slips her tenders' grasping hands and gets too close to the furry bundle. Her own hands form claws. She is almost on it when one of the smaller bats pulls her back—but gently.

Ulyanova looks beyond Borden, along the ranks of Antags. "Don't let it die!" she says. "I want to watch it *suffer*."

DJ has a look in his eyes I haven't seen except in the thick of desperate battle. And Borden—

Borden has cropped her former agitation, her rage, and is studying the damp gray shape as she once studied me.

"Can you understand Keeper?" Bird Girl asks.

Ulyanova draws in her brows.

"She must tell," Bird Girl says.

Ulyanova gives her a quick, dagger glance. "I would go back to the way I was, if I could, but I can't. I know one thing now I did not know then. I cannot unknow it."

"What?" Borden asks.

"Why Gurus are here," Ulyanova says.

Borden gives DJ and me a side glance that seems strangely guilty. Was this why the commander came out here in the first place? Maybe not to test me or to hear what DJ or Kazak had to say—no care or concern at all for the bug archives—but to learn what had happened to the *starshina* out on the Red. Gaining access to a Guru mind, tapping into a direct feed through a channel they can't control—a channel planned by our forebears hundreds of millions of years ago, designed into the Ice Moon Tea. Bug vengeance or bug defense—ancient and with no regard for our young *starshina*'s mental health, or, I suspect, for her ultimate humanity.

What would that be worth?

Bird Girl points for us to grab the cables to again be yanked along like leashed puppies. "Take you back," she says through the translator. "All will be brought forward."

I haven't heard her interior voice for some time, but now I do:

She (I see a distorted view of the *starshina*) *is polluted. When this is done, we will kill her and the Keepers with her. Then we will take back the sky.*

At that, she puts up a wall. For the time being, no more questions, no answers.

It will be done.

A PAIR OF ACES

This is going south fast," I tell DJ and Borden while we are being led aft. "Once we help break down the door, we're no more use to any of them."

"Big surprise," DJ says. "Bad hand all around."

Ulyanova seems dazed. I'm not sure she hears us. She's listening to something else and I don't like the implications of that one bit. If she has a connection to a Guru or to a couple of Gurus, what's the guarantee they can't delude her, too? But to tell Ulyanova that seems to be as fraught as waking a sleepwalker. She might just explode.

We pass by the cage full of corpses. Leathery bits drift around us, as disgusting and pitiful as ever. From the corner of my eye, I see something floating near the mesh, a faint glint with a chain or wire attached. Borden, the closest, reaches out and grabs it.

We're taken by the railcar aft around the screw garden, then returned to the first hamster cage, where the rest of us wait. Bird Girl and two subordinate Antags escort us to the opening, unlock it, and swing it wide. We let go of the leash and pull ourselves through.

Inside, Ulyanova kicks away, grabs a stray mat, and then kicks off again, crossing the cage to get as far as she can from the rest of the squad. She wraps herself in the mat, then peeks up briefly, staring in our direction for a second or two. Her face is stolid, numb. Litvinov and Vera cross the cage to be with her. Bilyk keeps well away.

Borden explains to the rest where we were taken in the ship, what we saw, and the very little we were told. They learn there is at least one Guru on this ship and probably two.

"Antags want our help, her help mostly," Borden says. "This could be the endgame. They'll kill us if we're not useful, Ulyanova first. She's the most dangerous if she gets out of their control—if somehow she gets back to Earth."

"What chance of that?" Ishida asks.

Borden shakes her head.

"What else can we do?" Jacobi asks. She sounds hoarse and exhausted.

"This may have been Mushranji's plan all along," Kumar says.

"Your ignorance is awe-inspiring," Ishida says, and Tak gets between them, just to be careful.

———

Wrapped in a mat, I try to close my eyes, but there's too much going on behind my head, wherever that is, to let me sleep. Bird Girl truly believes that the *starshina* and likely their own exposed soldier are crucial to piercing the nightmare gate, taking control of this ship and getting the hell out of the solar system. Crucial to going home.

My eyelids disagree with my brain. They become too heavy. I drift off.

Comes a sudden jerk-up to full awareness. Ulyanova is floating a few feet from me, suspended in shadow and the last few drops of cage-cleaning spray from our attendant bats. She looks at me as if she would solve all her problems simply by figuring out how I work, what I mean. Turnabout.

"What?" I say.

"Do not need live Gurus. Will be problem."

"All right," I say.

"Do not want this," she murmurs. "I will not be me."

As I have never been quite sure who Ulyanova is in the time I've known her, what can I say that might help? Nothing.

"I feel *Antagonista* who is connected to Guru," she says. "Very unhappy. Others do not treat her well. Stupid, no?"

"Stupid," I agree. Her English has improved. Is that some sort of proof of her connection?

"All Antag fighters are female," she says, after a thoughtful pause.

"Interesting," I say.

"Once I thought females in charge, bottom to top, would be good. Now, not so much. Well, she needs me to finish this work. Can you tell her that? Your *Antagonista*, your steward?"

"I'll tell her." I decide against passing along Bird Girl's design for the *starshina*'s fate.

"Good," Ulyanova says, then presses her lips together, as if evenly spreading lipstick. At least that's familiar. She looks away, looks up, then focuses her pike-sharp gaze on me again. "Gurus know you," she says. "I know what they know."

"Okay," I say.

"You brought dead girl from Mexico." She gives me a disgusted look.

"True."

"You almost died walking on railway bridge."

"Yeah," I say.

"And you killed your father." She smiles with a sad, creepy kind of pride. "I stabbed my father. He did not die. Why I joined Skyrines. Anybody else know these things?"

Honesty is definitely the best policy here. "Joe Sanchez," I say.

She shakes her head. "He is not like you, the corporal, or me, right?"

"Right."

"Proof this comes from shithole Gurus. What they know, I know. Poor me! My soul is rotting. But is good." She moves closer and grabs my arm. Her broken fingernails dig in. "Bits of Guru inside you, like bombs. No others needed. We kill other Gurus, and *you* help open gate."

Before I can think of a response, she backs away, folding her arms. Joe moves into view as another volley of food is tossed through the cage. Nobody tries to catch the cakes. The bats watch, squeaking, then retreat. Maybe they need us fat.

"Borden's getting bored," Joe says, with a worried glance at the *starshina*. "Time for a conference."

QUESTIONS NEVER ASKED

Borden's bare feet just touch the mesh. She has reasonably long and grippy toes, handy under these circumstances. She folds her arms as Jacobi and Litvinov and their respective troops join us. Litvinov and Ulyanova are at the center of the cluster, Bilyk and Vera to one side. Vera seems deeply concerned about the *starshina*.

I'm curious about one big, important thing, especially after my conversation with her a few minutes earlier.

"Who set Ulyanova up for this?" I ask. I do not want to give Borden or Joe, or Kumar, control over the discussion. I'm not at all sure who's on the side of those exposed to the tea.

The commander lets out her breath in exasperation, whether at me or at the cards we're being dealt. She says to Ulyanova, "I'm not sure where we're all at now—but we'd like to know how this happened to you."

Ulyanova gives us a head-back, almost reptilian look, as if recovering from a punch in the jaw. Her brows draw together and she starts slow. "What I remember...On Mars, between big battles, we defend Voors and Muskies in station, when we are told important leaders, Wait Staff, come for visit."

"When was this?"

"Last season," she says, referring to the combat season I spent away from Mars, at Madigan. "They will inspect."

"Inspect what?" Borden asks.

"Drifter, Voor camps. And another piece of crystal on surface, exposed by sandstorm. We are ordered by *polkovnik* to escort leaders sixty kilometers to this place, wait for them, then take them to lander. There are six, including *polkovnik*. We stay in tractor. Hours later, visitors and soldiers return with heavy box. They order us, put it in cabin, take all to lander. They have for what they come. No more talk."

"They look human?" Borden asks.

For some reason, this seems to surprise Ulyanova. "They are Wait Staff!"

Jacobi looks back at Kumar, who as usual is staying a few meters from the group.

"An important pair of visitors, but just one tractor?" Borden asks. Ulyanova cocks an eyebrow at the commander. Is she the one who needs to explain the ways of rank?

"Only one," she says. "Big enough."

"Did they know about the other Drifter?" DJ asks.

"I think not. We carry them, try to make sure they get safe from Red. But strike happens—strong force, two millies, maybe one hundred *Antagonista*. Lander is in pieces when we arrive. We hear on radio is Russian force trying to reach us, join to repel enemy, but bolts strike tractor, throw bodies. Throw me on dust, but I am just shaken. Russians arrive, many die pushing back enemy." She folds her hands. "Box is broken open, full of crystal and powder. Pieces inside are black."

That sinks in. We experienced how dangerous the crystal is when it feels it's in danger.

Joe says. "If they carved off samples…"

Inevitably we all look Kumar's way. "Please continue," he says. "This is new to me."

Ulyanova resumes. "Around what is left of tractor, we find four of our dead and both Wait Staff. One visitor is in pieces, turned glass—other badly injured. Soon, he, too, is dead. All are covered in powder. Two soldiers are also glass."

DJ taps his head, then looks to me. "Hear any other Russians?"

"No." I watch the *starshina*.

"We carry remains to another tractor. Not touch pieces. Then—one last bolt. My helm loses suck. I breathe powder and blood before troopers put me in safety bag."

Litvinov looks haggard. "Unique orders from orbit," he says. "Collect all dead. Collect visitor body. Nobody allowed to inspect."

"Gurus," Kumar says.

"But they look human!" Vera says.

"They usually present as one form," Kumar says. "But can easily look human if they wish. Master Sergeant Venn has seen at least one such. However, I believe nobody, until that moment, had ever seen a *dead* Guru."

"If they can be whatever they want to be," Jacobi says, "they can look like a corpse, right? Fake us out?"

"And this one had turned glass, anyway," Ishida reminds us.

A brief pause as we absorb more awkward implications.

"What would the tea do to them?" DJ asks. "They're not part of our old family, like Antags—or are they?"

Nobody wanders up that sidetrack, but I've already figured it out. The crystals and the tea can be adjusted to do more than just absorb enemies. It can also link them into the bug network, with none of the advantages. A deep and dangerous espionage.

"Did Mushran arrange all that?" Borden asks Kumar. "Was there a plan to expose Gurus and humans to the tea together? To get a Guru to turn glass?"

Kumar considers. "I cannot deny that such a plan was a possibility, but I was not told of it, even after I arrived on Mars."

"What happened to the casualties? The Wait Staff bodies?" Ishikawa asks.

"They were shuttled to Earth," Litvinov says.

"More shit to turn Virginia Beach into black glass," DJ says.

"Sacrificing Russians!" Litvinov adds, giving DJ a warning glare.

Kumar folds his arms and grips his elbows, as if he's suddenly cold. "That must be when Ulyanova became important to the Antagonists," he says. Admirably restating the obvious, or just bringing the point home to slow Skyrines?

We don't bring back our dead. Scrap and stain forever. What changed, and who changed it? I try to imagine Ulyanova and Litvinov's Russian troops on the Red, traveling in the presence of Gurus who look human—with a box full of Ice Moon Tea. Close, breathing the same air. Going into a trap designed to mix them all together, just to see what happens. Was Joe already involved? Conspiring with rebel Antags to undercut Wait Staff on both sides, screwing with those monsters who found advantage in sending us far, far out to fight and die? Joe would have loved that. A real *upgrade*.

But I don't interrupt.

"Is Mushran really dead?" Ishida asks.

"He was in our Oscar," DJ says. "I didn't see him after we were dumped into the tanks."

"Nobody saw him after that," Litvinov says.

"Maybe he was a Guru after all," Ishida says.

"Not possible," Kumar says.

"How would you have known?" Ishida asks.

Kumar looks away. "Perhaps I would not," he admits.

My thoughts are almost too dense and rapid to hold on to, so I keep my attention on Ulyanova. The *starshina* seems to be warming to her situation as a strategic asset.

"You've known about this how long?" I ask Joe.

"Parts of it since last season," he says. "After I sent you home. But not the Guru bits."

"Planned it?"

"Not me," Joe says.

"Very likely, Mushran and a very few others in Division Four," Kumar says.

"But not you?" Jacobi asks.

"Not me," Kumar says.

Back to Joe. "You returned to Earth for a few months," I say, "but avoided me—I was in Madigan, right?"

"Yeah."

"Then you hopped a command shuttle to Mars. Who arranged that?"

"You saved the coin we found in the first Drifter," Joe says. "Hidden up your ass, as I recall. I took it back to Mars to open the second Drifter station. But for some reason, you seem to think I've been deceptive." He gets right up in my face. My turn to feel the burn. "Maybe you were the one who drew me in!"

"Fuck you," I say.

"Shut it," Borden says.

"We've known each other since day two, Vinnie, when I helped bury your fucking secrets. Look at me! I'm as confused and twisted as you are," Joe says, then backs off. "You give me way too much credit."

Borden pulls her way up between us. "Let's put two and two together," she says. "Mushran had to establish several things. One was that the Antags actually had their own Gurus—the ones they call Keepers—and that they were substantially the same as ours, maybe working to the same ends. He kept Kumar out of that loop. Kumar's job was to track Wait Staff and Gurus on Earth, figure out how they were reacting. Right?"

"That is so," Kumar says.

"Even before that, Mushran needed to confirm that the tea really gave you and Johnson and Kazak access to special knowledge and didn't just make you see stuff. With that confirmation, Kumar and I arranged to get you out of Madigan and back to Mars.

"After Mushran had established an element of trust with rebel Antags, he told them what had happened to some of our Skyrines. In turn, they relayed to him that they, too, were aware of the crystal archives."

DJ cocks his head. "We're like detectives in the last chapter of a fucking mystery!"

This actually draws out a smile from Borden, the first we've seen in a while.

"We could use some more clues," Ishida says. We've forgotten that not everyone in our group has the big picture, but now is not the time to fill in those details, and maybe they'll pick them up as we move forward.

"On Titan, the one you call Bird Girl was channeling an Antag who turned glass. Isn't that how it works?"

Makes sense to DJ and me.

"Keepers probably relayed that intelligence to Gurus on Earth," she says. "Division Four noticed that Wait Staff and Gurus were paying lots more attention to suspicious communications, looking for exchanges between humans and Antags." She looks to Kumar.

Kumar says, "When we weren't doing our best to kill each other."

"But how did Division Four, or the Antags, learn that Gurus could be hooked in?" I ask.

"I am not sure Mushran knew that was possible," Kumar says.

"So it was just dumb luck?" Jacobi asks.

"I don't think so," Joe says, hot on the trail. Watching him, I remember what he was like as a teenager, and have my doubts he is deep in the conspiracy. After all, the source of my only info on these matters is the Guru at Madigan—and Gurus lie, right? "The rebel Antags must have discovered that the tea could link their soldiers to Keepers—give them access to shit from deep inside a Keeper's mind, no filters, no sham. Gurus feared that prospect more than having humans dialed into ancient history. Mushran may have then set in motion the encounter on Mars."

Joe grabs my shoulder and spins me around. I'm being grabbed a lot lately, but I don't resist. Maybe I deserve this. "You've been blaming me since you came back from Madigan," he says. "And maybe I knew stuff I couldn't tell you right away. I put you into play, sure. But I never got clued into the big picture, just bits and pieces—orders with thin or no explanations. I doubt Mushran ever trusted any Skyrine. At the beginning, I had no idea you'd be so important. But it made things a lot easier."

"Because I'm a sap."

"Because you're reliable. I knew that given the opportunity on Mars, everything would be easier for all of us—because of you."

"I would like to have had a choice," I say.

"Me, too," DJ says.

"You knew pretty much when we knew," Borden says. "And on some matters, you knew before."

"What about Ulyanova?"

The *starshina* listens, eyes still narrow, lips tight.

"I can't speak to what the Russians knew," Borden says, "or when she awoke to her connection."

Ulyanova lifts her hand and one finger, then folds the finger and looks away as if bored. Or in control, waiting for us to figure all this out so she can get on with her life.

"Bird Girl knew before we did," I say. "She chose Ulyanova. Maybe *their* steward told them who to look for."

"Who's getting Wi-Fi and who's not," DJ says.

"Can you hear anything through her?" Joe asks DJ and me.

"Nothing substantial," DJ says. "More like static."

"Then nobody knows what she's actually tuned into."

Again her impatient, bored look.

"I do," I say. "She's been sharing some of my deepest secrets, and she could only get them through a Guru."

Joe looks uneasy. "Or me," he says.

"Yeah."

"How did the Antags find this ship?" Borden asks.

"Let's ask them later," DJ says. "I'm so tired I could croak and not know the difference."

"Right," Borden says. "We'll give it a rest for now."

I'd like to sort things out further, but have to agree that would not be productive.

"We are done?" Ulyanova asks.

"Done," Borden says.

Vera brings up a rolled mat and leads the *starshina* to another part of the cage. Bilyk looks like a lost little kid. Litvinov is paying him no attention, and the others are scrupulously avoiding Russians—all but DJ. DJ spreads his mat next to Bilyk and conks immediately. Bilyk soon joins him.

But I'm buzzing.

We haven't even got around to the caged dead and the gate.

SORROW AND PITY

We're allowed a few hours of nothing like peace but at least quiet, and the rest of us are starting to rouse. We take advantage of a stream of water shot through the cage by a trio of bats, then intercept baseball-sized lumps of the cakes we've been eating for days and now hate like fury. But we're hungry. We eat, then hold up mats as curtains. The bats obligingly wash away our by-products. I don't know where the water and shit goes, but it doesn't come back into our cage.

"More discussion, sir," I suggest to Joe. "Debrief on our trip forward."

He looks uneasy, as if his gut is bothering him, then says, "Let's do it."

Ishikawa and Vera escort the *starshina* to rejoin the main group. Litvinov and Bilyk flank them. Ulyanova's attitude is again cool and calm. Litvinov is almost obsequious toward her.

Everyone forms layers around DJ and Borden and me,

clutching arms and legs and rearranging until all can see and hear. Joe forms up beside Borden and they lead the brief/debrief.

DJ and I, Borden adding details, explain what we saw on the way forward, in the company of Bird Girl and her Antag commanders. We neglect to say much about the screw garden and its low, bushy forest—which nobody understands—but we do describe the tangle of human bodies in the second hamster cage. Borden's face takes on a brief pained expression, like she knows something we don't, and doesn't want to know it.

The explanations wind on. Not all our group is clued into the weird details about Bug Karnak, the steward, and DJ's and my off-and-on link with Bird Girl.

"Yeah, but why did they pick you four to go forward?" Ishikawa asks.

"Because you're clued in, right?" Ishida asserts.

"Commander Borden isn't," Tak says.

Jesus, we have to start all over again. Everyone asks pointed questions about who knows what, who's talking to whom, whose head is most busy and why. I doubt that most of our survivors believe deeply in any of this. Trust is going to be hard to maintain—after all, we're consorting with the enemy, one way or another, all of us, right? And some more deeply than others.

Slowly, with jumps and starts, everyone is brought up to a kind of pause point, the closest thing to exhaustion of topic we can manage for now—which I think should have happened back on Mars, but I wasn't making those decisions.

Then Borden raises her hand. She's clenching something. I

remember she grabbed a shiny little piece of metal outside the second hamster cage.

I get a sick feeling.

"On our way back, when we passed the corpses in the cage," she says, "I found this. It must have slipped through the mesh." She extends a dog tag smeared with dried blood and lets it float out on its crusted chain.

Joe pinches the tag between his fingers as it drifts his way and examines the stamped letters. It's a newer tag, with an embedded chip, but the letters are still stamped, and that means it belonged to a Skyrine. "Jesus!" he says, and looks at me as if he's finally had the very last of the air let out of his tires. He releases the tag and wipes his hand on his pajamas.

I grab it next. The blood is dark and crusted but I can still read the name: *MSGT Grover N. Sudbury*. Master Sergeant— my rank. Grover Sudbury—the rapist bastard several of us, including DJ, Joe, Kazak, and Tak, pounded to a pulp outside Hawthorne.

Bringing back another part of that moment in the dream, the instauration, about returning to Madigan—

Ask Joseph Sanchez about where he went with Grover Sudbury, and why.

I never asked. Too ridiculous.

Tak reads the tag and recoils in genuine horror—the kind of shuddering, supernatural horror you might feel in a nightmare or as a character in a scary movie. Which suddenly we all are. This could change everything—but how?

How does it make *anything* different?

"He can't be here," Tak says, his voice ragged. "We stomped

the shit out of him and we weren't brought up on charges or even asked why."

"Kazak helped," DJ says. "Just before we were sent to Socotra. We heard the shithead was given a dishonorable discharge. After that, he went away. Nobody saw him again."

Borden lets the tag and chain slowly swing between us. "Okay. You knew him. If he was no longer in the service, how did he get here?"

"And how the fuck did he earn rank?" DJ is sensitive about promotion, having been busted down a few times.

The others wait for a story, any story that brings them into the picture.

Litvinov inspects the tag and asks, "Who is this?"

"A psychopath," Tak says. "He assaulted a sister in a scuzzy apartment he kept just outside Hawthorne, while we were in training. Probably not his first, and we did our best to correct bad attitude."

"Why is he here?" Ishida asks.

"Was here," I correct.

"Kind of coincidental, finding his tags, don't you think?" Jacobi asks, but nobody can put together an explanation that makes sense. Knowledge of the past does not help us get to where we are now.

Ishida asks: "Is anybody sure this Sudbury was actually here?"

"No," Joe says, as if it might be more convenient.

But now it's Borden's turn. She found the dog tag, she's holding it again. She looks around at the accusing eyes. "I didn't stash this away and bring it out now to upset everybody," she says coldly. "One of us knows what happened to Sudbury. I think we all need to hear."

I look at Joe. Borden looks at Joe. Joe looks defeated, then defiant. "Goddammit," he says. "We beat the beans out of a fellow Skyrine."

"He deserved it," Tak says.

"Yeah, but we didn't kill him."

"He wasn't just kicked out, given a dishonorable discharge?" Borden asks.

"No," Joe says. "He went to the MPs and IG and pressed charges. Everybody I knew was about to be court-martialed. I had some connections already, so I went to the main office at Hawthorne. Told them what happened."

"Told who?"

"Our DI, as it turned out. I told him about Sudbury and what he did—to protect my squad. He took me to a side office in another building. Special Considerations, it was called. Inside, he volunteered Sudbury. Filled out papers and everything. We'd heard rumors about Guru attitudes toward sex criminals—violent offenders. Rapists. Child molesters. The rumor was, if they were reported, the Gurus and Wait Staff would make sure they were locked up. DI said only that it was rumored to be a death sentence. I didn't care."

"What happened?" Borden asks.

"Everything tidied up," Joe says. "Sudbury went away. Nobody was brought up on charges. The DI never mentioned it again, and I never went to that building again."

"The Gurus took charge?"

"I don't know," Joe said.

"*Didn't* know," Borden says. "Nobody let on that Sudbury would end up here?"

"Wherever here is, how could they?" DJ asks.

Joe shakes his head.

"Not just Skyrines," Borden says. "Similar deal in the Navy. Nobody wanted to talk about it."

Litvinov adds, with a firm nod, "Russian perverts, too."

"Gays, you mean?" Jacobi asks sharply, as if leading him into a trap.

"No. Still difficult in Russia, but not for Gurus. These were worst of cruel, vicious—sadists. Generals and colonels said they were made into Guru sausage. Never asked for more. Did not wish to know."

"Sausage!" Jacobi says. "Nothing wasted in this man's army."

The others take the tag from Borden and pass it around. Ishida, as if morbidly fascinated, holds on to it the longest. "No guns, no knives, no weapons, right?"

"Apparently," Borden says.

"Everyone fought with bare hands and teeth," Ishida says.

Ulyanova has been studiously avoiding entering the discussion until now. "Ugly bits of flesh. Sausage. Gurus find use."

"Just guessing?" Borden asks.

Ulyanova frowns. "See it. Remember it. They were put in cage, told they would not eat until, unless, they select meanest. Gurus want...how do you say it? Like skimming cream. Why humans deserve their doom, for film and broadcast. Audience love it. In the end, Gurus leave dead to rot."

"Sex monsters in the fight of their unholy lives," Ishida says. "For the director's cut." She clutches her metal arm with the opposite hand, knuckles white. "Almost makes you sorry for them."

"You didn't see what the bastard did to our sister," DJ says. "Got what he deserved."

Some of us nod in agreement, but Tak and Litvinov, Borden

and Ishikawa, have this dismayed look, as if even now they can't believe or even conceive of the depth of Guru depravity.

The dog tag hangs between us, loose. Nobody wants to hold it. Borden doesn't reach for it. It should just float away, like the guy it once belonged to.

"You see why I want Gurus dead?" Ulyanova asks.

"Aren't you one of them now?" Ishida asks.

Nobody defends Ulyanova, and she doesn't seem to care one way or the other. Nobody speaks for a time. Our tight little group has definite seams on this issue. Fascinating. I'm split myself—I could have killed Sudbury and enjoyed watching him die.

But this...

Makes him almost equal to us. Fodder for distant eyes.

"Might make it more convincing this is actually a Guru ship," Tak says. "What the hell would Antags care about human deviants?"

"What are they planning for *us*?" Ishikawa asks. "Same thing, different day?"

"Fuck!" DJ exclaims. "I did not need to hear that."

"You should ask your Bird Girl," Jacobi says. "You can do that, for us, to put our minds at ease—can't you?"

"Ask Ulyanova," Borden suggests. "She's right here."

"I do not see future," Ulyanova says, and turns sullen.

"Well then, who the fuck does?" Ishikawa asks. "If the Antags have Gurus—"

"We know that much," Borden says.

"—then what's happening with *them*? Is this all going to end up *interesting*, part of the movie extras—or a whole new show?"

Jacobi digs in. "What's the equivalent of Antag sexual deviancy? Breaking eggs? Making omelets?"

That's too much. The tension weirdly breaks. Joe snorts. Some of the others let air out of their noses, showing amusement and disdain.

DJ says, quietly enough, "Good question, though. Are there any cages here full of dead Antags? Or are humans just particularly nasty sons of bitches?"

"If you haven't noticed, we're already *in* a cage," Jacobi says. "Maybe they just have to get us mad enough and we'll put on a show. Maybe Vinnie is a camera—or DJ! Maybe they're filming us right now."

I hadn't thought about that. It is too fucking possible, maybe even likely.

"I'm ready for my close-up!" Jacobi says, leaning in.

My fists clench.

"Leave Venn alone," Ishida says. "We have to cut the *starshina* some slack, too." She returns Jacobi's hard look with a hard look of her own. "We have no idea what it's like to be hooked up to this shit."

"The bodies in that cage have only been dead a few months, not years," Borden says.

"They still smell," Jacobi says.

"Justice grinds slow," Tak says, following his own line of thinking, which doesn't get any response.

"How long has ship been hiding?" Litvinov asks.

"Does anybody know *anything* about this ship, other than what they've told us—and maybe what they've shown us?" Jacobi asks. "She's our only source on some of this! Give us the rest, goddammit!"

Ulyanova's turned sickly pale, almost green. She looks as

if she's digging around in a toilet and finding clogs and back-ups of the worst sort. "You want me to *know*?" she asks, tears coming to her eyes. "You want me to ask Guru what the fuck about all?"

"What *do* you know or feel?" DJ asks, only marginally more gentle. He and I, and Kazak, have been closest to the situation she's in now. Can the Gurus be any stranger than bugs or Antags?

"Is not good," Ulyanova says, holding her hands to her head. "Is not true, not correct. And not safe." Litvinov gathers up the wilting *starshina* and leads her away, weeping.

"She is done with answers," he says over his shoulder. Vera goes with them across the cage, and wraps Ulyanova again in her mat.

DJ embraces himself in his arms, as Kumar had done earlier. From behind, he looks like someone is hugging him—someone invisible. We've all had more than enough. As if reacting to yawns in a crowded room, pretty soon we're mostly asleep—exhausted and traumatized.

Before Joe joins us, he plucks the dog tag from the air and pokes it through the mesh, letting it slip out to become part of the water and the shit, cleaned up, moved out. "By itself, this is useless," he says. "We're going to ask a lot of pointed questions before we let Ulyanova probe a Guru. If that's what the Antags are planning."

I feel a twist. They're not mentioning me, but I know.

Kumar agrees. "Let us see what leverage we have."

Then they wrap up and at least pretend to join the rest. Perversely, as I grip the mesh and squeeze my eyes shut, I'm picturing how the fight went down in the second cage. How the teams formed and dissolved, sucking in victims, dispatching them, throwing them aside, then turning on one another until one or two remaining fighters simply bled out. A horrible way to go.

Who's showing me all this?

Just my fucked-up imagination.

Or maybe not.

Sweet.

THE SITUATION THAT PREVAILS

So it was phrased in a silly old cartoon about a real shithead who fought in World War II and sounded like Bugs Bunny and somehow never got himself killed. The phrase is bouncing around my head as I slide in and out of stupor. We are in the situation that prevails.

I hate sleeping in zero g. One can only hang on to wire for so long, before your fingers cramp and you let go and bounce off whatever's nearby. If it's another Skyrine, or Borden, they shove or kick you away, usually without even waking up.

But in zero g, I don't dream much—at least not here. One doesn't dream inside a dream, right? Maybe all I've been living through since I left Madigan is just another Guru instauration, and when I wake up I'll be back in my apartment in Virginia Beach, getting ready to take my car out for a squeal, maybe drive to Williamsburg for kidney pie and some old-fashioned, cozy history. Real history. Has human history ever been real? How long has this shit been going on? Looks like a long, long time. Lots of wars.

Have to ask: Which war was the most popular, ratings-wise?

I open my eyes and find myself looking through the mesh into Bird Girl's four purple-rimmed peepers. She's floating steady on the other side, watching me, just waiting, quiet inside and out—letting me enjoy my restless doze.

"Where are we going?" I ask.

"Forward. All of you. All of us. Through maze and fake eye shit." She's getting creative with her English.

"There's bad attitude brewing," I say.

"*Brewing*? Like beer?"

"Yeah, bad beer. We're not going to put up with being lowly assholes anymore. If the *starshina* is valuable to you, we want equality. Knowledge. Concessions. We have memories of dead friends, too. Tell your commanders that."

Long fucking speech, but inside it takes just instants and there are actually fewer words. More like thought balloons filled with emojis. That's the way it is, here in the land of deep mind-fuck. The madder one gets, the more the word balloons simplify.

But Bird Girl and I are closely enough related both in ancestry and employment that the message is clear. And when I look back at the others, watching my interaction with the Antag, I see they're awake and alert and have lined up in combat order. Borden and Joe and Litvinov and Jacobi are at the tip of a fighting formation, holding one another's hands like they're going steady. Wonder of wonders, we're together.

I try to find Ulyanova. There she is, in the charge of Ishida and Vera. Sisterhood of power. Cool to see, and cool to see that our *starshina* is neither weepy nor green.

Bird Girl brings her four eyes back to mine.

"I will say it," she tells me, and then moves off back into the darkness of the squash court. I see her shadow exit the cube.

A while later, she and three of the armored commanders return. Bird Girl says, out loud, "We join. No bad beer, right?"

I look back at our officers.

Joe and Borden say, simultaneously, "Agreed."

Litvinov says, "Agree."

The translator buzzes.

The cage door opens.

"All?" I ask.

"All," she says. "Keep together."

"Where are we going?"

"Forward. We will bring Keepers."

"And the connection?"

"Connection and Keepers. They will tell us Keeper thoughts."

"Right," I say. Doesn't sound too complicated, does it? I have no idea how Ulyanova is going to respond, how she'll involve me, or how precise and efficient she'll be. We're all new to this.

HORN AND IVORY, BLOOD AND BONE

Joe and Borden and Litvinov grip arms and share a tether, a leash, as we are led forward. Kumar is right behind them, listening as they evaluate our piss-poor options.

"They must feel vulnerable, to agree to this," Borden says.

"Duh," Jacobi says from behind. Borden doesn't even give her a look.

"They're feeling trapped, like us," Joe says.

DJ and I are paying more attention to Ulyanova than to our superior officers. She's being escorted on another tether by Vera and Ishida. Her lips are creased in a kind of dotty smile, as if we're on a country outing and she's listening to the birdies, so charming to be here. Jesus.

Without Ulyanova we're useless to the Antags, and while at the moment, despite the smile, she's strong enough to manage, to stay alert and keep up with us on the leashes as we're dragged forward, through the usual curving corridors and then along the screw garden on the rail system—just capacious enough to carry us all…

The strain she's under, she could still break at any moment. What if her soul crumbles? She's filled with Guru. Could happen, right?

And me?

DJ and I seem strong enough, we've lasted long enough, but are *we* reliable? Maybe I'm the main POV. I'd gladly ash-can my brain, or at least my imagination, just to be a dumb grunt again.

"Anything left of Titan?" I ask DJ.

"I think they've finished bombing. Good times down there."

He sounds uncertain, so I have to ask, like a kid probing to find out where the Christmas presents are hidden, "But you're still getting something?"

"Not really," DJ says. "Just shrapnel from earlier overloads."

"Right." DJ and I are a thin soup of residuals, peas and carrots in cooling broth.

Kumar drops back closer. "I do not believe that anyone can connect to a Guru and live long," he says in a low voice. "Even when they are right in front of me, talking to me, I have never found them the least accessible. They are masters of…" He breaks off. "What is this place we are going? How much do their Gurus and the connected one—how much do they understand about the ship? The systems involved?"

All good questions. DJ answers the first as best he can. "It's a puzzle lock. You have to solve a code to move forward. Without the code, it's a meat grinder."

"Are you sure you all saw the same situation, or the same version of that situation?" Kumar asks.

"You'll just have to see for yourself," DJ says with a crease of his cheek muscles.

We exit the transport. I've been staring out at the green,

brushy inclines of the screw garden and asking myself why Gurus would put such a thing at the rear of the ship. Having impossible problems to solve is what distracts me from how awful our situation is. I'm a nerd. Have been since I was a little kid. It's kept me sane before. I've been a killer since I was thirteen and not once did I enjoy it or feel anything less than shitty. Killing is putting an end to threatening stuff I don't understand, before I can ever understand it. Nerding out distracts from that essential emptiness.

The Antags flank us, all that remains of our pitiful little party, and guide us through the curvy alien regions to the hatch, which is presently shut tight. From behind us, out of glimmering shadow, emerge four more Antags in light armor. Between them are slung two squirming gray bags.

Through Bird Girl, I feel that another Antag is on her way to join us, with her own escort. The picture I'm getting is that this is the connected one, and she's a basket case.

Then we see her. She's spiked and awry, covered with a damp, sweaty sheen, wings drooping, feet and hands clenched. Her four eyes are crusted with snot and she's all twitch and quiver—in worse shape than Ulyanova. Maybe the Antags have been working her over, trying to force her to tell them what they need to know.

Bird Girl advances to the bulkhead that holds the mystery gate. The three commanders bring the droopy Antag toward the gate and hand her leash to two armored officers. DJ, Ulyanova, and I are urged forward by two more officers, who let us drift up next to the bags.

Our fellow Skyrines and Kumar and Borden hang back, for the moment, eyes wide, glad they're not us, not Ulyanova. The *starshina*'s previous calm, her dotty smile, has turned brittle. She's shivering, but that might be because we're all half-naked, in minimal pajamas, and the air around the gate is chilly.

The Antags unclasp and peel the bags, revealing two bundles of wet gray fur with floppy ears and wide, sleepy eyes. Here's the other that Ulyanova said was necessary—but isn't. Not if I'm around. Their sleepy eyes track us, humans and Antags, as if they would burrow deep into our heads. Eyes that do not concede any ground to our domination, our control.

God, I do hate them.

Ulyanova shudders but does not look away. She tilts her head back, curves her lips, and gives them a sharply angled look, as if she's a dragon about to spit fire. The Gurus jerk and try to shrink away.

"Look," Bird Girl announces, and presses a circular indentation to the left of the hatch. The hatch opens, six pieces sliding aside and back, all somehow very standard, very expected. We've been spending far too much time on alien spacecraft. Give me a simple pressure hatch anytime, give me a rocket, a capsule—

Then we all have to look, no choice—like facing the mouth of hell. But inside the gate, this time there's only a neutral beige emptiness, not easy to look at, to look into, since it seems to promise the nullity I'd like to avoid, thank you—but nothing like the horror we experienced before.

Ulyanova and the connected Antag are kept about two meters apart from the Gurus. Ulyanova's nose is bleeding. DJ tries to help, raising the back of his hand, offering to dab as blood flows down her lip and one side of her chin—but she punches his arm aside, then gives us a hard, steely look. The scruffy Antag doesn't do much of anything.

Then, as if waking from a nap, the beige nullity gets active. Spinning gears take shape, followed by knives, suggestions of endless misery in a variety of fates and forms.

Ulyanova's dragon flames fly now as furious words. "This place...is *disgraceful*," she rasps. "Push Gurus through, first one, then the other!"

The translators work for the armored commanders, but Ulyanova seems to be in charge, not them—they've given up that much in their desperation.

"Will that be enough?" Bird Girl asks.

"What do you care, really?" Ulyanova says. "If we do not feed them to puzzle, if we fail, all who look will be crazy. Try, or we are all mad!"

The scruffy Antag tries to lift a wing, makes sad scrutching noises, along with high-pitched wheeps. She apparently does not agree with Ulyanova.

And strangely, that tilts the game. Bird Girl makes a hatchet chop of one wingtip.

The Gurus squeak.

Kumar moans, then tries to break free of our group—

"Hold him!" Joe calls out.

The little rabbit bundles squeak again, but that doesn't stop two of the armored Antags from pushing one forward, sack trailing like an afterbirth, into the growing, awful gate. Sending a Guru into Guru hell. The squeaks rise to wailing shrieks. The illusion inside the hatchway seems to reach out and grab, pin the little rabbit bundle, yank it from the gripping hands of the Antags, almost dragging them in with it, but they let go—

Together, Ulyanova and the pitiful Antag make sick musical sounds, like a small orchestra about to throw up.

The other Guru squirms and suddenly changes shape without growing or shrinking, looking for a few seconds like a miniature Antag, then a small human, then something I've certainly never seen before—

The inner illusion of the hatch turns black as night—

And spits out pieces of flesh and fur. My God, is that magnificent! Isn't that absolutely what we need to see!

But then the dead puzzle returns. The madness starts all over again. We try to turn away and can't. "Fuck!" DJ says, drawing it out in classic DJ style. We're all on the line, or way over it.

Ulyanova makes a little *hmm*, then looks back at me, at Borden. "Does not seem good," she says. "Not convincing. There is more than two!"

And she's not talking about me.

The eyes of the second Guru sink back into its rabbit-puppy skull.

"It would be most interesting," Ulyanova says, "if both die, and there is a third that needs to die also before I can take their place. I have their minds, their thoughts. We do not need any of them."

Bird Girl and the Antags are not at all happy with these results, or this suggestion. I can't blame them, really. One Guru down, only one left that anyone can see, and the same thing seems very likely to happen if it's fed into the gate. After all, why would the Gurus allow one of their ships to be accessed by unauthorized personnel, even Gurus? And who knows what the Gurus think about personal death, about sacrifice?

The scruffy Antag seems entranced by Ulyanova's words. She reaches out as if to touch the *starshina*, but the armored officers deftly push aside her wing-hand. Ulyanova intervenes and to our surprise grasps that hand—clenches it tight, and surveys us all with her head drawn back.

"It is offering to *solve* puzzle," she says. "But we must not let it help us. If I am become what it is…"

Her eyes turn to mine.

I see the chamber vibrate like a remote that wants to change the channel but can't.

The scruffy Antag makes distressed, angry sounds that are not translated, but the other Antags listen close. Ulyanova says, "This is disgraceful. It is not *interesting*. The Guru says, it *thinks*, there is way to add to drama. We will be more entertaining if we let it teach and guide us. That must not happen. Instead," and she looks back over her shoulder at me, "if it lives, it will block everything we must do. There will be no Gurus on this ship! I *will become*!"

She's following through. She gestures for me to come forward, and this time she grabs my hand. The translator buzzes and makes strident musical notes. There's disagreement and confusion between Bird Girl and her commanders, and apparent concern that we're all about to make a huge mistake. This I get through the ragged connection with Bird Girl. They do not want to put control of this ship, even assuming we can take control, into human hands.

Bird Girl disagrees. We've gone this far. Not to go farther will mean defeat and death.

The last Guru puts up an awful, sad barrage of squeaks and guinea-pig growls, as if intent on making us all feel it's totally without resources or power. Inside my head, I feel those embedded chunks of suggestion vibrate as if in sympathy. And I'm not the only one.

"Agree with it!" Kumar says, aghast. "It's the only way!"

This doesn't convince any of us, least of all Joe. But our Antag counterparts have made up their minds. Bird Girl and her commanders pull the bag and shackles off the Guru. The Guru's squeaking becomes slower and deeper, like a toy whose batteries are running down. Then it makes a sound like a cat playing fiddle on its own sick guts.

What lies beyond the doors is nighttime black. Neutral. Waiting.

Maybe a little hungry.

"No pain if it is gone," Ulyanova says so softly she can barely be heard. "If it dies, I become—I think and solve right here. Right now. Kill the Guru. Kill it!"

Kumar shrieks, "No! It *wants to die!*"

With blinding speed, Bird Girl is handed a bolt weapon by one of her assistants, one of the pair holding the Guru. The commanders try to stop her, but she points it and fires point-blank into the damp, mewling gray bundle. At such short range, the bolt cooks and spatters. Half-baked blood flecks my face. I wipe it away, fascinated beyond disgust.

Then she turns the weapon on the scruffy Antag, their contact, and fires two more bolts into her chest. The unfortunate creature wilts like a spider in a candle flame. Her limbs shrink and curl, her chest caves in—her head wrinkles like a rotten apple.

Then—

She's gone.

None of us can believe what we've just seen.

"She is Keeper mind-fuck," Bird Girl says. The translator throws her words back verbatim. "*Yours* is real."

"You've done what the Guru wants!" Kumar shouts, furious. But nobody is listening. Instead, as if hypnotized, we're locked on to Ulyanova's face, her sharp eyes, her words.

"We go now!" she sings—and the pieces in my soul combine, spin, helpless—

"See and follow!" Ulyanova cries out.

I'm right behind her, we're linked by hand, the puzzle gate requires two Gurus, and suddenly, I'm good enough. Ulyanova is strong enough. We click all the tumblers together, melting the little bombs inside me, using all their energy. The nerd part of me just loves puzzles, doesn't it? And with all that extra, perverse energy—and Ulyanova's deep connection—

The Gurus are not necessary.

I feel the gate succumb and become very, very simple.

Empty air, really.

Bird Girl says something to her fellows and the Antag commanders grip Borden and Litvinov and violently shove them through the blackness, like shoving swimmers into a pool. The darkness swallows all. *That's it,* I'm thinking. *Nice knowing you.* They're going to be coughed out as mincemeat.

But the gate doesn't throw back anything. Again, it remains black, neutral—empty.

"All go, now!" Ulyanova sings again, hand releasing mine and waving like a wagon master's.

Our leashes are gathered; we're surrounded by Antags and kicked and shoved into the blackness. Our screaming gets kind of silly, really, like tourists on a roller coaster. I manage not to make much noise as I go through.

I briefly see Borden and Joe…

Kumar! Looking old and baffled.

But where are they? Where am I? Deep cold but no pain. No cutting or dicing.

When I emerge in a shimmering, shadowy space, not that different from the in-between, I'm still thinking and firmly believe I'm me, always my gold standard for feeling alive. Tak and DJ and Joe float limp beside me. Bird Girl is here, too. She's got a tight grip on the leash that holds Ulyanova. The *starshina* appears to be asleep.

The Antag commanders come through next, followed by the rest of our Skyrines, and what might be the last of the Antags. I'm astonished, as much as I can be astonished, in this condition, the condition that prevails—numb and cold and alive.

I never thought we would make it this far, or take it this far. I always assumed that somewhere between here and then Ulyanova would spark out, or I would, or the Antags would give up and kill us all. I did not know what to believe or think while passing through. Nor do I know what to think of where we are now. The problem with dealing with Gurus has always been that nothing is what it seems.

I try to look deep. Am I empty of those little instaurations, those buried bombs, all fused and used?

No time to know.

We're in a big, dark nothing. Okay. Got it. That makes me giggle. Only *nothing* is what it seems.

We killed all the Gurus we had, didn't we? And the scruffy Antag, who seems to have been an illusion, a deception, and a damned fine one to last so long.

Where's the glowing fog coming from? Our eyes are adjusting to a different kind of illumination, a grayish, dead-looking elf-light that surrounds the gate. At least I think it's the gate. The center is covered. No going back? Or can Ulyanova solve the puzzle whenever she wants?

Is she human now, or Guru?

Can she control what's in her mind?

Or control *me*?

DJ takes hold of his section of our leash and pulls himself into view. His face is as thin and pale as an El Greco saint. Tak and Joe are right behind him. Jacobi, Ishida, and Ishikawa are leashed up to Vera and Bilyk. In the back, Litvinov has Kumar by the shoulders. The elf-light seems to glue itself to everything that came through the gate, like plankton in a passing tide. Patches wrap us here and there and we all look like broken ghosts.

Parts of the glow break off as we move and gleam in the dark like flakes of mica in clouded moonlight. I'm reminded of the Spook's big steel tables and the quantum treatment. More of the same? All Guru tech, we've been told. How much more of this before we crumble like dolls made of dust?

But the Antags, and in particular Bird Girl, seem to still have it together, even after they destroyed two Gurus and bolted one of their own. Has this been their plan all along? A double deception right up until the crunch? Do they trust Ulyanova?

I don't.

They gather our leashes and arrange us like posies in a bouquet. We're all here, Kumar and Litvinov taking up the rear, and the way the Antags are exercising their wings, I think we're about to be drafted to the forward parts of this godawful ship. For a time, I almost want to resist—to force them to bolt me, all of us, just to end the suspense.

But that's not an option.

"Up there," Bird Girl says, pointing with both wingtip hands into the forward darkness. "We hear searchers. Gurus take them as slaves. It is what we expected. What we have been told. Up there."

"What the hell is a 'searcher'?" Joe asks.

"She means the squids," DJ says. That's the image she's feeding us.

PART TWO

PLUTO AND BEYOND

The Antags beat against the thick, cold air. We're still in pajamas, of course, and now we're freezing. Antags don't care. We've made it this far, we'll go the distance. Valley Forge. Battle of the Bulge. Those soldiers had it worse. It was lots colder in those places than here. But we're still clacking and chattering and shivering. DJ is blue with cold, pale gray in the bad light—and maybe it *is* bad light, infected light. Who knows what the Gurus could use to punish intruders?

I don't hear any echoes, any fragment of sensation that could help me figure out what sort of space we're in, how big, how wide, whether it's empty or filled with invisible snares.

Joe's eyes must be sharper than mine. He tugs on my forearm. "Out there," he whispers.

I look. Very far away, no scale to judge how far, I see what could be tangles of silvery branches filled with those elfin lights. Striking two ghosts together could make sparks like that. No surprise to find a Guru ship is haunted, right? Not just our dead back in the hamster ball. So many wars, so many seasons, so many corpse entertainers hanging around to learn about their ratings, how they rank in the sum of history.

"Bamboo groves," Tak says. "All pushed together."

"Bigger than that," Jacobi says.

Ishida asks, "Wonder what could fit in there?"

Then the lights fade and for a time we can't see anything. The Antags are still pulsing and drafting, still silent, and I don't hear Bird Girl or anything else in my head. I thought getting beyond the gate would be some improvement, provide some sense of accomplishment, maybe a hint of our next destination, but so far no joy.

"Fuck this shit," says Bilyk. Bird Girl's translator goes to work. The Antags fluff their bristles, maybe in amusement. Maybe they agree. GI bitching is universal.

"We are okay for a while," Bird Girl then says through the translator, so that all of us can hear. The translator moves over to Russian.

Litvinov growls. "Progress!" he shouts. "We need progress!"

Old-man words, I think. He's the oldest of us, other than maybe Kumar, and he's fading. Doesn't make me happy. Litvinov is one of those people I'd like to sit down with and find out how they've lived their lives, where they've been, what they've done—outside of Mars and all this shit. We all have instincts about guys we'd like to ask personal questions or just listen to, no questions, over vodka.

Kumar is allowing himself to be dragged, not resisting, not protesting, hardly moving—maybe suffering from a hangover after giving in to his Guru conditioning. He said you had to be around Gurus for a long time to come fully under their spell. Maybe they lied to him about that as well. I don't want to think about Guru lies or illusions because that takes me straight back to what was or is in my head and how Ulyanova used me, used that. Let's pretend there really is progress, that we know what we're doing, at least a little.

What did Bird Girl mean by searchers used as slaves? Their slaves or Guru slaves? Would finding *them* mean progress? And if we do find them and hook up, and they mean progress, but only for Antags—are humans then disposable?

Ulyanova would be so disappointed. She's coming into her own, getting her own way, making this all work for Bird Girl. Her allegiances are getting complicated.

Joe and DJ try to separate their strands so they won't keep spinning around each other. I'm lucky enough to be untangled, my leash beginning with Ulyanova, right next to Bird Girl, then stretching back to Tak and Jacobi—all in a row. We're pretty good at using our parachute training to tug here and there and keep separate.

How long is this going to take? I don't like fucking big ships. I remember watching science fiction movies way back when I was ten or eleven, when my mother, between boyfriends, would make me watch with her, and even then marveling at how engineers could shove gigantic spaceships across the cosmos, even then wondering where they got all that energy, doubting the efficiencies, all those cathedral spaces being dragged around wherever you went, like driving a car the size of a city. Even as a kid, I doubted those movies made sense. Boy, was I wrong. The Gurus prove me wrong. Sure, all our transports leaving Earth and going to Mars are small enough, in the beginning, and efficient enough, given spent-matter drives.

But Spook and Box and now this…

Once I nerd out, I can amuse myself for hours. But over

time, and especially now, as I search for the open holes left by the melted and fused bombs, and not finding them—so are they still there?—the nerd impulses turn sour. I'm not a naturally cheerful and optimistic fellow. Had that beat out of me a long time ago, either at home or on the playground.

Maybe this isn't a spaceship at all. Maybe we've crossed over through the gate to another dimension, a dimension not of sight, but of mind—a distributed hell-space with no boundaries, no walls. Those specks of light up ahead—the decayed ghosts of previous visitors.

Maybe if I felt cheerful I'd know I was no longer me. I've gotten used to this poor battered kid-self. Not that I wouldn't like to be set free every now and then. With Joe's help, I veered from drugs and moderated my intake of booze. I could have easily sunk fast and not climbed out. I watched my mother go into that pit a couple of times. The last time, Joe and I helped her out. Got her into a program. I watched most of her boyfriends dive into dope and booze and never rise again. And not just the guy who taught me how to use guns, the guy I shot, but the bank robber she dated for a few weeks. He spent his whole life planning and doing jobs and then getting high. When my mother refused to get high with him, he beat her, he beat me—and then he left. Cops got him outside Barstow. He ended up minus a hand in Chino.

"We need to get somewhere!" DJ shouts to the Antags.

Amen, whatever he means. But they're still drafting. They still have hope.

And as for me...

I get metaphysical, inspired by all the weirdness. I've long since believed in God, but have never quite figured out what belief means, what God is, what God's plan is—what's in store, ultimately. What would it be like to actually cross over into a *good* dimension, into heaven itself? What would heaven be like? Would God be waiting to greet you, or would it be Grandma? My aunts? Former squad members? Veterans in full dress uniform, with their ribbons and medals and all? I'd like that, actually.

How terrific to know it's over, that I can stop sucking in my guts and relax. No more killing, no more strategy and tactics, no more awful grief and mind-bending shock—no more war. Death itself is behind me, over and done with. What would that be like? I'd be a fish out of water. Where in this other dimensional afterlife could I get an assignment, get a job? Who the hell would want to work with me? Maybe I'm not cut out for heaven. But it would be fun to give it a try. Nature's long, long vacation. Anything's better than staring ahead at the armored butts and pulsing wings of a bunch of Antags.

"Where the hell are we?" Tak asks.

"Forward of the tail," DJ says.

"That big bulge, maybe," Jacobi says.

Ahead, the elf-lights outline another thicket, leafless but dense, a weave of long sticks or canes that surrounds our forward view.

I'm not getting any help from my Antag channel, probably because Bird Girl is intent on drafting this awkward crowd several dozen meters ahead. If the "searchers" and "slaves" Bird Girl mentioned are the squid we saw tending to the Antag transports, the double-hulled catamaran creature we saw through the walls of our tank...would this gym set of interlaced sticks allow them to traverse the larger spaces? Monkey bars for squid. They'd do better than us, certainly better than the Antags.

"Squid playground," DJ says, squinting ahead.

I slap his shoulder for stealing my comparison. Borden looks irritated at both of us but Joe says, "Let 'em yak. They're balance to the real crazy."

By which he probably means Ulyanova.

"Starting to close in," Ishida says. And she's right—the thicket is narrowing.

"Searchers!" Bird Girl calls over the translator.

Emerging from the thicket come nine catamaran squid, grappling around the outer reaches. We hear booming and clicking, answered by Antag music and chirps from Bird Girl and her commanders, who rein in our leashes and gather us into a dense, weightless cluster.

The booms grow louder. In the flickering, come-and-go clouds of moonlight flakes, dozens of squid fill the forward spaces, crowding and bumping as they compete for a view. Each is about three meters across, with arms on both outboard bodies that can stretch an additional three meters. On each "hull" they display two amazing eyes, each the size of a human head, gold-flecked sclera almost obscured by large, figure-eight pupils. Again, four eyes—does that mean they're related to the Antags? Other than the eyes, they could not be more different.

Then the sounds stop. The squid gather around us in silence. I have to think they're not happy. Their arms quiver and dart back as they reach out to touch Bird Girl, the armored commanders, and then—me, DJ, Borden. It's here that we all realize that the squid, the searchers, are pushing us gently aside, their attention centered on one individual in our bouquet of humans. Ulyanova.

Bird Girl drafts between us and the searchers and hovers,

wings beating slowly. "These are the ones we hoped to find, the ones we need," she says through the translator. "Keepers use searchers as drivers."

"Are they friendly?" DJ asks.

"To us, yes," Bird Girl says.

"What do they eat?"

"Not you."

DJ grins. Maybe he and the squid will get along.

Ulyanova pushes past us. "They think I am Guru." She smiles as if they aren't wrong. "They will take my orders!" The searchers part, then brush her with their tentacles as she passes through them, spreading her arms and pirouetting. Her self-assurance is startling. She seems to pass inspection. Dealing with Gurus, maybe you get used to all kinds of shapes.

I catch a closer look as we're cabled up again, matched in pairs and quads. Searcher skin seems to be covered with soft plates, like armadillos—a kind of exoskeleton. The plates interlock to stiffen an arm or part of the squid's body.

The Antags urge us forward, into a deeper and thicker forest of canes. Within the thicket, scattered through the spiral, lie shiny dark spheres, each maybe thirty meters wide. More hamster cages? I don't think so. More like living quarters. Searchers come and go, pulling and twisting around the spheres and through the canes.

Bird Girl decides it's time for details. "These searchers cannot fight. They uniquely serve," she says to DJ and me through our link. I get some of that—peaceable monsters—but what use are they to Gurus or Keepers?

"For Keepers, they know how to work this ship," she says. "And for us, they swim on Titan and access archives."

"But none came through the gate," I say. "Have these been here all along?"

"They are from Sun-Planet," she says, attached to an impression of wonder, hope, loss—and sadness. "They have been here for much time. But they remember our home, as well." Bird Girl and the Antags really do feel a relation, an indebtedness, to the searchers, not at all like owners to pets. The relation seems to have overtones of a blood debt. Obviously, when there's time, more needs to be asked and explored.

"Where are they taking us?" Jacobi asks DJ.

"Someplace where we can get a shave and a shower," he says, almost as if he believes it.

RUNNING ON EMPTY

Putting one's self in the arms of a squid requires a courage not expected or taught in basic. We all do it, however,
because it's hard to imagine getting through the canebrake
without searcher help—and because the Antags have sub-
mitted as well and are even now ahead of us. We don't talk
much. We're scared, scared to our very guts, in that way that
exhaustion makes worse.

It's dark, it's weird, it's Guru—and there are squid.

But nobody gets hurt, and in half an hour we're escorted
through the brake, and what's on the other side is more what
you might expect within a gigantic spaceship—genuine, mon-
umental architecture.

We're taken across a hollow big enough to hold an apartment high-rise, but filled instead by a wide, undulating coral
reef of spun and accreted metal. Judging from the occupants
coming and going, like bees flying in and out of a hive, this is
another low-g housing tract for searchers. Helping them get
around are rope ladders and twisted cane bridges, but more

open, with, at the center, a large concave blister that seems to reveal space, or at least blackness and stars. No sign of Titan or Saturn or any moons. About ten searchers are stationed inside the curve of the blister, paying no attention to what's behind them. They're on driver duty, I presume.

We're brought up short on our leashes and again arranged into a bouquet, keeping our distance with outstretched arms and gripping hands, pajamas hiding very little, while Bird Girl takes hold of Ulyanova's leash and leads her into a searcher congregation behind the starry blister. There, our prize pupil creates a minor sensation of movement, investigation, rearrangement.

"It's like an aquarium," Jacobi says.

"I thought squid are mollusks that live in water," Ishida says.

"We've eaten enough of those," Tak says, and Ishikawa looks unhappy.

"Don't tell them that," she says.

"But Bird Girl can read Vinnie like a book, can't she?" Ishida says.

"Never liked sushi," I say. "More a teriyaki kind of guy."

"What's she thinking?" Joe asks DJ and me.

"Who, Bird Girl or Guru Girl?" DJ asks.

"Either one," Joe says.

"Bird Girl is feeling pretty good," I say. "No specifics, but she's where she wants to be—a slow carrier wave of accomplishment, of good feeling."

"She's at the end point of a long strategy," Kumar says. We've all either ignored or tried to stay apart from him after his interlude, including me, hypocrite that I am.

"Maybe she really likes squid," Ishida says. "Old friends from home?"

"She's never been home," I say.

With Vera at her side, Ulyanova's submitting to a more thorough searcher examination, and maybe already being put to use. She's the only one of us that seems to have a real purpose. Yet Bird Girl hasn't stated to me, or to DJ, any change of heart regarding our *starshina* once her usefulness has ended. I hope it doesn't come to that. She's still human, still one of ours—until proven otherwise.

Like me.

Bird Girl leaves her surrounded by searchers to return and address us all. "We will find quarters," she says. "Will be better than hamster cage. And there is food."

"Good to know," DJ says. We look quizzically at each other, since we don't remember passing that comparison—the hamster cage—on to any of the Antags. Didn't go through *my* head. Maybe the bats were listening.

Where are the bats now? I'd forgotten about them. Bats. Birds. Squid. I'd like to shove a few of our DIs into this present situation. They'd go nuts. Serve them right.

"We bring others around, outside, from tail forward," Bird Girl says, and her eyes do not waver from mine.

"You trust this ship?" Joe asks.

"With searchers, yes," she says. "The one named Ulyanova outranks all of you, for the time. Are there mating pairs or other considerations?"

Borden asserts herself. "If possible, we'd like to be kept close—but no mating arrangements. Kumarji will explain ranks, if you set time aside."

"We do not like him," Bird Girl says. "We are not sure of him."

"Neither are we," Ishida says, but Borden gives her an elbow.

"We'd like a decent service and arrangements for the dead we found," Joe says.

"They will be incinerated, along with our dead."

"Dead from Titan?" Joe asks.

Bird Girl blinks all four eyes. "We are told by our searchers that games were arranged for us as well as you. These provoke feelings of guilt in searchers. Arrangements will be made."

"Thank you," Joe says. "I understand."

"Do you?" Bird Girl asks. "I have insight into two of you, and our searchers are, in your eyes, horrible."

Borden says quickly, "We hope to revise our opinions."

"Searchers always important, and these have been to our home, piloting this ship. I wish to learn from them and prepare for the journey. We have work to do, and all may be useful."

She drafts and pulls herself back to the concave, star-filled dish.

"That isn't the nose of the ship," DJ says in an aside to me. "Not a direct view."

"I got that," I say.

"Ship goes way beyond. Wonder what's up there—what they all used it for?"

"Kumar, come here," Borden says.

Kumar climbs forward.

"What's the chance that Ulyanova can remain independent while channeling a Guru?"

"Zero," he says. "I'm pitiful, and all I did was look at them, work with them. She has one in her head."

"Great to hear," Joe says.

DJ hunches his shoulders. "You know what I'd give anything for right now?"

"A blow job," Ishida says with rich sarcasm.

"Fuck no. That can wait. A tent on Mars, with some of those Russian food packs, those sausages, those little reindeer ones."

"Yeah," Tak says.

"Those were the best, weren't they?"

The Russians agree. "Blow job would be good, as well," Bilyk adds. He looks hopefully at Jacobi and Litvinov cuffs him.

INTO THE WEIRD

The arrangements for quarters are interesting. Beyond the starry dish there is indeed more ship. We get drafted through the centerline on our leashes, this time by two searchers, who brachiate like long-armed gibbons from one jutting cluster of canes to the next. I feel like Jane in Tarzan's arms, only a lot more arms. The canes seem to be arranged in a tube around the centerline, and the searchers move alternately on the outside of one tube, then cross to the inside of the next, deftly avoiding other squid on other tube highways coming and going toward the ship's unknown and distant prow.

In some places, the tubes are thin and we can see almost all the way to an outer wall, which in this segment has transparencies like very large windows, giving us glimpses of the outboard cylinders, which have their own transparencies. We're uninvolved enough in our transport that I try to peer through the canes and both transparencies. The outboard cylinders are filled with other screw gardens, lots of them, bigger than the one in the tail. Important. Nonsensically important.

The searchers smoothly shuttle us through an immense cavern. At first, I can only make out blurry patches shot through with flashes of that fairy light—but then I get a real sense of scale. We're being shuttled over a major e-ticket ride. Guru tech is on full display as we smoothly pass over what amounts to an immense four-leaf clover, the leaves pointing aft, the node, connecting the leaves, about two klicks forward of the trailing edges—the whole arrangement maybe two klicks across. Each leaf's inner surface is mapped by canals and geographies of walled-off rivers, along with what could pass for a lake, all teeming with hundreds of searchers going about their business, whatever that might be. Makes more sense than the screw gardens—they're the ship's drivers, right? They need a place for R&R.

Gravity is not apparent, but the water flowing along the rivers and lake doesn't drift away. The giant clover doesn't spin or do anything obvious, but the surfaces of the leaves seem to have their own sticky properties. The searchers in charge of our bouquet make no comments on these wonders, not that we'd understand if they did. DJ and I did not share tea with them and know nothing about their inner thoughts.

Near the node where the leaves come together, we're taken to a lumpy neighborhood of gray-brown mushrooms, spotted with holes, as if worms have been busy, and for all we know, they have. But we haven't met any—yet.

The searchers deliver us and deftly, silently move way, tail first, keeping their eyes on us like servants or guards in a royal palace.

"Our bunks," Borden says.

We untangle from the leashes and explore. The spaces within the holes are equipped with mats and net-bundles of cakes, along with succulent gluey beads about the size of grapes, but bright yellow-green. We're ravenous and try them all. Not terrible. Almost good.

The walls are spongy, soft, reasonably warm and comfortable—and glow with a soft, bluish sunset light. Best accommodations yet, but what I need most, what all of us need most, is sleep. So we divide along rank and friendship, crawl through different wormholes, wrap up in blankets, and rest easy. It's an instinct Skyrines have, sort of Greek battle-field wisdom—know what you can change, accept what you can't, and make do with whatever's handed to you.

But as I drift into a much-needed and reasonably sound slumber, I can't stop thinking about those impossible rivers, flowing along the huge, angled cloverleaves—searchers swimming, breaching, refreshing, enjoying themselves—all the while doing something apparently essential to this ship.

A little residual from Bug Karnak stirs and decides to take shape in my foggy thoughts. The searchers are familiar to the bugs—in reverse. Like the Antags, they were designed and assigned. "What's that even mean?" I murmur, with my hands reaching out as if to grasp these facts. "Bugs never met them, never knew them."

But bugs never met or knew human beings or anything on Earth. Reverse familiarity. Later manifestations of bug civilization helped seed the outer reaches of the solar system, far beyond Pluto, far indeed from the sun. In fact, that's where all the important stuff was happening, four billion years ago.

And the searchers, for the Antags at least, are among the most important.

But how did they become useful to the Gurus? They don't

fight. Can they defend themselves against anybody or anything? How can they be soldiers in a Guru-inspired war?

Maybe they provide a lagniappe of irony, pity, perspective. There's a theory so vague I withdraw my hand. The vision subsides. I'm warm, I'm surrounded, it's not much stranger—maybe slightly less strange, actually—than the quarters we occupied on the Spook, and there's no impending battle, no fight planned for the day, the month, maybe for years, How long will it take us to get where Bird Girl thinks we're going? Hundreds of billions of kilometers. Maybe a trillion. We're definitely out of action for this part of the season, probably for hundreds of seasons to come. Maybe we'll die inside this monster.

Inside. We've been eaten by an immense Guru ship populated by Captain Nemo's worst nightmares...but all in all, it's not too bad. A vacation break from the Red or Titan. Instant death delayed.

I can't hear Captain Coyle anymore, but I know what she'd tell me. She'd say, *When you get home, Venn, you're going to be one fucked-up dude.*

———

I EMERGE FROM my hole and almost bump into Borden. She's looking reasonably sharp, so I ask her where she got coffee. She gives me a chilly smile. "We need to talk."

"I'm still half-asleep."

"That's our problem, Venn. We've been sleepwalking ever since Titan. I need to talk to somebody about command structure and discipline."

Of course you do, I say to myself. "Happy to listen, Commander, but I'm not sure I'm the right guy."

"I'm conflicted about Sanchez. I don't like his story about Sudbury. Putting our soldiers, any kind of soldier, into the hands of monsters…"

"DJ and Tak and I wouldn't be here without him. He saved our bacon, ma'am, and Sudbury was one mean son of a bitch."

"Even so. I can't talk to Litvinov, he's too grief-stricken at the loss of Ulyanova."

"She's not dead, Commander."

"She might as well be. And she's taken one of the *efreitors* with her."

"Vera?"

"We haven't seen either of them since I don't know when. That's part of the problem…I have no idea when this is or where we are, and no actionable about where we're heading."

"Bird Girl says she and her fellow Antags are going home, but most or all of them have never been there. DJ thinks it's Planet X."

"I goddamned well can't talk to the corporal. He's too whacked for me."

"DJ is smart and he's straight, Commander."

"Maybe it's my lack, then, but I need to think about structure, about who we are, with somebody I think gives a damn."

"If you don't know where you are, you don't know who you are."

"Who said that—you?"

"A writer named Wendell Berry."

"You read a lot, Venn?"

"I like to read. My mother read a lot, sometimes to me."
Borden is the current puzzle, I tell myself. Constrained rage, trying to appear so calm on the outside…What does she

think we can do? We're so reduced we could all hole up in a nutshell and leave room for the nut.

"What about Kumar?" I say. "He's the civilian authority, right?"

"I haven't trusted Wait Staff since before I broke you out of Madigan."

"Well, he's been pretty straight with us—except for that moment trying to remember what the Gurus meant to him. I've had my own lapses that way."

"Venn, I want to gain traction here."

"Tell me what you need, Commander."

"We need to reestablish. We've long since exceeded our mission, and we're down to Hershey squirts for orders."

"Jesus," I say, and laugh.

"I mean it. If we don't get it together soon, we'll go fucking native, and that is not any sort of option…is it?"

"Our enemy is in charge, but they're no longer our enemy. Maybe you need to speak with Bird Girl."

"That's what I'm saying, goddammit! What's her real name? What's her rank?"

"I'll ask next time we get together," I say. Borden's face is a mask of little-girl disappointment. I did not think she was capable of reviving her inner child, but here it is, she's in pain, and there's not a meaningful thing I can do. She's my superior officer. We shouldn't even be having this conversation.

Which proves her point.

"We need to have a mission," she says, her voice falling off. She gives me a hard look. I have to think outside the box— that's a direct order, isn't it? All my life I've assigned leadership and planning to others—to Joe or people like Borden—to our DIs or battlefield commanders.

"Maybe it's right in front of us," I say. "We need to follow the Antags to their home world, get as much information as we can about their relationship to their own Gurus—their Keepers—and acquire as much intel as we can about where the Antags come from and what they have to offer in our effort to free Earth from all this bullshit."

She looks squarely at me. "Like you say, obvious. But I'm maybe the least informed of anyone on this ship, the least sophisticated on things Guru and Antag—all book and paper training, right?"

I don't respond to that. I'm still pondering what her highest directive was when she sprang me from Madigan. Was she already anticipating—along with Kumar and Mushran—that there would be a Guru mimic in their future?

"What do *you* suggest?" she asks.

"Litvinov and Joe and Jacobi could work with you to create a new set of directives. New orders reflective of our circumstances."

"Where would Bird Girl fit in?"

"Maybe she wants us to contribute to their game plan, their new mission—but so far she's just providing minimal education...and trying to overcome her hatred."

"What about her commanders? Do we have any sense of how they work, militarily, socially?"

I make a wry face. "I'm not sure, but when we communicate, there's something not stated—some place inside her thinking where I'm not allowed to go."

"Can she wander in your head?" Borden asks.

"I don't think so." *Can she? Would I feel it if she did?*

"How many shoes can an Antag drop?" Borden asks, seriously enough, but with more wit than I thought she was capable of. We're not often allowed to think such thoughts of our sisters in the military, and particularly not of rank, but for the first time, I can conceive of maybe enjoying a social occasion with Commander Borden—going out for drinks if not an actual date. She might laugh at my jokes. I might laugh at hers.

I've been out here a long, long time.

"Well, the big shoe that hasn't been dropped is, where are the men?" I say. "Antag males, I mean."

"They're all females?" Borden seems surprised.

"That's what Ulyanova says. Even rank is female. But there might be something more to the picture."

"A different command structure?"

"Something odd." *Something big.*

"Odd how?" Borden asks.

"I do not know, Commander."

"Surely not as odd as the squid, right?"

I shake my head.

She looks alarmed, then disgusted. "You're thinking the squid are the males?"

"No, they're definitely from a different part of whatever world they all come from. The bugs knew about them in reverse, I mean, the bugs laid down some of the possibilities for the searchers way back when, but…no. They're more different from Antags than we are."

"Thank God," Borden says.

And I have to agree. But what's lurking in my scattered shrapnel of knowledge, now that we're so far from anything like Bug Karnak? Now that Bug Karnak has been hammered into silence…Where *are* the Antag males, and what are they like?

"Thanks for a sympathetic ear, Venn."

"Not a problem, Commander."

"Keep me in the loop, okay?"

"Will do. And sir, I'd be happy to help you understand DJ. He's a valuable member of our team."

She shudders delicately. But then she sucks it up. "Sure," she says. "We need more understanding, if we're going to keep it together."

———

BIRD GIRL CONVENES us all in view of the maze of supports and machinery forward of the node where the cloverleaves come together. She's been joined by two searchers. I can't keep my eyes off the way they grip and glide smoothly through the canes and a spiderweb of flexible cords. They help Bird Girl find her place at our center and even offer to help arrange us. Once again, we're treated like flowers, and the squid seem to enjoy the little flourishes of who is planted next to whom, which some of us accept with tense reserve and others with a growing sense of perverse humor. Who can be most cooperative? After you, ma'am. May I pull up an arm, a tentacle? No, I insist.

Borden takes it all with relative calm. Maybe our talk did some good. Who can suss out what's really going on, what's really about to happen?

Tak is a master of his own sort of calm introspection. I would have expected no less. Jacobi is perhaps the least at ease. Litvinov and the remaining Russian, Bilyk, show little more than resignation. Vera and Ulyanova are still not present.

One of the searchers accesses a satchel looped around its starboard hull and draws out replacement clothes. The outfits seem tailor-made—by squid? They could be excellent seam-stresses, right? The outfits are handed to us as individuals, and while searcher "faces" and gestures are still impossible to read, there's a kind of tenderness to the whole ceremony, mixed, maybe, with Bird Girl's display of what might be observant humor. I've noticed in our connection that there is humor in her, though it's tightly bound to embarrassment—ours, not hers—and the potential for falling out of line, for humiliation, losing social position—not fitting into a per-fectly obvious status quo.

Ishida and Ishikawa speak in Japanese, cocking glances at the squid, at Bird Girl, and nodding sagely. I wonder what they're saying? Tak joins them and they seem to enjoy a joke on all of us. This irritates Borden.

Then I see the similarities—cockeyed similarities. Borden's only human. Bird Girl is also human. Being called *human* is funny that way—a stretchable label that covers a multitude of common sins. Our Antag representative is not deliber-ately cruel, not sadistic, but there's a touch of the challenger and even the bully about her, as if she'd rather be anyplace but here, tending to us, despite our clueless clumsiness—our evil nature! We who used to be killers of her kind and who still are, back around Mars and Saturn. How far she'll go to arrange for and enjoy our embarrassment has yet to be determined.

In their natural habitats, and outside of protective armor, neither searchers nor Antags need or wear clothes. Do they think us weak for our shivering nakedness? Weak and funny? But they're accommodating our obvious needs for the first time, replacing the near-useless pajamas and arranging for us to be covered.

There's surprise among our group as we realize the new clothes fit and are comfortable. We struggle to put them on, but only against the necessity of weightless motion. The new duds are comfy enough, but they're still just pajamas. I'd feel better in fatigues, but little chance of that.

"We are leaving Saturn space," Bird Girl tells us all through the translator. "What we both came to Saturn to study has been destroyed. Both sides will take credit."

She's getting that sarcastic tone down pretty well. I wonder if Antags are just naturally a little angry. That would make them even more *human*, no? Easier to understand.

"Can you still feel the old knowledge?" DJ asks her.

Bird Girl looks at me—is this a question it will be useful to answer, maybe for the others? I try to nod my approval. She's still not very good at reading human expression. But then, I can't read her well without retreating into our link, which is not always open.

"I no longer feel the old knowledge," Bird Girl answers. "Do you?"

DJ seems to try to listen. "Nope," he says.

Nothing, not even shrapnel. The last residuals are melting in my head like ice crystals in a warm breeze. I might miss those bits, but I won't miss the Guru bombs—if they're still there, which...

They do not seem to be.

"As we move out to where comets are made, there will be study of one outer world. You call that Pluto, small, like a lost moon."

"Always happy to learn more about Planet X," DJ says.

"Pluto isn't Planet X," I say.

"Not now," DJ agrees.

Joe is quiet. Stealth Sanchez. Even as a teen, there were days when he went away, hid out, only to pop up when I least expected him. He'd usually say something about having a girlfriend or going to a party in the Valley, but I never knew what to believe. My attitude toward Joe has softened quite a bit.

I ask Bird Girl what Ulyanova's doing.

"Ship has schedule: Pluto, then the transmitters, then Sun-Planet. Your companion helps guide ship's planning."

Still Guru. But where? Is there a wheelhouse on this monster?

I ask Bird Girl how long such a journey will take.

"I am told, for Earth, five times around the sun."

"Who tells you that?" No answer. "What'll we do to pass the time?"

"We will not notice the time."

"How's that done?"

"That is what searchers tell me," Bird Girl says. "They have done this often and often. We will learn."

Then she shows us another projected chart of the outer regions, swooping us out to Pluto, which is accompanied by one large moon and a handful of smaller moons.

At this stage in the delivery of her data, her impressions, all Bird Girl is receiving from the searchers and maybe from Ulyanova, something unexpected and even a little scary, for her, crawls up between us, interrupting the impressions of Pluto.

This object, on the projected chart, is an unlabeled, wavering smudge, not presently active in any obvious way—and definitely not alive or carrying living things. Whatever it is, it's not far from Pluto, doesn't do much, may not seem important, but has no explanation. According to the orbital track, after we reach Pluto, but before we reach the transmitter, we'll come quite close to this mystery smudge.

"Is it a Guru object?" I ask.

No answer. Our squad is taken back to quarters. We resume what passes for routine, going from sleep to sleep, being fed by squid, watched by their huge eyes as we emerge from our mushroom hole nests to chat and stare pointlessly at the stars in the star dish, telling one another we're making history, which impresses nobody, not even me, because the distances and the numbers are so far beyond anything humans can work with, and we're not anywhere near traveling between the stars, which supposedly the Antags had done, part of the big lie we have been fed since the Gurus arrived—arrived this time around—and when I tell that to Bird Girl, she experiences something like amusement, crossed with guilt and self-judgment, because her enemies have been so deluded and ignorant, and that is not honorable—

And we sleep and eat and sleep again, and gather and separate, and gather again, and I guess it's been about four weeks since we passed through the gate, and I wonder what's happened to Ulyanova, whom none of us have seen since.

All of which seems to mush up and fade from memory.

And suddenly—

Months have passed. Things feel very different out in the canebrake, around the searcher quarters and our quarters. We're fed, repeat our dull routines, and most of us believe nothing new has happened, nothing at all has happened.

But I know different. Lately there's a touch of Ulyanova in my thoughts, something about an apartment and steam heat, Moscow winter—as if she's teasing her only contacts now other than her internal Guru and the ship's squid. But then again, what I'm feeling may not be her at all. It might be me imagining what her life was like, once.

Maybe there's been a Guru on this ship all along and it's pretending to be Ulyanova. At this point, would I know the difference? *Could* I know?

But we're far, far from where we had been during our last "briefing," and when we look at the concave "window," we seem to slide through star-backed, dusty darkness at very high speed. We see at least the simulations of nebular cloud structure. Looks compelling and cool, broadly 3-D, which makes me doubt it's straight-out real.

Likely this display is simulated for the benefit of the searchers' big, wide-spaced eyes.

———

BIRD GIRL APPROACHES DJ and me in the tangle around the window, escorted by three searchers. "We do not like this ship," she says. "It is not honest."

"Figured that out, have you?" DJ asks, and I elbow him in the ribs. She's trying to be forthright.

"What's Ulyanova doing now?" I ask.

"She is behind curtain. She does not communicate with us."

Curtain? Okay. Strangely, I don't feel concern, because this much is becoming clear to me: Ulyanova is still on this ship, she's still in control, active, and she's going to call DJ and me forward soon. The last few hours, I can hear her in my head like a distant song.

I feel another cold, deep concern, worse than that gut-level fear I had earlier, before the confused passage of ship time.

Pluto is coming. The Guru transmitter is coming—a dangerous and important moment. And we'll soon be near that silent
smudge that nobody knows anything about—unknown to
Gurus or Antags. Unknown to the searchers.

Why go there at all? I don't like it.

———

WE'RE IN OUR soft, warm quarters, half-asleep, when a
searcher appears at the entrance. Its tentacles twinkle in the
dim light. No surprise, in darkness they, too, kind of glow.
They could be responsible for all the elf-light residue, bits
and pieces of squid skin, squid dust. Humans shed, too, but it
isn't nearly as weirdly pretty.

Wonder what they look like when they're at home? Maybe
not very different from the way they look swimming along
the cloverleaf waterways. Peaceful, graceful—dedicated and
working away for the Gurus. Wonder if Bird Girl can per-
suade them to work for us. Maybe she already has.

There are several of them outside the hole. DJ and I are
gathered up, gently but no nonsense. Not that he and I are
prone to offer objections. DJ looks resigned to anything as
long as it's over with soon.

The searchers have Bird Girl in tow as well. She's not moving, not in charge, not drafting us forward with her wings.
I miss that, somehow, and wonder what's changed. They've
wrapped her in a cinched cover or blanket. All of her four
eyes are tightly closed. Unconscious? No link. No information from her about what might be next.

"We're going forward, aren't we?" DJ asks me.

"If that's where Ulyanova is."

"Christ, she scares the fuck out of me," he says.

"Why?"

He snorts and gives me a grim smile. Nobody else from our squad is going with us. They're sleeping like cozy little dormice.

The searchers do their arm-nest thing and sedan-chair us beyond the node, through more canebrakes, following an internal highway that spirals and arches forward. I wish I could have a moment with Joe or even Borden to express my last will and testament—give my love and a soldier's farewell to Mom if you make it, Commander, won't you? The tear-jerking moment of every half-assed war movie, because you know this poor SOB is doomed—all he has to do is ask and you know he's about to fly right out of the frame, right out of the screenplay. The Gurus, expert craftsmen, would plan it that way to keep their audience happy, right? Maximum interest.

But this is a tougher kind of epic. Not much in the way of sentiment. Pure scrap and stain. We should be accustomed to simply and violently ending it all. A lot of our dismembered, carbonized, vaporized friends are out there waiting for us. But this *feels* different. What can Ulyanova possibly be or do that scares us both so bad?

———

WE'VE BEEN TRAVELING with the searchers, right behind them, for quite some time. Big fucking ship. None so big as this one, and here it's filled with screw gardens bigger than any we've seen earlier, if size can be estimated in the dim light—and if they are gardens, really, because they seem to enjoy the dark.

More spherical cages become evident, hiding back in

other squash courts, other cubical recesses, filled with skel-
etons, some possibly human, many not—like abandoned and
uncleansed graveyards in an old city—proud Guru trophies.
Imagine the categories! *Best performance with cruelty. Most
satisfying vengeance. Most popular caged slaughter.*

It's sobering to think (or to hope) that all these bodies,
these dead, were once monsters like Grover Sudbury. Per-
versity is everywhere. But where did they all come from?
There aren't enough planets, I'm thinking, DJ is thinking.
And none of our melted soup of leftover knowledge helps us
understand.

That's all we've got to distract us—screw gardens and
cages filled with corpses. DJ and I keep silent out of respect,
but maybe as much out of terror. Surely these charnel houses
carry their own ghosts! What would the ghost of a nonhuman be like? How would it differ from our own spirits of
the dead—which of course we all know don't exist? They're
figments of our imagination. I've never seen a ghost, right?
Except that I have. And not just Captain Coyle, who wasn't
really a ghost anyway.

Ghosts seem to be able to get around. I don't know how.
Maybe the dead humans up here have already returned to
Earth. Maybe they're lost, drifting in between, dissolving,
evaporating. That leads me down more highways of dark
speculation—anything to keep alert. Fear and anger are good
for keeping alert, though maybe not the best for clear thinking.
But I have to wonder—when they destroyed Titan's archives,
and Mars's, did they destroy Captain Coyle's last existence?

Maybe now she can become a *real* ghost. Will that be
better?

Enough spooky shit. We have to concentrate on what is

immediately apparent and important—that there are dead things aboard this ship that do not come from Earth or anyplace like Earth, that are not Antag or anything like Antag. So who most recently supplied these cages with victims? And are more on the way?

"Maybe they won prizes," DJ says softly as we're moved forward, echoing my own theories. "Big ship carries a shit-load of fine Guru memories."

Maybe. But still no explanation for the screw gardens, why so large, why so many?—dozens and dozens arrayed in the dark volumes. Maybe the screw gardens are spooky, too. How the fuck would we know what's spooky and what isn't?

This is the Guru's Rolls-Royce, the limo that takes the most important Gurus where they want to go, their personal conveyance around and beyond the solar system—the way they connect with every show they're producing for their faithful audience of interstellar couch potatoes.

The show must go on, but who could hold an audience's interest for hundreds of millions, much less billions, of years? We're none of us all that charming, all that interesting and suspenseful. We're none of us movie star material! Maybe it's in the writing. The Gurus have to be masters of suspense and plot to make our petty little dramas popular.

———

FINALLY WE COME to an opening in the cane highway, something the searchers can pass through, carrying DJ and Bird Girl and me. The architecture changes. My eyes have a difficult time tracking, and I'm not sure I understand our present surroundings, but that turns out to be because I'm dizzy. My heart is thumping out of rhythm. Something in the air smells sweet. Could be airborne persuasion or nutrients for searchers—not so good for us. To distract myself, I pay attention to searcher skin and how the segments link as they move. These are nothing like terrestrial mollusks.

My heart steadies, my eyes stop trying to cross—and it all clicks into place. Up ahead, nine searchers in charge of a large, dark bundle give scale to a distant bulkhead. The bulkhead is flat gray and hundreds of meters wide. The bundle the searchers have surrounded is wrapped in a tight gray blanket, maybe eight meters long. At their poking, the bulk flexes. A big Guru? No...and in silhouette, it doesn't look like a searcher, either—more like an Antag, but larger than any we've met.

Bird Girl's eyes open. She blinks and spreads her wings. Two searchers attend to her now, grooming her fine feathers with the tips of their arms. She's smoother, less frazzled—being dolled up for something, I guess, some major introduction or presentation, but who could possibly care how she looks, way up here?

Our link is back but it's filled with emotions and scrambled information I can't make sense of. I try to sort and filter the emotions—and then realize they're both intensely political and intensely romantic.

Bird Girl is terrified. And she's in love.

The searchers move away. She straightens her shoulders and spreads her wings with a pride and presence I've never seen or felt from her—like a princess entering court for the first time. The searchers allow us to float free, but we aren't nearly as good at drafting as the Antags, and the canes are out of reach. Then they remove and roll up the big blanket, revealing what could be a huge, shiny black slug with purple highlights. But it spreads a wide set of wings, as if waking, or as a welcome...dwarfing Bird Girl, the searchers, us. Wingspan of at least ten meters.

Bird Girl speaks. DJ and I hear a raspy version of what she's saying, in both English and Russian. "Thank you for witnessing. This is my husband—*our* husband. We are together again. Isn't he *beautiful*?"

The emotion pouring through our link is extraordinary— immense relief that this huge Antag is still alive, that the family they trained and fought with has been rejoined, ready to resume something approaching a normal life—along with a sense of completion. Where did they keep him? Somewhere on Titan, I presume, and then carried here...asleep, waiting for a safer moment to return and take charge.

"We are together, we have come this far, and we are going home!" Bird Girl announces.

The big male's head is at least twice as wide as hers, his four eyes farther apart but roughly the same size and color. He surveys the searchers and Bird Girl with a sleepy calm, all is well, all is in order, he approves—but then his four purple-rimmed eyes light on DJ and me. With apparent surprise, he scrutinizes us, feathers rising around his massive shoulders. I gather that we're unexpected, unwanted—why are we here?

And that could be a problem. Based on the emotions coursing through our connection, to Bird Girl—and no doubt to the other female Antags on this hijacked ship—he's the ultimate reference point, their mentor and mate, mate to all...

Scares me, really, because to him, we're completely disgusting. We're still the enemy.

THE SECRET WORLD OF PLANTS

The big male speaks to Bird Girl in a high voice that belies his size—more screech-rasp, untranslated. This goes on for a few minutes, with DJ and I out of the loop and way out of our depth, but happy to be ignored.

"She's filling him in," I say.

"I don't think he likes us," DJ says.

Nothing on our link except a smothering mask of affection, not meant for us. Bird Girl is truly enamored.

"They should get a room," DJ says. "Is she going to keep him all to herself?"

He had to ask. From behind, we hear more Antag music, chirps and rasps and soaring notes. I rotate by waving my arms and see five searchers escorting seven more females, including three of the formerly oh-so-superior armored commanders, singing their appreciation like groupies. All of them have folded their wings, leaving Bird Girl as the only female to spread them wide. Clearly this is a great moment for the larger family. We know our enemies not at all.

Two searchers spray something from their tails at the canebrakes. From the shadows we hear rustling and rattling and watch as more canes grow and weave to shape arched thickets, which then fan to connect with the bulkhead, a spiral of climbing ways and bridges.

"That's cool," DJ murmurs.

The searchers take hold of us, gentle but no nonsense, and Bird Girl slowly folds her wings, then allows herself to be conveyed by her fellow females away from the big male. Her moment with the paterfamilias seems to be over. Her grief is obvious even without our link—and overwhelming when I dip in. Separation is such sweet sorrow. What a guy. What a species in which to be male! What's required of the big boy when he's at home? Is he tasked with a head-butting competition to win his place in the herd? Alpha male sports? Keeping a rolling orgy going 24/7?

DJ and I keep silent on all frequencies as our escorts guide Bird Girl and us toward a spiral bridge of fresh canes.

"Ever seen a dead cell?" DJ whispers.

"Plenty, after a bare-knuckle fight."

"In microscopes, I mean! Cells got a skeleton made of fibers just like these bamboo bridges—grow at the tips when the cell wants to move, shrink back when it's not needed." DJ can be full of surprises. Not all porn and old movies in that noggin. "Kill the cell and the gunk, the gel, shrivels, and leaves a pile of sticks. This ship is a giant cell!"

Good to know. I don't believe it for a moment, but it's better than anything I've got. We've been sedan-chaired around that internal skeleton for half an hour or more, and now, through gaps in the canes we see spaces accessible by other arches and bridges—dark, empty spaces. Maybe Gurus once slept there. Maybe they kept sporting victims up here and pulled them out when needed to fight and die.

I once got into a classroom argument with a teacher about the plural of the name Spartacus. The other kids ragged me all day, on the playground or walking home. Now we're surrounded by cages and maybe holes that were once filled with Spartacuses. Spartaci. Spartacoi. Fuck it.

Echoes tell me our surround is narrowing. It's become completely dark. Not even the searchers are illuminating. Not at all reassuring that Bird Girl is with us, because based on what's passing through our link, her deadly sadness and lovebird grief, she might happily be going to her doom, having displeased the big male with our presence, her dealings with the enemy. No way to know how smart the big male is or what they said to each other. He might have given her instructions to gut herself and us besides.

As the lights come back up we can see that we've reached a much slimmer portion of the ship's hull, perhaps closer to the actual bow. Bird Girl isn't committing suicide. She's taking us to Ulyanova. Big male (I'm going to call him Budgie) may not like us, but that hasn't changed the basic plans.

"Why aren't the showrunners doing something about us? Why haven't they learned?" DJ whispers.

"Showrunners? Learned what?"

"Gurus!" DJ says with a critical scowl. "Ship's been hijacked. Shouldn't there be a fail-safe, some sort of dead Guru switch, that would blow it up if it's hijacked?

"Damned obvious," I whisper back. "Ulyanova's convincing. Or maybe—" And this hurts to both think and say, I almost want to shut up and just curl into a ball. "Maybe the plan hasn't changed. We won't matter a great goddamned toothpick to this ship unless we get boring."

DJ plays out my drift. "So we're doing exactly what it wants—and this is our third act!"

I have to admit I was bored back in the tail, for a while, but this is definitely more and more interesting. *I'd* fucking stay tuned. What do we say to Ulyanova when we meet up? Wonder what Budgie will say once he's brought up to date?

Somehow these awkward thoughts leak to Bird Girl. She directs her searchers to move her and favors us with close examination. Four eyes bore into my two. I'm outmatched.

"Show respect," she says.

"Yes, ma'am," I say.

"We have left the mimic alone. Now she makes request for your presence."

DJ and I look at each other.

She raises a ridge between her shoulders and shakes it out with a shuffling noise. The searchers link up, grip our hands, and reach us out to a ladder of large, U-shaped grips mounted on one face of a long, sinuous beam. They release us to the grips, cold and hard, then swing off to one side. DJ and I cling as the beam pushes forward—grows forward!—and twists, spiraling us like a steel vine toward a diffuse haze, like moonlight in a cathedral.

Bird Girl has crossed with us and grips the rungs behind, wings folded. "Climb," she says.

The beam carries us into a narrower, longer chamber, like a pipe or a needle, filled with long ribbons about as broad as my forearm. The ribbons cross over in a kind of braid every five or six meters and are alternately dark, then bright again, illumination flowing aft as if carrying signals to the rest of the ship—like fiber-optic cables. The beam pushes and twists up the middle of these ribbons, contorting to avoid the braids. Searchers are moving up along the outside, keeping up with us and following more arches of canes.

As the ribbons twist along to an end, we see just beyond their conclusion four oblong panels, as colorful as stained-glass windows, but arranged in a wide quadrangle, like the faces in a clock tower. From where we are, each of the four faces appears divided into multicolored wedges, like pie charts—but sprinkled with stars.

As we grow up to and then through the faces, two searchers hiding in the angles between retreat into shadow like shy schoolchildren. The faces have painted themselves with thousands of cryptic symbols, red and blue against a silvery background like a clear dusk sky. Every few blinks, the symbols lift and rearrange—impossible to read or understand.

"Any constellations?" DJ asks from below. The beam—the vine—pushes and twists on.

"No," I say. "Some sort of diagram."

Maybe this is Ulyanova's playroom and these are her mirrors, where she's pasted Day-Glo stickers to remind herself of a human childhood. But the stars that flock in the surrounding mosquito cloud are pinpoint brilliances, like stars in a clear night sky. Not at all like stickers.

Beyond the ribbons and inboard from the faces, more searchers are spraying to encourage canes to grow, giving access to another swallow's nest of shiny black spheres—different in color, but not unlike our present habitats.

"The mimic asks that you will all move here," Bird Girl says. I detect a seething kind of hatred in her, and not just for

Ulyanova—for us as well. Meeting up with Budgie seems to have stiffened her anger—maybe bent her thoughts. At any rate, I'm not feeling any sense of partnership, much less affection.

"Better accommodations?" DJ asks.

"Closer to where the mimic hides." She stretches out a wing.

Starboard from the clock faces, about fifty meters forward of our new domiciles, I make out a slowly undulating curtain, like a tapestry woven from strands of smoke. I turn to communicate this discovery to DJ and Bird Girl when, without warning, Ulyanova and Vera appear through the curtain and surge up before us.

Bird Girl retreats a few rungs, feathers spiked, and DJ lets out a shuddering groan, but the *starshina* looks only at me.

"Long time!" she says, and tries for a charming smile. Epic fail. My God, she's nothing but skin and bones! In this light, her face stretches across her skull like frog skin, moist and shiny, eyes large and brilliantly empty. "I am glad you are here," she says. "I need to think again like human." I cringe as something from her probes my mind, like frozen fingers touching my thoughts, my memories. Ulyanova cocks her head, trying perhaps for coyness, but appearing toothy, feral. "So many strange days. Vera and I make new home. It will be beautiful when finished."

"It is already beautiful," Vera says. "It could be more *useful*."

"I know ship well," the *starshina* says. "I *dream* it. Work is difficult! They fight me, question me, all the time. Here—move closer and help me stay human, will you? Before long trips begin."

DJ climbs closer, starts to speak, maybe to save me from the full brunt of that brightly dead look, but Ulyanova simply glances his way—and he's knocked from the rungs into a nearby cane thicket, where he waves his arms and legs like a fly in a web.

Nobody dares to move. What more could she do if we actually crossed her?

She takes a shuddering breath. Then, at her permissive gesture, Vera and I link hands to pull DJ back to the rungs. He favors his elbow, which has been scraped by a broken cane.

Vera backs off a few rungs and watches DJ and me like a hawk. Literally. As if we're mice trying to hide.

"You have questions...?" Ulyanova asks.

"Where are we?" I ask.

"In needle at tip of ship," she says. "Like hypo that will inject us to stars."

"Is this a control room?" I ask.

"It is part of ship's eyes. Often, brain shows me what it is seeing. I control—but dead Gurus still try to return, take power, change things—and worst of all, *talk*." She looks both amused and sad—easy enough in her present condition. "I keep them in brain's closet. They are not happy!"

"Ship treats us well," Vera says brightly, as if that justifies everything.

"I do not stand in ship's way," Ulyanova says. "None of us are problem, not you, not me—not yet. We *amuse*."

"Can you tell the brain, the ship, where to go? Take us back to Earth—now?"

"Ship goes where it has gone, back and forth and around comet clouds, for thousands of years. This trip, after last delivery, after long journey out to *Antagonista* planet, it will return to Mars and Earth and maybe Titan, to pick up remaining Gurus."

"They're leaving?"

This seems to humor her. "They plan different." Ulyanova favors me again with that ghastly smile. I feel sick with guilt, empathy—not good emotions for a soldier. I remind myself if she fails, or if she turns against us, the *starshina* could kill us all. It wouldn't be her fault, but what would it matter?

I don't know whether to pity or fear her, but what I do not want to do is tick her off.

DJ climbs close again, coming back for more. I always knew he had courage but this is exceptional. "We're on our way to Planet X, right?" he asks.

She has eyes only for me but answers him anyway. "Next stop is near Pluto, for delivery. Then out to *Antagonista* world. Then return to Earth. They failed."

"Who failed?"

"Dead Gurus."

"Failed how?"

"Their deliveries did not amuse. But still they hide and plan."

"Nasty things," Vera says. "They are canceled, but always hope."

"I tell them what they want to hear. They pay attention. So for now, I control."

"Fine," I say, and brace for her response. "But if we can't control the ship and take it home, or wherever we want to go—what have you accomplished?"

Ulyanova regards me with sad triumph. "I stop ship from blowing out air and killing you like rats," she says. "Is that good thing?"

"She is Queen," Vera says, and pats her shoulder, then reassures her, "It is *good* thing. It is *very good*."

Is Vera truly a friend, an advocate—or a kind of pet?

"Come with," the *starshina* says. "Bring up searchers to help." She swings toward the nest of spheres. "This is where squad will live," she says. "Antags will also soon move closer, farther forward, where we can protect from ones we have set free."

"Set free?" I ask.

"Our shame," Ulyanova says. "When we opened gate, we opened cages. Fighters are free."

"But they're dead!" DJ says.

Ulyanova lifts an almost bald eyebrow. "Some still live, spread in dark places. Ours and others. Watch for them. They may be on look for you, yes?"

"Shit," DJ says. He's as gray as his overalls.

"How many?" I ask.

"Fifty-three," Vera says.

Ulyanova shakes her head. "Not so many. More have died, killing each other. They are like wild dogs."

This is a fight we don't need and certainly don't want. Makes my spine freeze thinking about it. "Can't you keep us clear of them?"

Ulyanova looks at us with real sympathy, but suddenly, her smile is wicked. "*You* are more interesting to ship when you fight." She shakes her head stubbornly. "I will not change that. It will help keep you alive."

Gurus and their ghosts know too fucking much about all of us. They know how to arouse fear, anger, violence—which might as well be complete mastery. It's their script. It's their stock on the market. And it's what makes us worth keeping around.

For a while, at least.

Three searchers move up and link arms.

"This way, please," Vera says.

CLOSER TO THE PALACE

It takes a few hours for the searchers to transfer the rest of our squad from the ship's midsection, beyond the cloverleaf water park, through the screw gardens and past the ancient cages, all open now, then along the steel vine and into the needle, where we advance along the ribbons, through the clock faces, and slightly outboard to the new black nests.

Borden and Jacobi assign the cubbies to pairs, except for Kumar, who gets his own. Judging from the reactions, our squad will soon exercise its own choices for nest buddies. Without her Queen, Vera is in attendance off and on, enjoying a break, or just enjoying human company...

As if in reward, one of the searchers that are always in attendance around the clock faces moves toward our new quarters, reaches into its slung pouch, and supplies us with more "grapes" and cakes and another round of blankets.

For the time being, most of the Antags will remain close to the hangars where their ships have been moved and re-stowed.

As the others move in, DJ and I gather Borden, Kumar,

and Jacobi in the ribbon space and tell them about the cage fighters. The air seems suddenly frigid, as if the cold of outer space has been sucked into the hull along with the starlight.

Kumar maintains a studious silence, as he nearly always does. Then he asks, "The searchers will keep lookout?"

"They don't fight," Jacobi reminds us, needlessly.

"I don't know," I say. "But they'll be in the way if the fighters come forward. Ulyanova commands them—but we still don't know what they can do for her."

"What's she look like?" Borden asks.

"She's a wreck," I say.

"How long can she keep it up?"

No way I can answer that.

Three of the searchers return aft, leaving two to take up station between the clock faces, arms barely rippling, intent on instructions and details.

"Perfect sailors of a starry sea!" Vera marvels.

We set up watches around the ribbon space to regularly sweep the five empty cubbies.

———

BARELY SETTLED IN, we're summoned.

We've grown quite adept at moving along the canes and ribbons. The searchers have slung more rubbery cables, so now we hardly need their help. The squad gathers in the ribbon space, where Vera and Ulyanova wait. Forward, two searchers swivel to listen and observe—possibly to protect us, though we all have doubts about what they can do in that regard.

"Show us where we are," Ulyanova tells the ship, and the ribbons expand as if carving great slices out of the hull—

opening up dozens of long, skewed views to vast clouds of stars—the nebulosities of the Milky Way.

My God, how long has it been since I last stared up at that great bridge!

Inside me, something strains—and snaps. I start to laugh. The others look with sour expressions. I can't explain myself—it's all colliding in my head, years of walking different worlds, becoming different boys, different men—looking up at the same sky.

Rediscovering a singular moment…

As a grunt on Socotra, studying that arch of a billion suns, I threw away my last tiny fragment of atheism, my last arrogant assurance that I was righteously alone.

I did not want to be alone, and then…I wasn't.

No way to explain it.

But at that time, the God I believed in was a violent, deadly God.

There were times on Socotra, at the end of basic, knowing I was going to be a warrior, when I tried to think my way to a suitable death—if I died in battle, or in space, out there! Looking up at the night sky, with hardly any lights for hundreds of miles around, I tried to turn the Milky Way into a direct stairway to Fiddler's Green, the actual Fiddler's Green—grunt heaven, Valhalla. Where all heroes go when they die.

I silently prayed to my new masters, to this violent god, to the generals and Wait Staff and Gurus, the threatened billions of Earth: Send me all the way out there. Send me on a mission to find the place where brave soldiers can fight forever, but when we are grievously wounded, when the guts hang out and blood gushes, the guts get shoved back in, new blood steams lava red in our veins—wounds stitch up, bones knit, and we return to our comrades, our fellow soldiers, to toast the pain, the victory or the loss, and fight again.

I'd already killed a man, but back then I did not know what actual battle was, certainly did not know what it was like to fight and die in near-vacuum. Eternal war seemed cool. I don't think that now.

I stop laughing, catch myself in a single hiccup, try to sober up. "Who sees things in these long strips?" I ask Ulyanova.

"The searchers," Vera answers. Ulyanova nods. "It works for their eyes. They can stretch over two strips and see everything. But we can adjust, as well."

I look into the widespread four eyes of the closest searcher, trying to estimate the parallax, the distance, but somehow also sensing the intelligence that might be there, might be set free, if it could only get home…

It does not hate us. It serves and does not resent its service. There's something potential in that wide, deep gaze—something that could be terribly useful and important—but then the searcher swivels and our moment is lost.

"Hey," DJ says, pointing along one wide ribbon, then another. We look where he directs, tilting on cords to adjust our view, and I make out, cutting a crescent from the starry bridge, a faded brownish-gray shadow. For a moment I can almost feel it suspended below our dangling legs. It's a planet. Looks vaguely familiar, but we're not used to this close view, or this way of seeing.

The crescent has a mottled, chunky, mountainous surface thrust between rough expanses of rubbled gray broad plains or maria of smooth white, marked by even bigger, isolated angular mountains like bobbing ice cubes dropped into a sundae. It's Pluto! We seem to be thirty or forty thousand clicks below its southern polar regions.

Moving back and forth between a few ribbons, like kids in a planetarium, we point out the crusty borders of large, icy peaks—trying to remember those lectures on Socotra. We recover the names: Cthulhu Regio, Sputnik Planum, Tombaugh—

But the light is so dim, the sun so far away.

"Old moon," Ulyanova says dismissively, then gestures for us to look forward, to where the strips converge, creating a kind of asterisk. Something large blanks the stars out there, in front of the ship, no way of knowing how far. The silhouette is all we've got to go on.

"Looks like a gift pack of railroad ties," DJ says. "But how big?"

"Is that the transmitter?" I ask Ulyanova.

"No," she says. "This not even Gurus know—*I* do not know. Something interested only by comets, moons, sometimes planets. Every few thousand years, it moves them around—but nothing else. Brain has records of its activity going back a billion years."

"Who made it?"

She shakes her head. "Ship does not know," she says.

"Really?" DJ says. "None of you know all there is to know?"

She diverts her glare but does not push him away. "*Really,*" she says. "It is always here—always avoided. Brain does not like it. Old ghosts do not like it, either."

"How big is it?" I ask.

"No size," she says. "We see it, maybe it sees us—but it has always ignored everything Guru, all the little wars—ignored even bugs, the ghosts say."

"Older than the bugs?"

"Much older."

"Cool!" DJ says. "I like it. Maybe it explains Planet X."

I shiver, and not just because of the cold. Something to deal with even if we shed the Gurus?

Or something that makes all of this, all of *us*, possible?

Looking between DJ's enthusiasm and my dismay, Ulyanova seems to soften. She raises her hand to touch and comb her straw-stiff hair. "All will sleep soon," she says. "Ship will make leap to transmitter, then to *Antagonista* world. Long leaps. Out beyond is realm of madness—madness and birth."

———

DRIFTING BETWEEN THE ribbons and staring forward at the asterisk where the ribbons meet, for no reason I can fathom, I spend my relaxation time keeping track of that unknown object.

"Are you God?" I murmur.

No answer. The object is alone. It does not care. It does what it does, nothing more.

Keep looking, grunt.

Joe joins me and I try to explain, but he shakes his head. "I'm full up with weird shit," he says. I know he's not an atheist, but he's never told me what he thinks or believes.

"Ulyanova says it isn't Guru," I say. "That's got to be important!"

"Maybe she's lying. Maybe it's *all* Guru."

"What do you want, out here?" I ask, angry.

He touches my shoulder. "There's so much shit I got wrong," he says. "It's going to take a while, I know, but I just want to make it right and get us home."

AFTERBIRTH

Days, maybe a week. Who can keep track?

For the time being, we're still parked tens of thousands of klicks beyond Pluto, in sight of that ancient mystery. Looking doesn't give me any more information, though that moon-shifter out there does look remarkably like a Christmas ornament assembled from model railroad parts.

No motion, no alarms.

Bird Girl has been gone for some time and no other Antags have come forward to visit. Maybe Budgie is keeping them busy.

The squad has been rearranging quarters, as I thought we would, as if that might help pass the time and make a difference. DJ and I share one sphere, where he appears to be fast asleep, curled up in a ball. But his eyes are flicking. Neither of us is sleeping if we can avoid it. We're waiting for that forced sleep that hasn't arrived. We all want to be awake when it comes.

Every few hours, I emerge from our cubby to study the

views available through the ribbons, which keep us from being completely blind, like cave fish, up in this needle snout. The clock faces, even when not occupied by a searcher or two, are too cluttered, too abstract—not for the likes of us.

DJ joins me, rubbing his eyes.

"Shit, I fell asleep," he says. "Anything different?"

"Not a thing."

More of the squad emerges, or returns from excursions aft. Going aft makes all of us nervous. Jacobi returns first and looks around with her sharp-eyed squint. She shakes her head. Nothing new there, either. No threats.

"No sign of fighters," she says.

"Tracking Antags?"

"They're busy down south somewhere, close to the clover lake. Still not interacting."

Negatives are mostly good, I think.

Now Kumar, Tak, Joe, and Litvinov join us. Kumar's quiet, as usual. Litvinov just seems depressed.

"Do *starshina* and *efreitor* still control?" he asks for the third or fourth time. "Behind smoke?"

I say, also for the third or fourth time, "Probably."

"Great and powerful wizard," DJ says.

A searcher waits nearby, in case we need help. We don't.

Borden joins us next. "Doesn't seem solid," she says, looking at the curtain. "Probably not hard to penetrate. Anybody been behind?"

Ninth or tenth time for that question. As if we won't announce it loud and clear, when—if—it happens.

"Not yet," I say.

"And you don't want to force the issue?" the commander asks.

"She allows us to see a little of what they're doing, not much," I say.

"They're redecorating," DJ says, and makes room between the ribbons for Ishida and Ishikawa. We're a knot of people holding hands and footing off against the ribbons.

"Steam heat and hot soup," I say. "I think we'll be invited in when Ulyanova is happy with the results."

"Do you guys understand how irritating this is?" Borden asks. "Having to get everything through you!"

"I've never believed it would work," Jacobi says.

Kumar says, "Using the Ice Moon Tea and crystals, taking a chance that one of us could channel a Guru, was the best hope we had."

"Did *that* work?" Jacobi asks, facetious.

"Maybe," I say after a long silence. "We have to trust that the bugs knew more about Gurus than we do."

"A hundred billion years ago!" Ishida says.

"Not that long," DJ murmurs.

"Well, then, you tell me!"

He shrugs. "A long time, not that much."

"This ship has been cruising around the solar system, and outside, for ages," I say. "The most important question is whether the bugs rid themselves of the Gurus way back when...and if they did, whether their tactics can work again."

"Any sign we're being watched by cage dudes?" Joe asks.

"Nothing yet," Borden says.

Litvinov says, "I am curious about screw gardens. Whole ship is filled with them. Maybe we become fertilizer for all the green."

That's a new idea, to me at least. I don't like it, but it touches key biological points well enough.

"Any idea what they are?" Borden asks us.

I shake my head, to her disgust.

Joe says, "If the bugs got rid of the Gurus, how did they come back? Where are they from originally? What can Ulyanova tell us about that?"

"She's communicated bits and pieces about the ship," I say. "But there's lots of stuff that either the Gurus don't know or the ship doesn't know."

"I find that truly dismaying," Kumar says.

"Huh!" Jacobi says.

"How closely connected are the Gurus and this ship?" Borden asks. "How much do they need it to get around and survive?" That may be the smartest question yet.

A long pause. Nobody can answer—but I tuck the question away.

"Heads up," Tak says, looking to the curtain.

Without warning, Vera has passed through. She moves in the spooky fashion she and Ulyanova have mastered, then clambers down the canes to the ribbons, very like a spider, to where we are.

"From now, take searcher if you go aft," she cautions. "They know how to return. Never try to go near or pass through puzzle gate. During next leap, it will be very bad back there. We leave Pluto soon. Next stop, transmitter."

She turns to Litvinov. "*Polkovnik*, gardens on screws are how we move so quick through space. Some plants on Earth plot ahead, all together, to maximize quantum chemistry and bind sunlight. But now they plot, think ahead, to change how slippery space is." She slices her hand out. "Whoosh! Why we sleep. You and me, at least. Where plants go, is difficult for us, since we cannot follow."

"What about the *starshina*?" Litvinov asks.

"Brain needs Queen awake." Vera makes a face and kicks away before we can ask follow-up. A searcher slings itself out from between the clock faces and firmly but politely blocks us from any attempt to go after her.

We haven't been invited. Not yet.

"Servant to 'Queen,'" Litvinov says, shaking his head. "Crazy scheme. And plants! Crazy idea."

"Every ship we've traveled on is different," Jacobi says. "Maybe they're just fucking with us to keep us confused."

"You don't use a bicycle to cross the ocean," Joe says. That's either profound, or profoundly stupid. "Every ship works on a different scale."

"What's that even *mean*?" Jacobi asks.

Ishikawa and Ishida listen to this back-and-forth with unhappy glances. Bilyk seems fascinated. With nobody to converse with in Russian but Litvinov—who doesn't seem interested—the *efreitor* has tried to join our Skyrines, but he's being frozen out by the sisters, possible payback for his comment about blow jobs.

Or maybe they think he's ugly.

———

JACOBI, JOE, MYSELF, and a searcher have ventured aft to see the situation that prevails. Following the cane bridges and with an occasional assist from a helpful searcher, we discover that the Antags have now moved into quarters about a klick behind us, aft and inboard of the nearest screw gardens. We aren't invited to inspect, and make contact with only one or two of them, both armored, both not particularly forthcoming—and after these sentinels send us back, with obvious irritation, our report to the rest of the squad brings up crude speculation, or extended wish fulfillment, that the birds are all engaged in a prolonged, wild orgy.

"Yeah, feathers everywhere," DJ says.

Bilyk laughs too loudly, which brings scorn from Ishikawa and Jacobi. I'm starting to like Bilyk.

Joe and I, with Kumar's tacit approval, say we think it's more likely the Antags are reassembling the social structure they once enjoyed on Mars and Titan, and maybe back home as well. How many males there once were, I don't know. How important the males are to military planning and discipline, I also don't know. Maybe the male is reasserting an aggressive posture and they're planning to come forward and take control of Ulyanova. Her crucial importance is no doubt a sore point with Budgie.

Of course, they could be preparing defenses against the remaining fighters—but we haven't seen any signs of them, either. Bird Girl is being remarkably thorough at staying offline. Maybe they want to keep our channels clear so we can listen for Ulyanova.

Would that mean we're still essential, even to Budgie?

REMEMBRANCE PAST

More hours, more days—more weeks.

Really hard to track.

Vera wasn't being straight with us. Or maybe her Queen wasn't being straight with her.

I've retreated from the cubby, where I now reside alone, to the ribbons, moving aimlessly from ribbon to ribbon. Only about half are illuminated and showing images I can understand—Pluto and occasionally its big moon, Charon. Forward, still visible in the quincunx, the asterisk—there's our mystery ornament, still blocking stars, and otherwise doing nothing.

I keep trying to find refuge in nerding out, but that part of my intellect has become very thin. Bilyk says he once read an article in a Russian science magazine about the quantum capabilities of plants—choosing chemical pathways, planning ahead based on some sort of botanical intuition, a quantum double-down on their chances of fixing photons...So how much weirder is it that the screw gardens can also look ahead and double down on making space *slippery*?

Yeah, it's weirder. Past is no preparation for present. When you keep stepping off the edge of the page and skipping over to another book, it's hard to keep track of the story.

How many months until we take the leap and push the plants in the screw gardens to their limits?

How long until the cage fighters decide to reappear?

I'm just around the corner from stir crazy when DJ and Kumar echo up near. I hide behind a twisted, dark ribbon. I do not want company, not now—certainly not Wait Staff.

They're quietly discussing Planet X—DJ's favorite topic. Another from our squad spiders from the cubbies along the canes to the ribbons, where I recognize him; it's the lonely Russian *efreitor*. Like DJ, Bilyk seems to be a fount of knowledge about science, about astronomy. His English is poor, but they manage to make themselves understood, and I envy them.

They murmur ideas and theories like kids, discussing the surface of our former ninth planet. Kumar listens quietly. Kumar rarely says anything since the Gurus were slaughtered.

Russian scientists (according to Bilyk) tried to figure out what had happened to Pluto, and what might still be happening—tried to understand what smoothed and rearranged those features even into modern geologic times. Pluto had either been subjected to tidal stress or had substantial sources of internal heat—radioactive thorium, possibly, which still keeps Earth warm. One of our Socotra professors described thorium as the atomic battery of creation.

Some speculated that maybe the planet and its moons

had swung close to Neptune during one of Pluto's inward passes—too close, on the edge of the Roche limit, below which the bodies would have broken up completely, joining another set of rings. The grazing orbit would definitely have stressed Pluto, and could have added or subtracted moons for both worlds.

Something had definitely messed with Neptune's big moon Triton, the only satellite in our system with a retrograde orbit. Physically, Triton looks a lot like Pluto—with a supercold nitrogen surface. Could have been imported from the Kuiper belt, just like Pluto.

And whatever pushed Triton around might have tilted Neptune itself into its weird orientation, pole aligned with the planet's orbit. But was Pluto responsible for these disruptions?

Not likely.

Something even larger, farther out—

Big enough to rearrange everything.

Bilyk insists that Russian scientists had long suspected a massive world with an eccentric orbit, way out beyond the edge of the solar system.

DJ enthusiastically agrees.

"Yeah, I'll bet on it—Bird Girl's planet could have made a pass through our system," he says. "It really is Planet X, rolling around the big old billiard table!"

WINTER DREAMS

'm alone in the nest, still trying not to sleep—too many bad dreams—but drifting off anyway, when I feel a light touch on my wrist and open my eyes with a startled moan. Ishida hangs on a stretched cord a meter away, her metal arm and the metal half of her face gleaming in the light from a strip outside the round opening. Her hand hovers over my wrist, shining fingers suspended, silent, no quiver or betrayal of flesh—steady hand, steady body. One of the most steady of our Skyrines.

"What's it like?" she asks after a murmured apology for waking me.

"What's what like?"

"Being dosed with tea."

I stretch a little. Exercise is difficult under these conditions, consisting mostly of choosing a partner—usually Tak or Joe—and trying to run in a circle inside a nest, or wrestle while hanging on to canes. I feel stiff and unsure. This isn't the first time I've noticed Ishida paying attention to me, and I've certainly paid attention to her, but there was a kind of lost cause about the whole situation, the attraction, for so many reasons, and now I'm embarrassed that she's made the first move. We haven't exactly violated any code, but I always thought a beautiful woman should have the luxury of not having to make the first approach—if this is an approach.

Truth is, she *is* beautiful—strange and strong and beautiful. I've never known what to make of her or her situation. But now she's neatly reversed the puzzle.

"Kind of like dreaming while awake," I say. "There's a part…" I pause, not sure she wants details.

"Go on," she says, not actually touching my wrist.

"There's a part that's separate." I tell her about the sensation of word balloons being filled, which was true for both Captain Coyle and often enough for Bird Girl. "But they aren't actually word balloons, just parts of me that aren't really from me." I shrug.

"I get it," she says. "Can I tell you what I feel, sometimes?"

"Sure," I say.

"After I was hurt—in training on Socotra—I was taken to a field hospital and things sort of blanked out."

I nod. "Yeah," I say.

"When I woke up, the surgeons and the mechanics were eager to talk to me. They were Japanese, and very proud of what they had done."

"It looks like fine work," I say. "And you're still here."

"But everything felt different. They'd saved most of my internal organs, but hooked them up to a layer of what they called false tissue, to pad the metal parts when I bumped around. Plastic buffers and slings. Combat-ready, they said. I could do anything I wanted. I'd live a good, long, active life."

"Wow," I say.

"Felt strange to move."

"I bet."

"But none of them wanted to spend much time with me," she says. "Always busy. Moving on. They spoke Japanese, not English, but used an inflection, like they were speaking to a servant, an untouchable. A *Korean*. That made me sad, but I had seen it before. Female soldiers... We get kind of lost, even in the new Japan."

"Wow," I say. Tak had never mentioned such attitudes, but we'd heard about them.

"Do you have things that protect you, cushion you, when you speak with Bird Girl or the bugs?"

"I don't speak with the archives now. That was back on Titan, and we—I mean, humans—pretty much wiped out those voices."

"I always thought that part was fascinating. Captain Jacobi gets weirded out, but we—the Japanese sisters—we feel a little more familiar with the idea—with being hooked up to *kami*. Maybe just from anime, but... more familiar."

"I remember the markings on your suits. *Senketsu* and *Junketsu*. Anime?"

"Old anime, old-fashioned. Lots of jiggle. Nothing like that in Japan now. Mostly heroes and history and emperors and such."

"Right," I say. Oddly, my sense of discomfort is fading. I'm next to her, she's talking to me, more than ice has been broken—a new protocol is being established.

Technically, Skyrines are not supposed to open up to the possibility of anything sexual or romantic, but of course we do. Some of us get in trouble, but usually only when rank is

involved, or one of a pair or team gets out of bounds, pro-
fessionally and emotionally, and feels left out, badly used.
Because of that, and because my stations have been hard
and desperate, I've never established anything I could call a
romance with a Skyrine. I've thought about it in a vague way,
of course, but it's never come up.

And now it seems to be coming up, starting out as a letting
down of the barriers, telling stories—enjoying company. While
alone. Which I am. My roommates have all cleared out, or I've
left them in the other cubbies and set out on my own. Maybe
they knew before I did.

Other than to DJ or Joe or Tak, I haven't talked much at
all about the links, what it's like to be dosed with the tea...
not much at all.

Ishida asks, "When you interact with Bird Girl, what do
you see?"

"Mostly hear, rarely see," I say. "Sometimes there are hints
of deep stuff, but mostly it's what she wants me to hear. When
Captain Coyle faded, she handed me over to Bird Girl, and
she served as bug steward, hooked me up to the archives on
Titan, which she knew pretty well by then. DJ got hooked up
to her as well, but Bird Girl seems to favor dealing with me."

"I like DJ, but you're different," Ishida says.

"DJ is okay," I say, as if giving her an out. "We've served
together a long time. He's a real friend, and he's funnier
than me."

"But you're the one I'm talking to," Ishida says. My level
of embarrassment returns. It would be very bad for my
long-term opinion of myself if I said something awkward to
this fellow Skyrine, either about her being Japanese, about
those difficulties—we hear so many stories, and not all of

them are true, probably—or being a Winter Soldier. Same there. So many points where I could get things very wrong. I do know it's hard for female soldiers in Japan now, as everything has gotten so conservative, reverting to historical norms—but I have no idea what to say about that, what I know, and what crap I've just heard that's all wrong.

And then her being half-metal. Sort of. Metal and colloid and plastic and all kinds of synthetics. Half-organic. She's almost like an angel from Fiddler's Green, most of her organs intact, saved, stuffed back in, fully functional.

I'm far more ignorant about all that.

So I stop talking and just tilt my head, big eyes, sad smile, like a real asshole. She skips past all this, cutting me substantial slack, and gets to her point.

"I need to talk to somebody who's male and who I respect," she says, "and who knows what it means to hook up with something that isn't you. Something essential—but really different."

"I'm listening," I say. I've always preferred listening. The last girlfriend I had, back in Virginia Beach—and where is she now?—left me because she thought I didn't care. I just listened more than I talked, and it turned out she took that all wrong. So off she went. We'd been together for two weeks. Longest I've ever been involved. Joe always seems to do better with women.

"Don't take this wrong, the wrong way, but I'm not all there," Ishida says with a kind of hiccup. "Not yet. I'm scheduled to be attached—that's what they call it, but it hasn't happened yet, there hasn't been time. Does that bother you?"

I don't know whether it does or not. Again, what boundaries can I cross and cause pain by so doing?

"You're beautiful, I know that much," I say.

She keeps staring at me, with one natural eye and one mechanical eye.

"It's like a new kind of beauty," I say. "I don't know about all the rest. Maybe it's not important right now."

"But it will be, right? If I'm going to stay human. And that's...that's what I think about you. Are you still human?"

"Mostly," I say, as if it's a joke.

"I don't think it's a funny question," Ishida says. "I thought I was no longer a woman, but that turned out to be wrong." Still watching me. "I feel *everything*, I feel the old... parts...as if they were still there. But I reach down and they aren't. Just skin and metal."

"I've heard about that," I say. "Phantom limbs."

"Phantom cunt!" Ishida says, with the most brilliant shy smile on half of her face, lighting up her eye and seeming like a prelude to something sadder, more direct and painful. "I dream about it. And someday, I'll go back to Madigan or Sasebo or somewhere and get the plumbing finished off. Get hooked up. I'll stop being half a female and be a whole one. They say I can even have kids, through caesarean—through a hatch!" She raises her hand and giggles behind it. "I'd enjoy having a family. I come from a big family."

"Best of luck," I say.

"I don't think any Japanese man will have me," she says.

"Try a Skyrine," I say. "They've seen a lot."

"Yeah. Wonder if that would ever work." She smiles... at me. "What I miss most is just talking. Relaxing. Holding. Until I get hooked up again, right?"

Her need, her expression, her words—so direct. So human and appropriate. I slowly reach out and pull her toward me.

We hold each other for a few minutes, nothing much more, and she snuggles into my arm, flesh face against my skin, keeping the metal side away.

"My God," she murmurs. "You're hard. That is sweet. That is special."

I touch her face with one hand, stroking lightly along the boundary between metal and flesh, and then, touching the metal.

"I feel that, too," she says. "I feel all of my other half. It's almost normal to me now. Is that Guru tech?"

"I don't know," I say. "Maybe. But we'd have found it eventually."

"Sometimes I wake up and think it's all just the old me. And sometimes when I sleep...I think the metal half is dreaming. I can never remember, but that's what I think."

"Then you understand me," I say.

"It's like that?"

I nod and keep stroking her faces. Her face. The metal side is warm and...

I get lost in my thoughts.

DAYS OF FUTURE PAST

For days now, Joe's scalp, DJ's scalp, Tak's scalp, and my scalp have all been itching, and we don't think it's lice. Feels like team spirit.

Feels like fucking *change*.

The waiting has become nasty, unbearable. We've been making plans to gather up what weapons we can and head aft to find the cage fighters, or whatever's left of them. Why haven't they made their move? Any move? We're bored out of our minds! We're about to unveil those plans to Jacobi and Borden when everything suddenly speeds up.

It's Jacobi's turn to study the "asterisk" and the mystery ornament, and she sees the change first.

Change *outside* the ship.

"Hey," she says, softly at first, as if in awe—then louder. "*Hey!* It's different."

DJ and Bilyk and I join her.

"Different how?" DJ asks.

"Major!" she says. "Now it's hollow in the center, like a donut. What the hell does that mean?"

We study the ornament's silhouette, the way stars appear around and behind it, and have to agree.

Kumar joins us. He studies the changes with a frown, and shakes his head. "It means nothing," he murmurs. "It has no meaning!"

"Hasn't it been out here forever?" Jacobi asks. "Since before the bugs?"

Kumar shudders. "*She* is here," he says, and turns.

For the first time in weeks, Ulyanova emerges from behind the curtain, surprising us all. Vera is right behind her, as if carrying her invisible train.

We make space for the pair. "You see that?" I prompt the *starshina*.

"Brain of ship sees," Ulyanova says. She spins slowly.

"Brain have an opinion?" DJ asks.

"Planets will be put in motion," she says. "Soon, one large world, but many, maybe dozens."

"When?"

"Hundreds of thousands of years."

None of us knows what to make of that. DJ looks at Bilyk, then at me. Both shrug.

"Has ship seen this sort of thing before?" I ask.

"Yes. Is old."

"Are there other things out there, like this?" DJ asks.

"In most systems, is at least one."

"You mean, systems with planets?" DJ asks.

"They move moons and planets," Ulyanova says coldly. "That is all they do."

"Got to have power for that!" DJ says.

"Is most powerful thing here, but for sun," Ulyanova says. Vera is impatient. She wants to get back behind the curtain. "Let us leave," she says.

Ulyanova says, "Come to tell you, decades ago, mission before Mars and Titan, ship went out to other warm world in Kuiper belt, collected another population—and moved them to Sun-Planet."

"What sort of population?"

"Excellent warriors. Ship became large to hold them. Soon, it will grow inside, as it grew before bringing humans and Antags to war. It will make more and different weapons, to please larger and different audience. Dangerous times! Brain is restless, eager to return last of Antags, give them chance to fight before all die. Be ready for sleep."

She and Vera—Vera is immensely relieved—rotate to slip back behind the curtain, leaving us shrouded in mystery without context—except that something has changed that never does, and the Gurus are full of surprises.

Sun-Planet may already be under siege. Does Bird Girl know? Budgie? Do we tell them?

Perhaps not if we value our lives.

Joe looks right at me. Right through me.

"God*dammit*," he says.

We make a desperate move for the cubbies, but before we can all hide away . . .

Something strange, something wicked.

The leap.

SLEEP OF REASON

There's no sleep like bad sleep. Just because the universe doesn't count the total trip time against us, so far as we know, that doesn't mean it doesn't pass somewhere, somehow. What's it like to be half-aware of blind blankness for ten thousand years? I'd like to tell you, but there aren't words.

When we come awake again—fully awake and not just numbly miserable—most of us are scattered, some in the cubbies, a few in the canes, Bilyk and DJ jammed between ribbons—squirming. We pull our squad together and inspect ourselves, creepily convinced we've shriveled like the corpses in the cages. But we don't seem to have changed at all.

"Join the Skyrines and tour hell," Jacobi says.

Tak comments how different this is from the trip on *Lady of Yue*, where we came awake fresh and raring to go. Every scale has a different feel, brings a new set of questions.

Like, what's this thin layer of sparkling dust on our skin and clothes? We all start rubbing, as if we could wipe away everything that's happened.

"Searcher dust," Jacobi says. The searchers attend to us like patient servants, silent, respectful. Jacobi isn't happy with them, however. As they try to help her brush away the dust, she hits them with clenched fists—an exercise in futility. They back off, but do not otherwise react.

"I hate how they just don't get mad!" Jacobi says.

"Let them be," Tak says. "They're not hurting anyone."

"They're fucking squids, goddammit!" Jacobi says. We've all gone so far from discipline and training that anything can happen to us, around us, and we wouldn't know how to react.

Ishida holds up her metal hand, covered with little bright points. We watch them fade. After the sparkling dust evaporates, leaving only a cool tingle, we wonder if it was ever there at all.

"Anybody want to swear off having kids?" Ishikawa asks.

"Solemnly," Ishida says.

DELIVERY AND REJECTION

Ornament is gone, but something else is out there," Borden says, kicking off a ribbon, rotating around her abdominal axis to search what she can see of the sky. "Not the mover. Don't see that anymore."

We can barely make out a dim pair of gray fans, subtending several degrees of the big sky. Ship is either very close, or the fans are very large.

"That must be the transmitter," Kumar says.

"What are those?" Borden asks.

Possibly even more surprising, smaller vessels have departed from our monster ship and move toward the gray fans. They're too far away already and too small to make out details.

"Are those Antag ships?" Ishikawa asks.

"Don't think so," Borden says.

"This thing can make other ships?" Ishikawa asks, almost hopeful.

"No surprise," Tak says. "They taught us how to build Spook and the centipedes, right?"

"Are they doing maintenance or dropping off supplies?" Jacobi asks.

"Maybe they're delivering tapes for broadcast," DJ says. Bilyk, who regards Ulyanova and Vera, when they're around, as if they inhabit some sort of movable nightmare—friends he no longer knows—goggles at this.

"You still don't get it, do you, man?" DJ chides him.

Bilyk shakes his head. "We are for movies?" he asks.

"Yeah, for movies," DJ says.

"Anybody notice we're no longer necessary for anything?" Ishida asks, her voice small. She's keeping close to me, as if I can supply some sort of comfort, or at least a solid center.

I wish.

Kumar joins Borden and they almost touch the crowns of their heads as they spread out along a ribbon, trying to survey everything that can be seen—a long, narrow slice of sky way beyond the sun, the bridge of stars cutting across the slice, cold and steady—just the same as when we departed. Parallax nil despite our journey.

"When are we leaving to find the fighters?" Tak asks Joe as we move off from the ribbons, back to the cubbies.

Joe makes a face. "When we're through with these fucking leaps and sleeps," he said.

"We don't make our own schedule?" Tak asks. "What if they move before we do?"

"You want to go blank, up against a monster?"

Tak kicks away, disgusted.

LEAVE NOTICE AT THE DOOR

A few hours later, the outbound ships have finished their mission. They grow to specks and seem to be trying to return, but one by one blossom into small, brilliant clouds of plasma.

"Jesus!" Borden says and grips a searcher arm as if for assurance. The searcher sighs like a teakettle but otherwise neither moves, resists, or reacts. The clouds flash brilliant colors, then fade to gray—and spread out until they're gone.

"Expendable?" Litvinov asks.

"Maybe not even real," Kumar muses.

"What if they tried to deliver something—and somebody interfered?" Borden asks. She's got a funny look on her face and starts to hand-over to the cubbies.

"What if they tried to deliver...and nobody wanted it?" I ask.

"What are you saying, Venn—we're no longer A-list?" Jacobi asks.

"Jesus, my scalp again," Joe says.

The others agree.

"Get ready!"

Again, except for Borden, no time to get to our cubbies. Our Skyrines hug like koalas. They do not want to make the leap while the searchers are touching them. As if we could get jumbled up with a catamaran squid or two and come out looking like a plate of sushi. Who knows?

"Crap!" Jacobi says as the blankness descends.

SUN-PLANET

My mind slowly tries to boot up. I think I remember the ribbons, expect the waking bodies of my squad, three or four of them arranged loosely around me...

But first, there's a funny, dreamlike state where I'm back at Hawthorne, in the bar, listening to Joe half-drunkenly try to explain his views about the giant F-bomb reserves kept stored in tanks near Los Angeles and New York.

The other grunts and soldiers in the bar are skeptical.

"Sure, it's true," Joe says. "Before the war—the Second World War—F-bombs were strictly limited to military use. Illegal to use them in print or in movies, or in public—unless you were a criminal and didn't care."

"Didn't *fucking* care," says one of our fellow recruits. Might be DJ, but I can't see him clearly.

"Right," Joe says. "But the reservoirs holding the F-bombs were badly constructed. They were porous. Some leaked out into the water supply in New York, and then in Los Angeles. The plume of F-words didn't get very far, but by the 1960s it was too late—everyone was drinking that water and dropping F-bombs twenty-four/seven. The military couldn't stop it. So now, not just soldiers—everybody uses them."

"But what was the point?" asks another grunt I don't really want to think about—Grover Sudbury. We're back before he did his awful thing and we did ours, and then Joe did his. He's just another grunt in this bar, no better or worse than any other.

"Soldiers use F-bombs to keep themselves grounded, to remind themselves they're human, to remind them what they give up when they fight and die," Joe says. "Helps blow off some of the violence and weird crap that violence shoves into our brains. We use them, and we become better at managing a shitty situation."

Sudbury is still skeptical.

"Now everybody uses them, and look where we are," Joe says.

"Where the *fuck* we are," says the other soldier.

I linger on Sudbury's face. I want to talk to him, to warn him not to act out being a cruel asshole, but the memory-state, dream-state fragments into glassy shards of pain in my jaw, my arms, my chest.

Now I'm awake, but I don't believe it. I don't want to believe. I've been dragged from the others and tangled in a cane wall. A few of the canes have penetrated my pajamas and pin me like an insect in a museum. I hurt all over. Worse, my arms and legs, my hands, look lumpy. My entire *skin* feels hot and bruised.

I extricate myself from the brake, pull out the canes that poke through my clothes, and after a few minutes, float free— but my confusion is total. I don't see anyone else. I think

I'm alone, but then, I make a half turn and see a searcher a few meters away, slowly rotating in the half dark. It's been butchered—arms hacked away and hanging by the outer plates, midsection almost cut in half, eyes gouged out. More than one attacker, I think—the squid may be peaceful, but they're also strong.

It's taking me much longer than before to assemble my conscious self, and it's all tangled with memories I can't place, like dreams being edited and erased.

Then a voice rises from a buzzing pool of memory. It's the first thing I'm absolutely sure about—harsh, hoarse, angry, and putting an emphasis on every single thump I'm receiving. *"Never…thought…I'd find…YOU, did you? After what you guys…DID to me."*

I know that voice. But from where, from when? Was it my mother's boyfriend? The one I shot? I doubt it. But in my haze I remember Mom lying in bed covered with bruises after he beat her up, and I'm thinking, *No more of this—no more of him, not ever, why does she put up with it?*

And now—

Vera has awakened some of us personally. There's a look of concern on her face as she shakes us one by one. It takes hard shaking for some—for DJ in particular, but also for Joe and Tak.

We've all just had the crap beaten out of us.

"What the hell happened?" Joe asks. "Christ, I'm bloody! So are you."

"Yeah," Tak says ruefully. "I couldn't fight back."

He looks at me as he tries to flex life into his limbs. I touch my own face, feeling the swollen lips and cheeks, the crusted blood. We examine DJ. Blood and bruises all over. My sight is returning in a spotty manner, as if I'm looking through a slatted window.

How did I let it happen? What is this, some sort of sympathetic response, welting and pain as my mind is probed by Gurus? Feels wrong, feels crazy. They say you don't remember pain, but new pain flares with every move I make. Something or someone struck me repeatedly. Someone I once knew.

Someone almost human.

So I lean into the memories and bring it *all* back—the smiling, heavily scarred face leaning over me in the gloom, the same piggy eyes and interrupted eyebrows, but now with nose almost smashed flat. Long since healed but pug-uglier than I remember him.

"Did you see him?" DJ asks. "He was laughing. Really enjoying himself. Then the squids moved in and tried to separate everybody. Man, you wouldn't know they can't fight."

"Someone we knew," I say. "I couldn't wake up."

"Sudbury! Fucking Grover Sudbury!" DJ shouts, expelling a fine spray of blood. "He and some other fuckers."

"Some human, some not," Joe says through broken lips. He holds his head as if it needs to be glued back together. "The searchers stopped them from killing us."

The smile, the words, the delight Sudbury took in striking me with the back of his gnarly hand, over and over.

Ishida approaches carefully out of the fairy light. She points to the cubbies and cane bridges. "A lot of searchers. Looks like they tried to protect us."

"They fought?" Tak asks.

"They died."

Borden emerges from her cubby, the entrance of which

has almost been blocked by a dead searcher. She shoves it into a slow, broken-armed spin. "What the hell happened here?"

"I knew we shouldn't have waited!" Tak cries out.

"What do you think, Venn?" Borden asks.

"It was Sudbury," I confirm. "Not alone. Another human and as DJ says, a couple of *things*. Not human."

"Not Antag?"

I shake my head. "Didn't see any."

There are maybe five dead searchers in the ribbon space, up between the clock faces, in the canes—hacked, carved, gouged. Three more are spaced before the curtain, still alive, sighing and flexing. One isn't moving and is being examined by its fellows. The plates along its skin are flaccid, peeling away. Who would be strong enough to kill a squid? I've felt the grip of their arms and can imagine what they could do to defend themselves.

Tak runs another inventory on DJ's face, his hands. Then me. "Did a real number," he murmurs, flexing my jaw, prodding my cheek. My whole face seems to explode, and I jerk away, but he says, "Nothing broken I can feel."

Ishikawa and Jacobi seem barely touched. Ishida checks over Litvinov and Bilyk, but Bilyk shakes her off with an accusing look.

"Four of you seem to have borne the brunt of injuries," Kumar says.

"I still don't remember," Joe says.

Vera shakes her head with cold anger. Then she takes me by the arm. Her hand is tight and wiry, firm. "She will speak with you, if you can go, if you can move."

"Just me?"

"Just you," Vera says. The others watch suspiciously.

"I'll go," I say. "I can move."

"I'd like to come," Borden says.

"No," Vera says, and leads me toward the curtain. The searchers move the bodies and themselves aside. I try to keep from crying out in pain, but Tak's right, there are no broken bones—I think.

The curtain gets closer. After what I've been through, I don't want to touch it, or it to touch me. I turn my face aside, lean my head back, and one hand grips the other, to keep it from flailing.

"No fear," Vera says.

We pass through. Feels like thin cotton wool, like a warm breeze. Vera tugs my arm again. "Rules change. Queen can explain!"

Rules change? Now the rules allow Grover Sudbury to come back from the dead and beat the crap out of me, out of us, and start murdering searchers? Is the ship's brain breaking free of Ulyanova and trying to kill us all and regain control?

Vera seems to read my mind. "Ship does not care," she says. "Ship goes, ship makes. It makes for Queen, for *starshina*. She is waiting."

The smoky fog swirls and for a second I feel my stomach heave up emptiness…but then my feet touch floor. Flat floor. Things have reliable direction, up and down. I stand. The nausea fades. Ahead, a plaster wall shapes itself and corners with the floor. The floor spreads before me a paint of cracked, chipped, dirty black-and-white ceramic tile. The tile acquires a shallow depth and detail. What's left of the grout is dark with dirt, as if it's never been scrubbed.

Arrives before us a wainscot with a beat-up wooden strip and worn wallpaper printed with tiny flowers. The floor and wall become part of a long hallway that smells of cabbage and bacon. I hear voices from down the hallway, tinny laughter—children shouting.

"Ship cares not much about us," Vera says. "But *she* is still Queen. You cannot know how much it hurts her!"

Vera opens a wood-panel door. We step through. Beyond lies a small apartment: three tiny, overheated rooms, a kitchen to the right, half-hidden in dark orange light, where someone makes sharp noises with pots and dishes. An old refrigerator sticks out of the kitchen, humming and buzzing. Through another door, half-open, I see a bedroom, a small bed on a gray pipe frame, paint flaking.

I'm more than half-convinced I'm going through another instauration—but this time, perhaps not mine. Maybe Ulyanova's or Vera's.

I tongue my mouth and realize I've lost a couple of teeth. Through all of my childhood and my adventures with Joe, through Mars and training back on Earth, I never lost teeth. Fuck, that's a mortal insult.

Shoes are neatly paired beside the foot of the bed, men's shoes, and a short, flower-print dress has been draped across the gray and pink quilted cover. A dress suitable for a party.

Ulyanova emerges from the kitchen, holding a pot filled with steaming potatoes. "Hard journey!" she says, with a pale, stressed-out smile. "You don't know how wicked ship can be." She raises her arms—and the pot goes away. Some of the steam remains. Then she wipes her hand on a towel. She's looking, if that's possible, even worse. Like me, she's lost some teeth—but not through being beaten. I think she's malnourished, despite the potatoes. What's real here and what isn't?

"We have arrived around *Antagonista* home," Vera says. "Nobody knows we are here—again, we are invisible."

Ulyanova avoids meeting my eyes. Gray, finely wrinkled around her face and neck—as if she has grown old here! And Vera is looking older as well. They're becoming part of this apartment, this life—this instauration.

"Look at him, he is hurt!" Vera says, and suddenly, as if our Guru Queen has seen me for the first time, she notices the blood and swelling.

"Get him ice and a rag," she tells Vera, her voice deadly calm.

Vera goes to the kitchen and brings back ice wrapped in a worn towel. Both of them apply it to my face, my neck, my forearms. Feels cold. Soothes—a little.

"Do you know what's happened?" I ask. "The cage fighters—"

"I know," she says. "Like I said, when I opened gate. Did you not watch for them?"

"They came during the leap, while we were still... stunned."

"Ah," she says. "They learn not to sleep, like me. Vera, find chair for Vinnie. We must talk."

"The ship didn't tell you they would find us, attack us... that way, that time?"

She shakes her head. "Ship has its motives. Vera! Chair!"

Vera brings forward a cheap dining chair, made of deal and pine. As I sit, I look left. Filmy white drapes billow before a narrow glass door that opens to a shallow patio with cheap iron rails. Through the drapes, as they slowly flap and spread, I see that beyond and across a narrow street, other apartment buildings rise gray and stolid.

How far does the illusion go? How real is it out there? How far can she walk across town, to the park, up and down the streets—when she wants to relax? Queen of the apartment. Of the world outside. Queen of the voices and the children, of the blocks that could very well be out there, if I wanted to look.

"Queen of the city," I say.

"It is what I tell her!" Vera says. "Queen of Moscow, of all we see. Here Gurus once live and dream of other lifes. But now—only her."

"I am not entirely queen," Ulyanova says, with an irritated glance at Vera. "Wrong move, *boring* move, and ship knows, brain knows—everything will change. All will die."

"How many human fighters were in the cages?" I ask.

"Fifteen. Some have died since. Humans not best at cage fighting, it seems."

"Where did the others come from?"

"From where ship has been."

"Between stars?" I ask.

"No. Big planets out where comets are born. Ship has already carried beings not from Earth, out to *Antagonista* planet. I warned you."

"Right."

I want to get back, organize...warn Bird Girl and the Antags. If they don't already know.

"A few planets swing down through system every thousand centuries," Vera says, as if reciting from a textbook. What sorts of beings would grow up on all these worlds? The cold ones, the warm ones? How much more complicated can this get?

"What's all that to this ship? To the Gurus?"

"Victors of long fights in cages explore, find you. I lose searchers. Do fighters know you? *Hate* you?" She nearly aspirates the word.

"One does," I say.

"Male?"

"Yeah. Barely. A monster."

"Why does this one want to kill you?"

"Four of us helped put him on this ship, indirectly, ignorantly—years ago."

"The cage fighters kill Antags, searchers—kill with much pain. Pain as they have experienced, and more."

Her face is so like the face of my mother the morning after she woke up and her boyfriend was gone. Quiet. Not in the least curious. Almost dead-looking. She cooked eggs and made me breakfast.

"Why do you let them move around?" I ask her. "Why not just cage them again?"

"Think!" Vera cries. "She tells you! Even now, she plays game with ship. She builds walls inside. Ghosts cannot cross. Brain cannot hear."

Ulyanova gives me her own sadly critical look. "Brain and ghosts are fascinated by revenge. And so am I. When I open gate, as if to test me, cages open as well. I can do nothing. I cannot protect! I must not. I must not show you are important to me."

Despite the ice, my whole body aches. I dread the thought of what I might find if we go aft...if we do what we have to do.

"You are more *interesting* if you fight," Ulyanova says softly, moving near the window. She seems to want to lean into the sunlight, the breeze through the filmy white drapes.

"And you will live…if you fight. Be as brave as searchers, who do not fight—but protect, and die."

This discussion has long since crossed the line to scaring the shit out of me. So casual, so isolated—behind the curtain. How much time does Ulyanova have before the brain, the ship, the *ghosts* catch on to our little ruse?

She's playing with me. She's making my life more interesting by making me think she controls. How long can that be enough of an excuse? Until we get boring. Then we'll just be fused like those fucking ships coming back from the transmitter. Maybe the cage fighters are just prelude to that.

Ulyanova straightens and walks around a beat-up coffee table. "Worse is done by Gurus, by ship, before we come. Years before battle seasons on Mars, on Titan, ship grew, ship traveled to a large moon. This moon orbits two worlds, tossed and heated for billions of years… Kept alive without sun, not made by bugs, but older, with very strong inhabitants. Ship auditioned them in little wars, then gathered them by tens of thousands…and carried them to Sun-Planet. It supplied them with arms and landed them…to eliminate *Antagonista* and searchers. New soldiers, new species—not affected by bug archives. Very popular for Gurus. New show begins."

Vera says sadly, "*Antagonista* have no home. Nearly all have died. For those we carry, there will be one last, short war, short fight…death."

"What if you help them?" I ask, my heart suddenly made of lead.

"I will confirm this mask. And then, ship will cancel us."

The heat in the fake Russian apartment is muggy, oppressive. "What happens to us, then? If we kill the cage fighters, stay interesting...Are we going to leave the ship and fight down there, on Sun-Planet, with them?" I ask.

"Antags will leave ship. It is their duty," Ulyanova says. "Hard part comes after."

"We must not let Guru plans finish," Vera says.

"I tell Verushka. If I do not stay Queen, ship will gather fighters from yet more moons, more worlds—also not from bugs. Ship will deliver them to Earth. Many, many of them. Soon it will prepare by growing for them new weapons, interesting weapons, evenly matched—and more ships.

"These new recruits, brought to Earth, will be told story, like what Gurus told us—and they will fight to kill humans, all humans, and then, will be set up for long war against those victorious on Sun-Planet. Not *Antagonista*. Those will already be dead.

"But I have my own plan. If I stay in control, if I do not make stupid move! First, we will go to Mars and Earth and gather up last of Gurus, and last of those Wait Staff and leaders who live only for Gurus. They will be brought into ship and receive promotions, live as we do. For days, they will be happy." She points out the window at the long, hot summer of Moscow.

"Brain and ghosts will be happy. If I convince, if I am *interesting*, they may do what I say. I will send you off on ships that carried Gurus and traitors, and you will return to Earth. Then Guru ship will begin trip to far place, to opposite system—three hundred billion klicks. Very long leap."

In my head, she's helping me see that path, that grazing, high-speed journey out beyond everything we know, out to the far side of the Kuiper belt.

And I see her opportunity quite clearly. Just a twitch, really. A very small deviation.

"I will help ship finish well," she says.

Vera shivers.

"I will stay," Ulyanova says. "To finish my work. Vera…"

"I will stay, too," Vera says.

"But now, Antag ships are free to go home," Ulyanova says. "There is nothing for them to return to. So they will die sadly, valiantly. They have honor. Ghosts and brain love tragic homecoming."

I'm so lost now in useless backtracking that I start asking really dumb questions. "What about the Gurus who died? How does the ship, the brain react to that?"

"Ship can make more Gurus, if there is need. Ship can even replace itself, given warning. But not in sun." Her smile is maddening. "You heard *Antagonista* female," Ulyanova says. "She wants I will die, after I am used."

I can't think how Ulyanova heard that. Perhaps the ship ratted us out. Maybe those of us on the tea have no secrets— boring, lost, all our stories nearing their sad ends.

"You think the rest of us want to kill you?" I ask. "Rather than take a risk you'll fail?"

"Yes," Ulyanova says. "Would ship make new me, I wonder? Can you *see*, Vinnie? I dance on edge of knife. We play with brain. Brain plays with us. All to make story. Audiences wait. We might be popular again—as popular as those who fought on ship for years, fought and died. You sent them here, from Earth—and so did we."

"So did *Antagonista*," Vera says. "Many worlds contribute."

"How did the cage fighters stay awake?" I ask. "Why didn't they sleep, like us?"

"Many trips. If they not awake, others kill them. So… they adapt. They learn, do not sleep, no matter how long the time, how hard the trip. Like me. If I sleep, ship knows me to my soul…For now, plan is good. Ship is happy to return to Earth, to Mars, to pick up Gurus, then travel far and start new big show."

Vera's expression is that of a deeply puzzled child, as if this is finally getting to her. Madness leads. Reason sleeps. And sitting on the knife's edge, two of our own, willing to do—what?

It seems to me they've got it good here. A waking dream of home.

"You help me open gate," Ulyanova says. She waggles her fingers and the pot with potatoes reappears. "I remove Guru bombs from your head, use them…All but one. There is one more time I will reach out and use it to speak to you. And after that, one more time we will see each other here."

She carries the pot back to the kitchen.

"Now go," Vera says, shooing me. "Tell others Queen is tired. Being Guru is difficult." With a quick backward glance, Vera follows me out the door to the hallway and then through the curtain, into the ribbon space; still dark, empty now— where have the others gone?—but for the drifting shadow of another dead searcher, its arms hacked away, blood drifting in beads and fist-sized green-brown gobs around the blinded ribbons. The blood has formed a wrinkled crust, making the gobs look like big raisins. I wonder how it got here—killed recently, another fight?

But the blood is old. This one has drifted forward, more likely.

Vera inspects the corpse and *hmms* sad sympathy. Then

she takes my arm and spins me around, as if we're dancing in the dark, between the drops of searcher blood. "I do not know how, or even if, Queen fools ship, brain, ghosts. They make hard time. She never sleeps, not to let them in."

"But she's back home—you're back, too, right? This is the best you've had in years. What would you give to keep it this way?"

Vera looks at me as if I am some sort of vermin, a spider, a filthy mouse.

"Do you get out and go for walks on the streets, through the city?" I ask. "Do you live a normal life? Enjoy the weather? Is it all out there, a *solid* dream?"

I can't shake the layers of illusion, both the ones behind the curtain and the ones that wrap my own thoughts. Maybe we're all still caught up in Guru mind shit. Maybe everything is no more or less real than Ulyanova's apartment, her pot of potatoes.

Is it possible for me, for any of us, to break free of whatever has been ordained by the Gurus or by their great resource, their master, their reservoir—this fucking ship?

"What is that to you?" Vera says, keeping her voice low.

"Do you know it isn't real?"

"Queen knows," Vera says tightly. "This life will end soon enough. Now go!"

She shoos me again, then returns to the curtain.

———

"How is she?" Borden asks.

"They seem strung-out but in control, for the time being," I say.

Kumar joins us at the asterisk. The ribbons are still dark.

All we can see is the illumination from a thin coat of searcher skin juice, probably from the beaten and murdered, scattering deep-ocean guidance around our living spaces.

"How long have I been gone?" I ask.

"Hours!" Kumar says.

"Didn't feel that long."

"DJ, Sanchez, and Jacobi have gone aft," Borden says. Makes me feel a little sick, that they didn't wait. "They should be back any time now. I've ordered Tak and Ishida and Ishikawa to keep guard aft of the ribbon space, in case Antags come forward and try to catch us by surprise."

"Why would they do that?" I ask.

"We've already found dead Antags. They might blame us."

Litvinov returns from going forward, along the nose. "Is nothing but hollow," he says. "Empty. What about Ulyanova and Verushka? Is still sane?"

I try to describe their situation—the apartment, the warmth, the familiar comforts of home.

"Life of Gurus!" Litvinov says. "Are they in danger from fighters? From criminals?"

"I don't think so. But both are looking older. There's definitely a cost. Ulyanova says the Antags are about to be badly disappointed." I tell them more about the ship's past journeys, the rearrangements and transfers from far worlds to Sun-Planet. "The Gurus have been planning for some time to get rid of bug influence."

Kumar listens intently. "We have failed them, I suppose," he says, still groggy. Nobody's paying much attention to him, not even Borden. I check him over but there doesn't seem to be any particular injury—his bruising is light. "I am fine," he insists, waving me aside. "Do you still connect with Bird Girl?"

"Just more of that baseline signal. They're alive, they're busy, they don't seem to want to interact...and the big male is the core of their efforts. They want to take him home. They all just want to go home."

"But they do not know the situation?" Kumar asks.

"If what Ulyanova says is true," Borden says.

"If they don't," I say, "they could learn very soon."

Joe, DJ, and Jacobi return to the ribbon space. All are looking more than a little out of it, as if the scale of what they've seen takes time to absorb, and there is no time.

"Ship is changing all the way back," DJ says, taking a deep breath.

"Fighters?"

"Three dead ones," DJ says.

"All nonhuman," Jacobi says.

"Hurray for our side," Borden says.

"There are dead searchers and a few Antags all along the route we took, trying to follow the spine of the ship," Joe says. "The cage fighters must have caught them by surprise—like us."

"You can't believe what's going on back there," DJ says. "There's a gigantic tree-thing growing down the center-line, between the screw gardens and over the clover lake— branching and fruiting all sorts of mechanical shit, like making apples!"

"Armaments for our new opposition," Kumar says. "I would like to see those growths. We might understand what sort of creatures they're hoping to use to extinguish us."

"The searchers aren't being much help," DJ says. "All we saw are dead—dozens of them. But remember that transport we used around the screw garden?" He seems unwilling to continue until we admit we remember that much.

"Well," he says, weirdly satisfied, as if he's sounding out our sanity, "there's something like that along the tree, maybe half a dozen tracks moving in and around the branches, carrying shit forward and back—fruit, half-formed weapons, ships."

"Some of those ships look like ones we've used," Joe says. "Others are new and different. And as for weapons...I can't understand any of them."

"You won't be using them," Kumar observes.

"Anyway, we hitched a ride on one of those railcars going aft," Joe says. "About three klicks from here, past where the squid ponds used to be, the rest of the Antags have got four ships in an outboard hangar. They seem to think they're enough to get all of them down to the surface. They want the hell off this hulk."

"Can't blame them, if they're home," Ishida says.

"Have you seen the surface?" I ask.

DJ says, "Sort of, in the big star dish. There aren't any squids there now, either. Whole ship seems empty."

"Could they *all* be dead?" Ishida asks.

"They could have withdrawn. No way of knowing."

"Maybe they're going to be shipped home as well," Borden says. "Evacuating."

"Optimistic appraisal, at best." Kumar says.

"Is Ulyanova ours or the ship's?" Joe asks. "I really need to know."

"She's putting everything she's got into staying human, and Vera is helping where she can," I say. "But I'm thinking we gave her a fucking impossible task."

Litvinov curses under his breath and looks ghostly pale. He's contemplating the loss of almost every soldier he trained and fought with, one way or another. And we're no consolation. After all, we might have helped Sudbury become our worst enemy.

"Focus on what we need to know!" Borden insists.

"We're orbiting a big dark planet," Joe says. "That much we can confirm."

"But how can we be sure we're actually there?" Borden asks.

"The Antags should know, right?" Jacobi asks.

"Sun-Planet!" DJ says in wonder. "Planet X."

"There are a lot of Planet X's out around the Kuiper belt," I say. "Big and small. Maybe warm, maybe cold—in the hundreds. I don't know how many are as large as Bird Girl's world, or how many were tinkered with by the bugs, but they and the Gurus have been playing with extrasolar planets for a long, long time."

"And that Christmas ornament, too," DJ says. "Moving shit around."

Joe shakes his head. "I'm not even going to think about that."

Borden says, "Job one, we have to put together something like weapons, go back in force, and kill the rest of the cage fighters. And we have to make sure the Antags are happy to leave without killing us—or Ulyanova."

"Might be walking into a hornet's nest," Jacobi says.

DJ observes that Sudbury never did have leadership skills. "He could barely understand orders."

"Maybe so, but since then he's gone through a whole new level of fight club," I say.

"Doesn't matter," Joe says. He's trying to pare the mission down to something we can all understand. Borden seems to approve. "I assume what Ulyanova told you is that the mice are loose in the cheese shop and the cats don't fucking care. Happy to watch us all fight it out."

Long pause. I tongue the gaps where my teeth used to be. Wonder if they're floating around here somewhere…

Without warning, the ribbons begin to glow, then to alternate between lighting the darkness and giving us a look outside. Instinctively, we rotate and crane to get a full view of where we are—above and below.

Above is another terrific view of stars, including the ever-glorious Milky Way. Again, parallax unchanged. Below—

A great suggestive curve of shadow, dark brown and pewter, wreathed like a Christmas tree with flickering aurorae strung between hovering, glowing spheres. Too big to see all at once, the likely equator is divided by a thick belt of what could be ice, green or blue under the spheres, pale gray beneath the aurora.

Out here, tens of thousands of millions of klicks from the sun, there's no sunlight, just the illumination from those rippling, ever-refreshing aurorae, moving like ocean breakers above the surface, defining segments of bright and dark—a twilight-only version of night and day.

As described.

Sun-Planet.

"It's split in half," Jacobi says.

DJ looks caught up in it all, smug at the confirmation. His mind is absorbing the new details. As is mine. It's beautiful and strange down there. "Divided planet," he says. "Antags grew up in the northern hemisphere, searchers in the southern. Separated by thousands of klicks of ice! Brilliant. Bugs had a hand in this, right? Two species separated until they were ready."

"Bad news for the searchers," I say. "At first."

"Yeah...But then they learned how to get along." His voice trails off at these strange, impersonal memories of Antag history, exploitation. They behaved so much like humans.

The mention of bugs provokes a weird sensation inside me of yet again being examined by an outside interest—curious in a fixed way, insistent but gentle. Something very old and disturbingly familiar is rummaging through my head and picking out words, maybe trying to learn my language—but then it comes upon fragments of my interactions with the archives on Mars and on Titan. Bug memories. I contain history I never lived, history I couldn't possibly know, along with the serial numbers, the identifying marks left by those archives.

DJ isn't looking smug now. "It's back!" he says.

"What?" Ishida asks.

"There's an archive nearby," I say.

"It's fucking *huge*," DJ says. "Bigger than anything we've found so far."

I confirm he's correct.

The others absorb this with their own weary familiarity. We've been jerked around by history and by our ugly ancestors too many times to take great cheer at this news, but at least it gets us moving. At least it could promise more interesting developments.

"Let's go," Joe says.

Bilyk suddenly doesn't look good. His arms and legs hang limp, his skin is pale, and his eyes have rolled back. Ishida intervenes and Litvinov doesn't object. She carefully rotates him to show us the spreading bruise along his neck and the back of his head. Our attackers must have sapped him, cracking his spine.

"Is he alive?" Ishikawa asks.

"Barely," Ishida says.

He didn't complain at first. Now he can't.

Litvinov looks at all of us as if this is the last straw and escorts the *efreitor* back to their nest. DJ tries to go with Bilyk, but Litvinov blocks him. "He must heal himself," Litvinov murmurs. "He is strong."

"And what if the fighters return?"

"I am staying here," Litvinov says. "I am old and too slow to matter back there. We will watch and try to protect curtain, Bilyk—last of my soldiers. I ask Kumar to stay with us."

Kumar agrees with a nod, then looks at the rest of us, as if he will soon be a dead man.

"We don't have real weapons," Borden says.

DJ and Tak brandish their canes, rather pitifully—though the tips are sharp, if they're used correctly.

"And by now," she continues, "I presume they know the territory better than we do. They might just play with us until we're all dead. Or they could capture and torture us one by one."

"If the Gurus stocked the cages with Sudbury's type," Joe says, "from all sorts of species, we're not dealing with soldiers but with homicidal maniacs. They may not have any strategy. They may not care how many of their own they lose."

"Where would they go? Where would they hide—back in the hamster balls?" Ishikawa asks, looking at me as if I know.

"Too obvious and exposed," Joe says. "We started this. We have to finish it."

"Would the Gurus have given them bolt weapons?" Jacobi asks.

"In the cages? I doubt it," Tak says. "Not a good show, and besides, they could blast their way out."

"What I'm asking," Jacobi continues, "is whether they've captured weapons *since* they got loose."

"Antag bolt weapons have ID locks," Tak says. "I doubt humans of any sort could fire them."

"What if the fighters include Antags?"

"ID'd to the *owner*," Tak says.

"So probably not," Joe says.

"Antags may have recovered our weapons from the Oscars," DJ says.

"We don't know that, and I don't want to think they'd hand them over to cage fighters," Joe says, with a glance my direction: *Would they?*

"Then we might be evenly matched, up to a point," Borden concludes. "Question is, have they ever had the run of the ship before?"

"I don't know," I say. "This is just the sort of thing Gurus would do to stir the pot."

"But Ulyanova doesn't say that, does she?" Tak asks.

I shake my head.

"What's she think we should do?"

For the third time, I explain what she told me—that the Antags are about to get the shock of their lives, and that Earth could be next. I don't get into the balancing act she's involved in with the ship. She's not worried about the cage fighters. She has bigger issues.

"We've done reconnaissance many times," Tak says, clearly ready, even eager, to go on a mission to search and destroy. "We practiced at Hawthorne. We ran multiple exercises on Socotra, and we did it for real on Mars—first season."

"Against Antags," I say.

"Antags caught in a bad drop of their own," Joe reminds. "But we're definitely prime in tough situations, in strange territory."

"Doesn't make it easier," Borden says.

"Commander, have you had that sort of training?" Tak asks, forthright as always.

"Similar," she says. "Twenty weeks of SEAL training in Cuba."

"Jesus!" DJ says.

"Not many sandy beaches here," Borden says.

"Borden's in charge," Jacobi says. Nobody disagrees. Everyone falls in behind her.

We work our way back along the ribbons and the spiraling cane bridges. Without the searchers to grow and maintain them, the canes are already decaying. There are fragments everywhere, and dust, getting into our lungs, our throats, our eyes.

Borden, DJ, Jacobi, and Tak stick close to me, forming a kind of arrowhead. Joe, Ishida, and Ishikawa take up the rear.

The ship ahead of the bulge is very different from when we moved forward. There's that long, thick central tree DJ and Joe saw, made of the same featureless hard stuff as the rest of the ship, stretching back over the leaf lake (now dry and cracked) and producing strange fruit. War fruit—weapons and ships, nascent, nasty, ready to fill out for new recruits on the other side of the solar system.

Then—there's another tug on our ancient string telephone.

"Feel that?" DJ says to me. "Think they'll let us in?"

As if in answer, the probing presence tempts me with a nugget of information. I see through a deep eye, an eye that temporarily blocks everything around me, a more personal panorama of Sun-Planet, as if I've lived there a very long time—broad, icy regions decked in low, scudding clouds, great sheets and glaciers stretching tens of thousands of klicks to a livid glowing horizon—and on the margin, the border between the southern hemisphere and the belt of ice: a swirling black ocean filled with searchers, feeding, diving like whales—millions of them.

The archives are in the southern hemisphere, under kilometers of ocean. The searchers dive deep and touch them, access them. That's why they're called searchers. They're more important to the archives than the Antags, even. Searchers are wiser. Smarter.

And no goddamned good for war.

And then this glorious nugget of history and insight is supplemented by a permission, a demand—another offering.

Inquire.

ANCIENT OF DAYS

I ask, "How old are you?"

DJ agrees that's a good place to start. We seem to sit beside each other in a steady stream of give-and-take, sensual exploration, study. The rest are momentarily irrelevant. I don't see them. I feel a nudge, hear a word, but do not respond.

I'm deep.

How old are you?

"Not very old," I answer, along with DJ.

Inquire.

"Do you recognize where we got our education, our training?"

Down near the sun. An old planet or moon.

Inquire.

"Are you older than the archives on that moon?"

Probably not older. Perhaps more complete. Was there damage to those archives?

"We think they've been destroyed. Archives on a planet

even closer to the sun have either been destroyed or severely damaged."

Who is responsible for this damage?

"We are, partly. But we've been influenced, instructed, by the Gurus."

We see that. Here they are called Keepers.

"You let them take control of the Antags?"

Follows a search through our memories for associations. Apparently we aren't going to have any privacy, and that could save a lot of time.

Until recent time, the Antagonists, as you call them, were not aware of the existence of these archives. The Antagonists are from the northern hemisphere. They are the only ones to be infested with Keepers. The searchers are from the southern hemisphere, mostly around the polar regions. They are scholars and aware of the archives, of our history, but neither the Antagonists nor the Keepers have enlisted them as fighters because they are not suited.

They resemble animals familiar to you?

"Yes. Squid."

Not closely related to you, these squid—*perhaps enigmatic?*

"Yeah. And probably not great scholars."

DJ chips in. "We call this world Planet X. What's your name for it?"

Too old to be important.

Inquire.

"Is this planet natural?"

You know already it is not.

"How old is it?"

Comes a number so vast I stumble around in my head

trying to control it. Then I realize the units: vibrations of an atomic particle, maybe an electron in orbit around a proton— a hydrogen atom. Everything in these archives is measured by those beats, those vibrations. Very rational. Could be close to universal. But we're not that sophisticated.

"What's that in years?" DJ asks.

The steward of the archives digs deeper into our heads and understands. *Four and a half billion years.*

"Made by the bugs?" I project my memories of bug appearance and hope for the best.

They were key. Many species contributed to these archives, but the bugs, as you call them, as you show them to us—we recognize their form—completed and organized them.

Inquire.

"Are there any bugs left alive?"

No.

"The bugs were plagued by Gurus as well?"

They were.

"How did they get rid of them?"

They did not get rid of them. They cut the ties that existed at that time. It is very difficult to destroy the Keepers, and almost impossible to be rid of them forever.

"There were accidents, right? Bits of broken moons came down to the inner solar system and seeded Earth and Mars. Does that means that the Gurus, the Keepers, were indirectly responsible for us, as well?"

The bugs emulated an older force. That mysterious influence moves planets, and little else, and five billion years ago, moved several from the realm of comets downward, beginning life in the outer system.

After those long-ago acts, the "bugs" contributed by help-
ing seed the inner planets, by accident, through their long
wars with one another.

"Where do the Gurus come from?" DJ asks.

Not known. The Keepers are always looking for systems to
develop and preserve, in their way. You and Antagonists share
ancient origins, but "bugs" have nothing to do with the ori-
gins of Keepers.

"Who controls you now?" DJ asks.

Nobody controls. We work with searchers but they are far
fewer now than they once were. And the archives are them-
selves diminished.

"What's happening on Sun-Planet?"

Total destruction. We have seen it before. When this time is
finished, if the archives still exist, perhaps you can bring schol-
ars back to finish our studies...

The steward seems to fade in a haze of what might be
disappointment—if it can exhibit anything like emotion.

Can it?

Or does it echo our own feelings?

We come out of our reverie and look around us.

"Time to get the fuck out of here!" DJ says.

"Amen," Joe says.

———

WE RESUME OUR slow, awkward journey, Joe, DJ, and Jacobi
telling us what they know and helping smooth our learning curve. Without searchers, moving through the ship is an
involved process of trying to make out an available surface
in the twisted architecture behind and between decaying,
rickety canes, in deep shadow, then launch out with a kick—

sometimes connecting, sometimes painfully colliding. Ishida and Borden fly wide, miss the best gripping points, and get snagged in a crumbling spiral. It takes time to pluck them out.

———

THE VIEWING DISH is dark and now the space around it is crowded with dead searchers. The smell is fierce, like ammonia mixed with dead cat.

We find another Antag, also dead from cutting wounds. Not Bird Girl—to my relief.

"We won't follow the tree unless we can get on that rail line," Joe says. "Too much growth, too fast. And the rail is likely already carrying weapons away to stockpile them."

"Where's the line begin?" Borden asks.

"I thought it was at the tip of the tree," Joe says. Ishida agrees. "But everything's still changing."

Pretty soon, we're almost out of options. There's nothing but darkness, pieces and tangled clumps of canes blowing aft in the steady breeze, and searcher bodies—dozens of them, maybe hundreds. They're becoming a hazard, rolling aft or forming their own clumps, a hecatomb of astonishing proportions.

"Cage fighters couldn't have killed all of them," Borden says.

"Who, then? Ulyanova?"

I'm biting my inner cheek. I don't want to answer. I don't know the answer.

"Is she still human?" Ishikawa asks.

"She's playing a dangerous game," I say. "One move here, another there. If she does something really brash or stupid, the ship could flush us all into space—not just the searchers."

"Do you know that?" Borden asks, and for some reason that infuriates me, but I just hold it in—and keep biting until blood flows.

We've reached a section of this new ship where the last of the fragile cane thickets have spread as if to define a wider volume, only to be crushed by the shrinking hull. Last-minute adjustments by the searchers, before the great dying? Futile, either way.

One more body floats in shadows—spiked on a single jutting cane. This one is neither Antag nor human, like nothing we've seen before. Difficult from our distance to discern details, but it has a small, knobby head, large, almost froglike eyes, compact body with four ropy limbs—and its torso has nearly been seared in half. It's still clutching a bolt pistol.

DJ and Ishida move through the canes, swearing, to recover the pistol.

"It's an Antag weapon, all right," DJ says.

"Why was it carrying that, if it couldn't use it?" Ishikawa asks.

"Don't toss it," Tak says. "Maybe Bird Girl will let us arm ourselves."

"I doubt that," Ishida says.

Nothing but darkness ahead, no clues.

And then the breeze moving aft carries a swirling cloud of fairy glow. Searcher bodies have been sprinkling the surroundings.

"There!" Ishida says. Her eyes are sharper than ours. A few hundred meters ahead, we see a spray of branches blue-green with searcher dust. We grab hands to form a star, calculate how to kick off all at once, and fly across the intervening space. Joe and Borden snag a branch, then we all scramble inboard to what could be a rail line—a corkscrew curve pointing aft. But the corkscrew ends abruptly, and there's nothing obvious in the way of transport—nothing like the tram car around the screw garden.

We're contemplating our next move when we find another body—Antag, one of the armored commanders, caught up in an adjacent branch and mostly hidden by the withered arms of a dead searcher. The Antag's wings have been left half-spread. All four eyes are open and glazed. She apparently bled out through deep slices along her neck and shoulders— neatly skirting the armor on her breast and thorax.

"How many battles can we fight on this tub?" Joe asks in an undertone.

Borden and Jacobi move off a few slender branches to confer. In the light of more dead Antags and uncertainty aft, they're reassessing our situation, who to protect, who to reinforce—who to put in danger. I'm glad I'm not making those decisions, but I handicap their choices anyway, and I'm mostly correct.

"Four of us will go on," the commander says. "Three will return to the ribbon space. We don't know who's most in danger, or how protected Ulyanova really is. We can't risk both Johnson and Venn. I want someone who's linked to the *starshina* and Bird Girl with each party. I should have thought of that earlier, but…Fujimori, Johnson, Ishikawa. Back to the nests. Good luck."

We split up. Joe, Jacobi, Borden, Ishida, and I will continue aft. The pistol goes to Ishida.

"We'll hand it over to Bird Girl," Borden says. "Make it a peace offering."

THE LAST ENEMY

The great intertwine of tram lines, the foremost station, begins about a hundred meters behind the spike ball.

How many times before has this ship gone through metamorphosis? Across four billion years? I can't believe any ship could last so long. But the ship, as DJ pointed out, has aspects of a cell—a living thing. Maybe it's a cancer cell and can go on forever.

"Any idea how much Ulyanova had a hand in designing this?" Borden asks.

"I'd guess she's just letting the ship follow prior instructions."

"Which means sending the Antags down to Sun-Planet?"

"That's what she says."

"Where there's nothing left for them," Joe says.

"And after they're delivered?" Jacobi asks. "What happens to the ship then?"

"A long trip back to the other side of the Kuiper belt," I say. "Or... a short deviation, right into the sun."

"With or without Ulyanova?" Jacobi asks.

"Which would you bet on?" Borden says, and they look at each other with the sublime pessimism of having to anticipate the worst.

I don't like being put in this spot. "With," I say.

"All right, then," Borden says. "Brother and sister of the tea have exchanged confidences."

"Something's coming," Ishida says, and points down the shadowy, spiky center of the tree. A narrow, insectoid car with jointed, grasping limbs at each end is rolling in our direction. It pauses for a moment and reaches out to adjust the angle of a thicker branch, showing considerable persuasion or strength, and then more slowly approaches us. Faceted eyes at the end of long stalks seem to measure and observe.

The car stops a few meters away, ticking.

"Is it alive?" Borden asks.

Before I can hazard a guess, the car starts to move in the opposite direction—aft. We each take hold of a black arm and swing our legs into the cab, trying to hang on as the car picks up speed. We're on our way, slammed this way and that as it swerves to avoid the thickest and most productive branches.

All around us there's growth and noise, branches rearranging, more cars passing on the opposite side of the trunk, bundles of raw materials being ferried and delivered to the other branches…

The cell is metastasizing. The ship feels more and more like a gigantic, cancerous lump, producing death and destruction a million tons at a time.

Farther aft, huge objects, the embryonic beginnings of big ships, hang on the outer branches, some hundreds of meters long and still expanding, their hulls not yet closed over. Other, larger grapplers and industrial organelles move new components toward these ships, through gaps in their unfinished skins, and into what I have to assume are the proper positions.

The whole Guru war machine is in full gear, getting ready for a voyage across the solar system and beyond, to a far world where humanity's new enemies are being fed the old line of imminent conquest and domination...

Recycle whatever you can, right?

THE LAST INSTAURATION

Every second we risk being flayed. We're getting exhausted trying to avoid the rushing tangles, being brushed by nascent weapons or scraped along the rugged sides of half-finished ships.

Borden, seeing we've reached our physical limits, tells us to look for a relatively open space between branches and a slowdown in the tram car's spiraling, jerking passage—and when those are in congruence, we kick off, away from the branches and growths. The contraction of the ship's hull has pulled in outboard chambers we never saw until now, and we take refuge in one, if it can be called refuge, since it shudders and slowly spins, some of the walls growing long spikes, as if preparing to grab the other side and tug it shut—and may at any moment be absorbed, and us with it. But for a few minutes we find relative quiet and try to catch our breaths before resuming the trip aft.

I move off a few meters along a barely spiked curve and over a rim between the chambers.

"Going somewhere?" Borden asks from behind.

I wonder where I *am* going, and why. "In my head...I hear a little fly-buzz," I say.

"Ulyanova?"

"I'm not sure. Maybe."

"Mind if we come with?"

"No..."

The whole cluster of squeezed-down chambers is like the steely pith of a gigantic tropical fruit, with the big seeds removed. As we climb and echo along the walls, crossing over ridges where chambers join, we make sure to keep our bearings so we can find our way back.

According to the buzz in my thoughts, there's evidence nearby...evidence, and maybe something else.

Ishida, alert and sharp-eyed, spots the evidence first. "What is this crap? It's not Antag, right?"

Pulling aside a mass of broken canes pushed up against an inner chamber, like a cave inside a cave, we find shreds of fabric. I pull away what might be a decayed coverall. Its tatters reveal three pairs of armholes, two legs, and no neck hole, but an opening in the thorax, the chest, as if whatever wore this peered out from a central eye. The shards are torn, fading, and rotten—pushed around by cane growths like tattered laundry hung on a thousand poles.

The others observe in silence. This may be the migration the Gurus arranged before our war got under way—the previous episode in the season, so to speak, when they laid up a bitter, desperate end for the Antags.

Ishida looks at me.

I'm sweating.

"You all right?" she asks, as my eyesight fades. I hold up

my hand, feeling a deep unease spread through my body, as if I'll collapse or explode—

I can't help myself. Whatever's coming, I have to close my eyes.

The air around me changes, warms...

Seems more human. Fresher. I smell fresh detergent, soap, and feel the smooth surface of a sheet against my neck, my bare legs.

My body arranges itself, in gravity, on a bed.

I'm back at Madigan. I look up at the familiar ceiling, look left at the bathroom, look between my legs at where the main room was—is—beyond my bare feet...

And see Ulyanova walk through the door. She appears bright and fresh, untroubled, and at first peers around the bedroom as if she can't see me—as if the room is empty.

I want to shove off the bed, get away.

But her head turns and she finds me. "There you are," she says. "No going home for me, ever, but perhaps for you, Vinnie. Now, look...I show what happened on ship, where you are now, long ago."

She moves her hands with exaggerated elegance, as if she enjoys being a sorcerer, as if this, and creating an environment for herself and Vera, brings her the only joy she will ever feel.

As she performs these moves, the veil seems to fall away, and I see her as skeletal, ghostly, skin almost green—like a corpse in an old crypt.

Eyes large, staring.

And then, the instauration or vision or whatever rises from Madigan's ground floor to a higher, quicker level. I'm no longer human. I'm crowded with tens of thousands of others into a gigantic metal cavern, in attendance to fresh weapons, new ships, not exactly like the ones being grown along the tree. I perceive that every show must have fresh designs, novel architectures, new and innovative weapons in the hands or other appendages of new breeds of celebrity warrior, to meet and then sate the expectations of the far-flung, jaded audiences so important to the Guru showrunners...

Everything around me gets stirred, then laid out like leaves in a book, each leaf an experience.

I page through, no choice, and become one of the single-eyed, four-armed soldiers massed in drop-ships descending by the tens of thousands to Sun-Planet, our heads—or rather our chests—filled with training we experienced on our own home, one of those very far-flung, dark worlds in the Kuiper belt, far beyond Pluto, and even far beyond Sun-Planet—a remote, tortured world orbiting between three gas giants, constantly being heated and torqued, volcanoes everywhere—

No bugs were involved in this round of planetary evolution. Here is quite a different style. This world, part of a new initiative, was quickened by Gurus, and now its children have been carried to Sun-Planet, where they have done their very best to destroy the Antags, the searchers, and everything they value. All the current fashion in Guru-supplied entertainment. The couch potatoes out there have grown old and thirsty, in cruel need of newer, more ironic, angrier forms of destruction and apocalypse...

What we and the Antags provided for a time is now old-fashioned, no longer *interesting*. Betrayal and sabotage may be just what the audiences are expecting.

Time catches up.

I brush over the battles, all the wars on Sun-Planet, with dreamlike speed and precision—not just visual, but with snips of agony, flesh rending and bones splintering, wings shredded—feeling the anguish as the Antags lose cohesion when big males are gathered up and executed by ant-thick hordes of these single-eyed monsters...

The monsters then move on to the southern hemisphere and work to turn the archives into a library without readers.

I participate in the destruction of the crèches that support Antag eggs, each the size of a soccer ball and capable of hatching to produce multiple offspring—a male, several females, the necessary components for a seed-family that can also be integrated into other seed-families and raised as their own...

When the dream collapses and fades to a violent end, I roll up in the bedsheets, and through my tears, can barely make out Ulyanova, still standing in the doorway. I am horrified and blasted by the waft of her Guru psychology, her mask— but also the sad, almost hopeful presence of the *starshina* I first met on Mars, not so long ago. Protecting as she must. Challenging as she must to keep the ship from killing us.

No hope of anything more.

"This is what brain knows, what ghosts tell me," Ulyanova says. "I will speak to you one more time, but not as Guru. All your Guru bombs are removed. Even so, you are not out of danger, Vinnie. Ghosts and brain demand interest. If I do not oblige..."

She doesn't need to finish.

The room at Madigan vanishes like a soap bubble, and

I'm back in the decay and rubble of the old chambers that once contained many of the violent, one-eyed race even now awaiting our Antags down on Sun-Planet.

The great seed-pod chamber begins to split and crack, closing down, being recycled. The spikes join with their opposites and pull.

"We should get out of here," Borden says.

But we can't just go back the way we came. Four silhouettes appear briefly along our return route, difficult to see against the central shadows, the spinal tree's spin of growing branches, moving weapons, and vessels.

Ishida and Borden spot them first, Joe and I last. By this time, they're upon us, brandishing bladed weapons, canes, and nightmare faces—the two that have faces.

One kicks around the chamber, grabbing and tossing canes and other debris to keep itself pinned to the curve, until it's tangled with Ishida. A blade clangs on Ishida's metal arm, another silhouette moves in from another direction, swinging for her flesh half—

But I'm there with a clutch of canes wrapped in rotten fabric, something I've assembled in a fraction of a second, and my own trajectory as I kick puts that bundle between the blade and Ishida, soundly thunking her, but not carving.

I have the blade wielder in my hands now, groping up along a skinny chest for something like a neck, as I'm kicked and clawed by anatomy out of a seafood dinner, and then I wrench a tough outer shell almost half-circle below a rim of eyes, and acrid fluid shoots past my ear—

But this thing is almost impossible to get hold of. It's cutting at my hands when Joe recovers the wrapped canes and swings them over to Borden, who wedges her back against a curved wall, kicks down against Joe's body, and shoves the tip of the bundle between a scurry of legs and arms…

Prying loose the blade, the pike, or whatever it is, which Borden has used, apparently, in another form, to some effect in training—

She swings it around, still propped against Joe, who's sliding up a wall, about to fly free, when she passes the blade through the scurry and severs all the grasping legs, then somehow brings herself around as Ishida replaces Joe for prop and ballast—

The commander brings the pike down hard, starting to rise as she does so—and connects with the part I was trying, ineffectually, to strangle. Something flies free. I do not know what it is, because I've turned to take a barrage of twisting buck-kicks and sharp fist blows from a serpentine thing with a rippling haze of arms or legs, over three meters long, getting purchase by wrapping its hind portion around a spike growing from the wall. Thus anchored, it rises, long head of six eyes rotating in dismay, into Ishida's crunching metal grip. I hear but don't see what happens after that. Joe and I have wrapped our legs around the fourth silhouette, which is humanoid—is it Sudbury? More like a powerful ape with red and orange hair and tremendous hands, hands even now trying to rip off my arm, my legs, but without my cooperation, not quite managing to get a grip. I push in with thumbs and go for the eyes—two only—and rip at the flaps of the cheeks. It's amazing how much strength you have when you still care, and death is upon you—when Ishida and Joe and Borden are at stake—and where the fuck is Jacobi? The whole melee comes to an astonished, quivering, bloody halt when a bolt carves the serpent's half-crushed head away, and does double duty with the arm of the ape. The mass separates. Borden is on one side, Ishida and Joe on the other.

Jacobi is three meters away, clutching the pistol we recovered earlier—

And firing three more times before it whines that the charge is gone.

We stare at her in astonishment.

"Somebody made a mistake," she says. "Thought I'd make sure."

We push back from the corpses, surrounded not just by their main masses, but by twirling gobbets of flesh, revolving and rotating limbs, strings of internal organs.

None of them belong to us.

We've just engaged and taken down four cage fighters, and cannot believe that we're all intact and alive.

"Any more?" Ishida asks.

"None I can see," Joe says.

"Where's Sudbury?"

No sign. Maybe one more.

Jacobi and Borden do brief examinations of our opponents. They're all dead, but worse, are absolutely painted by old scars. The ape is missing fingers and a lower leg from a previous encounter, and every one of them looks as if they were once much stronger, more capable.

Before the cage matches.

Perhaps before they were all released.

No satisfaction comes with this victory. No glory, nothing but the chance to return to the spinning, fruiting branches and hitch on another car—completing our horror-train ride aft.

What a prize.

We feel barely alive when the car stops with a jerk and the

limbs fold away, threatening to pinch our hands. We let loose and hear, then see, Antags. They're drafting away from the ships in the hangar to intercept us. But they are hardly any sort of welcoming committee.

The air around us flashes with wings, grasping hands, bolt rifles, and pistols. The Antags take quick control of our group. Jacobi offers them our weapons. A bat intervenes to take them and moves off to join the busy mix around the interior of the hangar, where the big male is directing the loading of passengers and cargo. Preparing for departure. Two searchers move between the ships, interacting with the bats, helping carry cargo from one transport to another. Other Antags perch nearby, like a string of crows on a power line, wings folded, waiting. Looks as if they're packing to return to the planet. What's left of their home to return to?

I try to connect with Bird Girl, tell her we're here to deliver information—but the Antags tie us in cords and jerk us again into bouquets, not in the least gentle.

The big male interrupts his supervision to make a sweeping gesture with one wing. The armored officers and bats stop their own activity and move out of the hangar to surround us.

Then Bird Girl emerges from the hangar, assisted by several bats. Her wings are folded, but one is oddly bent as if dislocated. She's carrying her own bolt pistol and her shoulders are damply fluffled.

The crowd around us parts as she comes forward.

"You're going home?" I ask.

Her reaction is like a needle into my head. "There is nothing left, but there is an end," she says, pulling herself into something like dignity, her feathers smoothing. "Honor in completion." I get her impression of what will come after:

vast calm seas, warm lights glowing over water and land, over ice. No enemies except those chosen to bring glory and more honor. Bird Girl's Fiddler's Green.

"You have seen what our world has become," she says. "Who has told you this?"

"The mimic," I say. "I wouldn't wish it for any of you."

"I could feel your sadness," Bird Girl says. "After all we have done, and what we are now...Our husband wishes me to teach you, so you may teach others, what we were, what we are, and what we are about to become."

Joe and Jacobi have moved close, as if to protect me from the crowd—but there is no more anger, no more resentment. They have made their peace, and for these people, these races, that is remarkable.

What follows next between us is an internal dance, a remarkable exchange of what she anticipates for us—of where humans might go from here, the ship crossing to Mars and Earth, passing on to gather up Gurus and move to the next stage, whatever that will be...but leaving us to join those we feel are family.

This acknowledgment that we will live, that we might possibly go back to Earth, that Earth might still be there... this brings an end to many decades of deception and folly. The utter betrayal played upon them by the Gurus, the Keepers, is striking deep into the most conservative and warlike members of the families throughout the hangar.

"Our husband has changed," she says. "He will ask a favor."

For those not on our connection, a bat has set up the guts of an old human helm display to be shared—a kind of courtesy I would never have expected.

In one great painful sweep, Bird Girl feeds me what they have seen through remotes and the star dish. The surface of

Sun-Planet has undergone big changes. The topography is very different from what she was taught on Titan.

It seems Bird Girl was also something of a nerd, among her kind. Her favorite subjects rise above the rest, the phenomena and characters of home that she had most wanted to experience.

For the first time, I understand the equivalent of the Antag compass—the normal points and several other coordinates that Antags use, including where heat plumes are migrating way below the crust. Plumes and heat and magnetic field lines affect weather. Sun-Planet has external weather and internal weather. If the hot, pressurized inside fails, the outside fails not long after.

But the current reality overshadows her studies.

What they have seen:

Wide gray prairies and plains, low, layered mountain ranges, and…

Ruins. If these had once been cities, they seem to have fallen from a great height like chandeliers and shattered, then been kicked around. Walls, facets, fields of debris glisten like broken ice. The arcs of aurorae still flicker through the collapsed remnants of great arches. Apparently these cities once flew. Must have been a wonderful sight.

Directly below and stretching to the aurora-wrapped horizon, the eastern and western edges of two of the largest of six continents face each other across a narrow isthmus filled with swirling, muddy ribbons, flowing south toward the one great global sea, the watery wall between all the landmasses in the northern hemisphere and the huge equatorial belt of ice. That belt is more than fifty klicks thick in places—a daunting wall between the two ecosystems the bugs seeded here billions of years ago.

In Bird Girl's memory, the southern hemisphere is just the opposite of the northern—mostly water fingered with hundreds of rocky, ice-bound ridges of land. But we're not looking at that yet. We're surveying northern Antag territories, historical lands and their associated waterways—

Lands where millions of generations of Antags once swam and bred and fished, spread across the continents, discovered all the requisite technologies, built their communities, their farms and cities, and in time developed a civilization at least as old as our own.

Only to became entranced by the heart-wrenching stories of the Keepers.

Thousands of craters interrupt the old map of historical memory, often hundreds of klicks across, as if asteroids or small moons had been dropped from orbit. At Bird Girl's command, the screen outlines where major cities and government-designated regions once were. She mentally tries to convey some of their names—a phonetic murmur of her mind—and then, one by one, not finding them, scratches them out with blasts of reddish anger. They are amended on the screen as well—blotchy erasures. I flinch at her vigorous rage.

The destruction on most of the continents comes in the form of asteroid falls, followed by gigantic scorching runs across the landmasses, like claw marks—pointing to huge orbital weapons no longer in evidence. The small oceans now have very different outlines.

That part of the war seems to be over.

"Those brought here by Keepers have finished," Bird Girl says. "None of our cities remain. We find no living of our kind."

The big ship's orbit takes it once more over the belt of

thick ice, into a slow, low passage over the southern hemisphere. There's something cruel and mocking about these sweeps. Are the Guru ghosts, the ship's brain, squeezing the last reactions out of these heartbroken warriors, facing the bitter truth of their destruction?

Here, in the southern hemisphere, the display reveals that the clear blue-green oceans cover deep destruction. Trenches and plains are burned out, pitted—so deeply scored that the inner heat and pressures of Sun-Planet itself produce boiling cauldrons. Visible open trenches score the southern pole, spouting streams of plasma into space—replacing the benign and illuminating aurorae with grim prominences, overarching cascades of fire. The edges of these chasms glow orange in the eternal night, like angry welts around open wounds.

How much of the archives have been targeted? And who targeted them? The new warriors, or the Antags who followed the commands of the Keepers? The latter, I'm guessing, before they fell to the new warriors. After that, with the destruction of the searchers, the archives would have become irrelevant. Without those tuned to their libraries, their destruction is not important.

Nobody remains to listen. And the steward no longer serves Antags.

Which is why DJ and I, but not Bird Girl, can still hear its voice. The steward has only us to talk to, and soon, we will leave.

The one thought that floods me, overwhelming all indignity and anger, I can also see in the faces of our small band of Skyrine survivors.

Fear for what has happened on Earth since we left.

The display now shows the edge of the equatorial ice,

and zooms in to reveal fleets of submarines, ships arranged in starfish flotillas, linked with wave-frothing chains, their upper decks packed with both aircraft and spacecraft. Several of the spacecraft are launching on pillars of spent-matter fire.

"There they are," Bird Girl says. "That is our reception—a quick death. This is all that remains."

To see her home world in this monstrous disarray makes her shrink inside. "They fought for years. Some families, old and conservative, filled with honor, fought to keep the archives from changing our relation to the Keepers, our politics and historically revered policies. Cities built to exploit, then to support the searchers—they are gone. All of our unifying efforts seem to have been ignored. Searchers have nearly vanished."

"How many are left?" Borden asks.

"Wingfuls, if that. There must have been great fear, great hatred." Her four eyes seem to bore into mine. I can share those emotions, that combination of anger and dismay, because that's how we're most alike, Antags and humans—rage and disappointment. Maybe that's what made both of us attractive to the Gurus. Or that's how the Gurus shaped us.

"And now...they are gone. The good, the bad, the foolish, the deceived—the wise! All my people are gone. I am full of shame."

Borden silently studies the view. Ishida's tears, streaming down one side of her face, are the only sign of emotion in our group. Half of her was destroyed in our war. Strangely, she's the one with the most empathy for our former enemies.

"A decision is made," Bird Girl says. "The mimic has done what she promised. And so, after we depart, you will be left here to finish your tasks. There is no place for you down there. But we have duties to perform. Sacred obligations.

"In thousands of centuries, our world will once more travel through the inner space of the solar system. What Sun-Planet will be then...if it will even survive...who can know? But here, and on your world—we ask this of you..."

Three armored females in attendance to the big male are handed a black box about forty centimeters on a side, equipped with a battery pack and canisters. In turn, they give the box to the male, who summons me forward with a broad sweep of his wing.

I receive the box. Ishida and Borden join me and place their hands on the box, as if they know instinctively what's being given to our care.

I look at Bird Girl.

"We have dual births from each egg," she tells us through the translator. "Each egg can be configured to seed a family, and this one is so made. These children will be mine, my family's. You may let them live, if you understand...what we have done. What we are, and what we share. How we have both been deceived."

"We'll take care of them," I vow, and hope I can carry out that promise.

"I think you will raise them honorably."

"We'll try."

"Take what memories are in your heads, or will be when the archives finish with you, and remember what we did for you, in hope of peace."

We surround the egg.

"And take these as well," Bird Girl says, as another bag is

brought forward. Borden takes it, opens it, and peers inside. She looks up with a puzzled and pleased expression.

"Some of our bolt pistols," she says. "They look fully charged."

"Recovered by small cousins from your ships, your bases."

"I didn't know they could swim," Joe says.

"That is why you lost so many battles on Titan," Bird Girl says. "These, I am sure, will be used to protect."

She reaches out with a wingtip hand, as if for the last time, to caress the egg in its case. Ishida is crying freely now.

"Tell them how their family died," Bird Girl concludes, looking toward the transport, the other Antags, the bats, and the two searchers finishing the loading, moving in and out of the lone return vessel.

She raises her joint hand on her injured wing as best she can, and we each touch palms.

"Amen," Borden says, almost inaudible.

"Godspeed," Joe says.

Ishida hugs Bird Girl, somewhat to the alarm of the bats—and then releases her.

THE LONG HAUL HOME

The bats escort us back to the hangar and we are released. We watch the sealing away from the aft terminus of the spine-tree's tramway. Bulkheads are set in place and grow up between us and the Antag transport, beaten and battered, in the hangar. Follows a deep vibration that shivers the air.

The Antags are on their way.

"Suicide!" Borden says.

"Honor," Ishida says.

We begin the long journey forward.

"Keep your eyes peeled," Borden warns, as we each take a pistol and check it. All functional, all well maintained. I think I'd like to have some of those cousin bats go with us. "We're not out of this yet."

No place in our pajamas to hide or store the guns, so we carry them open. And between us, we protect the box containing the egg.

The tram vehicles are as tough to hang on to as before, and the journey is made even more arduous by more changes along the tree, plus what must be a major reshaping of the ship's hull, difficult to understand from our point of view—like rats on an ocean liner.

Throughout, spring-steel threads unwind along the branches and the trunk, filling the spaces between with a curly metallic fuzz—leaving swerving tunnels that barely allow the trams to move forward—while cradling the growth, the ships and weapons, as if they are seeds inside a gigantic pod cramming itself with death and destruction.

I wonder what Ulyanova is contributing, if anything, to these changes. I wonder if she's even still alive. I hear nothing from the bow, nothing from her world behind the dense curtain. The archives on Sun-Planet also have little to say now, fewer fragments to add—but for one overall impression, a kind of courtesy extended to visiting scholars—the confirmation that in time, Sun-Planet will survive, and will indeed pass through the lower system, between the orbits of Neptune and Uranus, and likely will once again scatter moons and rearrange human affairs. That's orbital mechanics—possibly set in place by the shifter of moons and worlds.

I hope DJ is hearing that as well. I hope Bilyk has improved and they can talk. Christ, I feel tiny. Tiny but inflated with huge emptiness where answers might be, perhaps should be—cavernous silences, presaging the ignorance and quiet to come.

I suppose in their own way the bugs were as arrogant and clueless as any gods. What an inheritance! What are we left with?

An egg. Jesus help us all.

We make our winding, devious, tortured passage from the hangar forward and see that the screw gardens are the only constants, obscured as they are by the winding fuzz. There are many more of them. The largest seem to have split and rearranged, perhaps to balance their influence around the ship. The few hamster cages we can make out through the metallic foliage, between the fruiting machines—the new growths and their packaging—the cages that had once been filled with death—have been crushed by growth, folded and crumpled, perhaps to be recycled. For now, they have no use.

The sets have been rearranged prior to the next production.

Every dragging bit of our journey forward fills me with an itching anticipation that the last of the cage fighters are waiting somewhere—hiding. They were never organized, I think. But that's no answer. I wonder if the last survivors are now the greatest fighters on this ship, perhaps between all the worlds—and the most ruthless. Or the most aware of what it means to fight a never-ending war.

Ishida is the first to see another body in the curling growth—caught up in the steel fuzz, being slowly propelled aft for whatever fate, recycling or expulsion, that has met the searchers and the other dead. This body is so decayed it is difficult to tell what it might have once been, or how it died.

We see only two more bodies as we cross through the regions once dominated by the lake, now obscured by stored material, machinery, ships, and thick fuzz. They look like crushed mosquitoes wrapped in gray cotton.

Joe moves closer. Borden turns to listen. "Can you hear DJ?" he asks.

"He's alive," I say. "I don't know what he's seeing or doing."

"Has he been attacked? Or any of the others?"

I shake my head. "I don't know," I say.

"Bird Girl?"

"They're already down on her world."

If she's dead, if they're all dead, then the package we're carrying, slung between us, may be the most precious thing on this godforsaken ship.

The mechanical vehicle, with all its manipulators folded, finally reaches the forward terminus, after we've long since gone numb, our hands and arms buzzing. It stops, rotates on the track, and seems to deliberately shiver us away, as if it's done with us. Then it makes a jerking movement in reverse, and we cooperate to join hands, leap, catch ourselves—leap again.

We're at the base of where the needle prow once began. The ribbon room is intact and seems unchanged. We climb along the bands of starry illumination, then pause before the asterisk, as if taking in that strange cathedral window one more time, for orientation, for instruction.

The ribbons now carry imagery from around the ship— the Milky Way, the slowly rotating shadow of Sun-Planet, its belt of ice still visible beneath the continually rolling breakers of the aurorae, like an ocean of light flooding over overwhelming darkness. The air has not changed.

Beyond the ribbons and the asterisk, the curtain is still there, looking tattered, oddly, as if reflecting the condition of our mimic, the master of all the illusions that hide behind it. This proves to me at least that Ulyanova is still in charge of the spaces and processes important to us.

We search the nests and find DJ, Ishikawa, Kumar. They emerge from a kind of dreaming nap and gather around us, hopeful we may know what's going to happen next. Litvinov and Bilyk are not in evidence. I assume the *polkovnik* is still tending to his *efreitor*, like a father devoted to his last son.

Kumar and Ishikawa take charge of the egg. "What do we do with it?" Ishikawa asks.

"Get it home," I say. "After that—whatever we can, wherever we end up."

"Looks like they've equipped it for a few months, at least," Ishikawa says.

Joe says to me, and aside to DJ, "You've got to learn what she plans."

Then they all embrace us, a most unexpected response, as if we're heading off to our own deaths.

I ask Ulyanova for permission.

Vera emerges and takes us behind the curtain, through the thick wool and fog. Despite the changes and death elsewhere in the ship, the illusions beyond the curtain are still there: the tile floor, the hallway, and now, cold winter sunlight through the window at the end of the hall. The air in the apartment has chill currents, mixing with the heat from the radiators.

We are greeted warmly by a skeletal Ulyanova, and spend time with both of them in that steam-heated apartment. The mood seems relaxed, casual, despite the *starshina*'s appearance. Vera watches me closely. Ulyanova sits me down in an overstuffed chair and pulls up a stool. She might as well be a corpse, with her lips drawn back, her eyes like those of a lemur, her skin pearly gray and showing signs of cracking. Vera looks only a tiny bit better.

They serve us soup and tinned fish, mackerel in tomato paste. Tastes good. Tastes real.

"I am here," Ulyanova says. "Ghosts are here. They still make plans, as if I agree, and I follow their plans."

"Right."

"Ship still listens as if I am Guru. But ship is about to do what it has been instructed for decades to do—make journey downsun, cross to other side of system, far quarter of Kuiper belt, to visit another new planet. Along the way, we will pass close to Mars and then Earth to pick up Gurus and their most favored Wait Staff. Once we retrieve all of the Wait Staff and Gurus, their ships will be available to carry you where you wish to go."

"Convenient," I say.

"I plan well, right?"

"You plan well. We are grateful."

"Do not be. I am now more than half monster. You cannot guess what knife edge I will fall from, any second, and slice plans. Verushka and I are both monsters—but we remember."

"We will stay here," Vera says sadly.

"To finish," Ulyanova says. "This is our home. We have friends, out there." She points through the window to the Russian winter, the lowering butter-colored sun and bunched, snow-packed clouds.

"It's a dream," I say.

"A good dream for old soldiers," she says. "Bilyk is very bad. He will not survive return to Earth. Tell Litvinov we have a place for both here. And a job he can do."

"I'll tell him," I say.

"Now this is what will happen around Mars, around Earth," Ulyanova says. "Ship will demand that all Gurus and their servants return, or destroy themselves, in preparation for new dispensation, new show."

"All the old shows have been canceled?" DJ asks.

They both nod.

"Fucking righteous," DJ says.

Vera smiles.

"This will be ship's last journey," Ulyanova says.

"As we discussed?" I ask.

"After you leave, I will fly into sun," she says. "Wait Staff, politicians, generals who never fought—men and women who made great money from wars and deaths—we will share big party behind curtain. Make fancy places for them to live, to feel they have escaped. Earth is moving away from their influence. Already there is anger. So last refugees of war wait for us to save them."

I mull this over, looking at the plate of cookies, the butter, the cup of tea.

DJ has put down his cup.

Almost against my will, I have to say, "Sometime back, you told me you knew the real reason the Gurus did all this. Can you tell me now?"

It seems that if one of us touched her, she would crumble. But she moves with grace, and her look toward Vera is still alive enough to convey affection.

"Yes," she says. "Ghosts tell me Gurus are like game wardens. They make little wars, allow little kills, to protect us against bigger passions. Without them, we would kill ourselves."

Vera adds, "But Gurus lie."

I squint at the watery sun outside the window. "Yeah."

Ulyanova rises from the stool. "Journey downsun will bring deep sleep, as before. Only I will feel the time. Time weighs heavy—bad memory."

Vera takes my arm, lifting me from the overstuffed chair. DJ gets up as well.

Gray and dusty, Ulyanova looks at us sadly. "Go home and tell," she says. "I hope you will land where you need to be. And I hope Earth is alive when we go back."

"You don't know?" I say.

She shakes her head. "No saying from brain, from ghosts. And at some point, ship must offload spent-matter reserves."

"Ship lets you do that?"

"Ship knows how to make more, if needed. But can travel without—and do not want it in sun."

I had forgotten about that. "Or Earth," I say.

"Will find best, safest place. Go now."

And we go. Back to the others, to the nests and to the ribbon spaces. So many more questions to ask the Queen! But we will not meet again. Perhaps she and Vera prefer the ship's illusions. I would, if I could convince myself…

All wars end in whimpers. And those who serve the Gurus most faithfully, most selfishly, never learn. They rise again and again to the emotions that lead to self-destruction. There is not nearly enough energy to exact vengeance.

We could say we were manipulated. Only true in part. We lie to ourselves like cocks in a pit. We bloody enjoy death and destruction. Sex is obscene. War is holy. We'll have only ourselves to blame when it's all over, humans and Antags, that we could be such fucking dupes.

But Gurus lie.

Maybe without them, we'll find a different balance, live a different history.

"How long have they been fucking us over?" DJ asks.

"Since caves," Vera says. "Long time."

The edge of the curtain is near. I hear groans, babble. We emerge and DJ is instantly on alert, pistol pointed at something unexpected, a shadowy broad X ahead of the asterisk, a figure—mostly naked, sprawled—

Human. Emaciated, bleeding, impaled from two directions. Litvinov emerges from behind the X, brandishing another long, sharpened cane, with a face of fury, about to finish the job, while Borden and Joe and Tak and Ishida and Ishikawa look on, unmoving, unmoved.

They, too, have blood on their arms and hands.

The figure stares at them with the last of its energy, its life. I don't want to recognize it, but I do. The flattened nose, thin, interrupted eyebrows, a rictus of long pain now sharp and undeniable, eyes almost colorless, as if having spent years in darkness...

And a nearly transparent body, showing all its bones and veins, not from darkness but from so many journeys, so many arduous adjustments to chemistry and physics just to stay alive. Champion of champions, the last gladiator on this awful ship, he holds up one hand. The other is pinned to his chest by one of Litvinov's canes. He clutches, at the last, a kind of knife, found or shaped somewhere, the chipped blade glittering. He lets go, and it spins off to chime harmlessly against a ribbon.

This is Grover Sudbury. Our nightmare, the man we condemned, the man Joe sent to this hell—

His head wobbles to see who else has arrived, and he greets DJ and me with a crooked half grin, of pain or recognition I will never know.

"I'm done," he says through bloody spittle, eyes like milky opal. "I'm the last one. I don't want to do it anymore. They're all dead, and I'm *done*."

Litvinov props his feet against a ribbon and shoves the final cane forward, into Sudbury's chest. The cane splits and shivers into fragments.

Sudbury spasms. His breath escapes with a sound like

sandpaper. He stops moving. Litvinov drifts back from the impact. We all seem to retreat from the awful mark, the pierced, racked, wretched example of soldier's justice.

Complete silence before the asterisk, the corpse's X.

"Bilyk died while you were aft," Borden whispers, as if we're in a church.

DJ says, "I think he came to give up."

"I think he wanted to go home," Borden adds.

"Fat chance," Tak says.

MARTIAN RETURN

Down around the sun, time and space are heavy. The screw gardens and their thoughts slumber, surrounded by the sins of warmth, light, and billions of years of closely watched history.

The ship slows, bogged by those densities, those changes. Takes forever.

And then—we're almost there.

After our first sleep, our longest jump, Ulyanova does as she said she would, and makes a pass close to Mars. We receive two transport ships, one for passengers, another for spent matter, which we witness from the ribbons.

We aren't told much about either, even when Vera appears outside the ribbon. She offers the opportunity to begin our departures here, to return to Mars, and to my surprise, Joe, DJ, and Jacobi are ready to go. They'll spread the word as best they can about what's happened, if they're allowed to survive.

Joe and DJ and I say our farewells quickly enough. Joe asserts we'll see one another again, that he plans on getting

back to Earth and beginning a new, more normal existence—
if Earth is still Earth, if we are still welcome anywhere. I hope
when do meet again that he'll explain it all to me, explain
what we've been to each other, but doubt any explanation
will make much sense to either of us.

DJ says he's heading down to the Red because we
might still get communiques—that's what he calls them,
communiques—from what's left of the archives down there,
but I doubt it. All I get are silences. Maybe that's good. Maybe
bug ancestry is nothing to be proud of. Bugs fought. We fight.
Maybe bug knowledge is something to be surpassed, grown
out of. Maybe we'll go it better without them or the Gurus.

Jacobi surveys us critically, then says, "Fuck it! No
excuses," and hugs us all, to my surprise. "Brothers and sisters," she adds, and departs with Joe and DJ.

Ulyanova gives the transports time to depart.

And then we're off.

HOME IS THE HUNTER

Kumar has vanished. Litvinov is nowhere to be found. I presume the Russian went through the curtain, as Vera had suggested. Maybe Kumar has gone through, as well. Maybe he does not want to live in a world without bugs or Gurus or some other influence—or he cannot bear the thought of having to explain.

That leaves the last of us Skyrines, and Commander Borden. The journey to Earth's orbit is brief enough. A nap, as it were. Who's there to wait for me? We're eager to be done with the fighting, the adventure—such as it was. I think we'll part ways as soon as we touch down.

On Earth, there's... Christ. What? A chance to get back to normal? There is no returning to what we were. Even if we know where we are, we still won't know *who* we are. The people I met, whom I could imagine living with after—so many changes! So much space between me and Teal and her child—and how old will they be? How much time between me and Alice? I think a lot about Ishida, but how could that ever work? We both share so many hard memories. What will we do, any of us?

I have no idea how much time I've spent out here, real or unreal.

HOME FROM THE STARS

Earth is still down there. It looks real. It looks alive. Borden suggests they probably can't see us, yet, but more transports are rising, dozens of them, some quite large—Hawksbills!

"Here come the Wait Staff and Gurus," Ishida says.

I think they're delivering their passengers near the new ship's midsection, where, perhaps, quarters similar to ours, or better, have been arranged, spun out of the steel wool—maybe displacing a few ships or weapons. Fancy digs for monsters.

Vera informs us that one transport is being readied to take passengers back to Earth. Maybe we can get down without being blown to pieces. Maybe they'll take us prisoner and debrief us at Madigan or wherever.

AND THE CHILD HOME FROM THE WARS

Right now, I'm a fraud. I do not want to have killed anyone or anything. I do not want to die like a soldier and end up in Fiddler's Green. I want to die the death of a dreaming child.

Someday, if God will honor a solemn request, I'd like us all to join up at Disneyland in Anaheim. A great big reunion of old enemies, old friends, old warriors. We'll meet in the parking lot, where I last saw my aunt Carrie, before she went off to die in the Middle East, and stroll between the ticket booths and up the steps, past the flower gardens, to climb aboard the old-fashioned steam train...

But first, I'd explore the train station and listen to the conductor's ghost—a balding mustached guy from a really old western, speaking behind a window, probably wearing a vest or an apron...telling us where we need to go next to have fun or just relax. "This way, boys and girls...to the happiest place on Earth!"

So sappy it's painful.

We'll shake hands and talk, and then just sit in silence

before strolling to the other rides, the other celebrations. The restaurants. The gift shops.

Silly idea.

Silly ideas keep me going.

————

WE HAVE THREE packages with us, cargos of life and death. We still have the egg, which is humming along happily in its battery-powered box. Borden is being quite protective. I think she may be making plans for her career after the wars.

And we have two bodies. We made bags from shed membranes around the terminus of the tree, using strips of cane, like natives on an island. Best we can do. We're bringing home Bilyk and we're bringing home Sudbury.

Tak helped us wrap them up.

Both of them.

We board the last transport, a Hawksbill, where we are met by a young, capable-looking pilot, whose name, we are told as he greets us at the portal, is Lieutenant JG Robin Farago.

"This has got to be the weirdest assignment ever," he tells us, then helps us move the box and the bags into the storage bay.

"Where are you coming from? What the *hell* kind of ship was that?" Farago asks. "I never even *saw* it—just got orders and instructions—and there the hangar was, and here you are!"

"What did you deliver?" Tak asks as the others wordlessly head to the couches to settle in, to lock themselves down and rotate.

"I have no idea. Transport command said all the ships

were full! I wasn't allowed to look back. But when I did—our passenger deck was empty. What the hell kind of operation is this?"

We pull out of the hangar, and after that, even we can't see the Guru ship.

I'll take it on faith that it's off to the sun.

I wonder if I will ever know.

The Earth is brown and blue and green and white, all swirled and touched with reflected gold. As we break atmosphere and the couches grow tight, I think back on the people we started with.

I'm still alive.

So many aren't.

SBLM

The landing field is empty, no defenses, no notice we're even here. Lieutenant Farago lands us with expert grace, cracks the hatch seals, and tells us he has no idea why, but there's nobody here to receive us.

"Sorry!" he says. "Those wars were so long ago, right?"

Then a truck pulls up and two Marines get out. Land-based, sea-based, not space. They look young and serious. Here it is, I think—we weren't expected and this is the first reaction.

But then the Marines solemnly tell us they're here to receive war casualties, and Tak, Borden, Ishikawa, Ishida, and I go to the hold with Farago and bring the bags forward. A couple of casualty gurneys are rolled up the Hawksbill ramp. The Marines carefully lay the bodies on the gurneys and drape them with flags—one Russian Federation, the other U.S. of A.

Ishida asks how they heard about us and what we were carrying. Farago says he didn't communicate.

"Radio transmission from orbit," the senior Marine, a sergeant, tells us. "Some Russian, we were told. Are there more Russians up there?"

We all acknowledge that.

"Anyway, we're also told you have a special artifact here, and that a deal has been made for it to be well cared for at a top science facility. We've asked for some people to meet us. Should be here shortly."

The two Marines look at each other, and then a large isolation vehicle, like those used to transport spent matter, rides up the runway and meets us at the ramp.

"Any idea what this is?" a female technician asks, tapping the box.

"A brave soldier gave it to us to take care of," I say. "We'll want to see the facility. We want maximum assurance it'll be well tended to."

Borden steps forward and says, "We're taking charge." She looks at Ishikawa, who moves up beside her. I knew nothing about this. Why should I?

"Absolutely, Commander," the sergeant says. "Uh…mind if we make sure you still hold that rank?"

"I'll wait."

We wait. Borden's rank and active-duty status are confirmed, her connections are confirmed—and she assures us Bird Girl's offspring will be their highest duty, their highest priority, from this point on. Neither Borden nor Ishikawa have ever given me real reason to doubt them.

And it could be a good career move, a good way to stay important and rise in the ranks. They might make admiral yet.

Other ambulances arrive and technicians supply us with civilian clothing—all in the proper sizes. And regulation underwear for males and females. Skivvies, modesty panties, sports bras. The pajamas made by the searchers are shed and collected by the technicians. We suit up, no modesty whatsoever, and then stand for a while in the shadow of the transport, not sure what to say. We've been through a lot and spent a lot of time together.

Farago finds a task he has to do back in the cabin. The technicians look embarrassed. They have no idea who we are or what we're going to do next.

It's awkward.

"It's like we've known each other our entire lives," Ishikawa says.

"I don't know what to do next," Tak says, with a long look at me. "Might go join Joe and DJ, if they let me. What about you?"

"I'm going to Seattle," I say. "If anyone will have me."

Farago is back in earshot, up in the hold.

"They still allow hitchhiking?" I ask him, leaning around the outer bulkhead.

"Sure!" he says. "If you don't like the ambulances, I could probably get you any kind of vehicle you want. Might take an hour. Base is on half-duty status, mostly empty now."

Borden shakes her head and crinkles the bridge of her nose, looking across the tarmac. We all know what she's feeling. We're done. We survived, but everybody on Earth has moved on and we're left out.

I nod and say that an ambulance is fine, to start.

Tak says he wants, needs, to go back to Japan. Ishida says she's going to stay stateside for the time being, feels more comfortable here. Borden and Ishikawa are going with the truck that will carry the egg.

And then, we just climb into our conveyances and spread out. We don't say good-bye, just let the truck and ambulances take us every which direction.

I'm intent on getting my Earth legs back as fast as I can, and that means walking, running, with as little help as possible. I tell the two technicians to drop me off at the demob.

The technicians, both young, both female, both Marines, look at each other before the senior in rank, a corporal, answers. "It isn't open anymore. Everybody's back who's coming back." They want to ask me, "Who the fuck are you, anyway?" But they don't.

"How long?" I ask.

"Seventeen years since they stopped shipping us up and out," the corporal says. "We think we should take you to Madigan and get you checked out."

"No thank you," I say. "I'd like to walk. Just let me out right over there. Okay?"

Another look. With no contradictory orders, they comply.

Pretty soon I realize that nobody down here cares one way or another. Earth, or at least Lewis-McCord, is no longer on alert. I walk. Grass grows in patches through cracks in the airstrip concrete and sidewalks. I don't run into anybody. There are people driving and walking, way far away, but the base is almost deserted.

I'm alone. For once, I'm alone and it feels good. No voices in my head.

I pass through the open gates, guard shack empty, and walk across an overpass to the businesses on the other side of the freeway. Not many people present there, either. It's early in the morning, traffic on the freeway is light, sun is just breaking through the clouds of the far eastern horizon. I can barely make out Rainier. It has its own spreading white mushroom cap, but that's breaking up and showing the snowy slopes of the very real and terrestrial volcano—still there.

Still here.

I walk along the marginal road. I can still walk. I can still take a breath. The air is unbelievably sweet and everything is so amazingly wide open. I want to cry, really want to cry, but the tears aren't there.

Not yet.

My head is…okay, for now. I'm as home as I'm ever going to be, and I'm going to have to figure out if that makes me happy, might ever make me whole again.

I wonder what Borden's going to arrange for the egg. I vow I'll check up on that as soon as I get my act together, my civilian act.

But I doubt she'll tell me.

Joe or Jacobi, or both, will get things done on Mars—maybe help them dispose of the spent-matter surplus out on some plain somewhere. But Joe won't stay there forever.

I should look up the others, too, wherever they've hauled off to. We'll probably run into each other in the next few months, one way or another. I need friends. I know that, but for the moment the luxury of being lonely, of walking with my own trembling legs along the asphalt and over the gravel, then breaking from the road and entering the unguarded scrub woods…

I wonder if I can find the Muskies.

More important for the moment, I wonder if somebody will give me a ride into downtown. Wonder if the apartment is still there, still ours, and will recognize me. Wonder if Pike Place Market is still open, still active. I'd love to grab a fresh bunch of celery and chow down. But I don't have any money.

No ID. I don't want to ask for help, but the technicians gave me a list of numbers to call, and some advice on how to pick up my last paycheck, if there are still accounts for former Skyrines.

If some cop stops me, I might spend the night in jail, as a vagrant.

I keep getting this falling sensation in my head, but I'm not falling. I'm walking and looking and breathing and everything's all right, nothing external is challenging me. Pretty soon I'm going to get hungry, and then I'll have to figure things out.

The marginal road goes on and on, past boarded-up businesses—fast food, payday loans, car dealerships—all closed. Effectively, no more SBLM.

The Hawksbill we rode back on has taken off from the cracked, overgrown runway, flown over me on the marginal road, leaving a smelly rainbow trail, flying off to I do not have the slightest idea where.

My God. I've seen it all, almost from the start and now past the finish. We've shed the Gurus, and while there's still a military—where are they stationed?

A small pink car whizzes by, like a grapefruit on wheels. I stick out my thumb. My beard is thick; I could be any sort of psycho. The grapefruit doesn't even slow.

But another car, an older green hybrid, slows, stops, backs up, and the passenger-side window rolls down.

"Where you heading?" a young woman asks, checking me over, not unkindly, as if I might have lice.

"Well, I'd like to get to Disneyland, eventually."

She looks at me with a squint. "Can't take you that far," she says. "How long you been hitching?"

"Long time," I say.

She unlocks the door and I climb into the kind woman's car. "You look like a soldier," she says.

"Am I that far gone?"

She smiles. "My father used to fly out of here." Then she looks at me more closely, with a frown. "There was that one ship this morning...But that can't be you. Can it? They were coming back from Mars or someplace. It was on the Net."

I shake my head. "What year is it?"

That same expression, but she tells me. I thought I heard seventeen years, but that didn't account for how long we'd been gone, overall, before the war was declared over and the Wait Staff and Gurus were cleared up, cleared out, handed over to the *starshina*'s ship.

Time has really been messed up for those who went to the limit and returned. It's been thirty years since we flew out to Mars.

There are still cars, but they don't fly—so I suppose we're on our own again, moving at our own human pace.

———

I GET OUT in downtown Seattle and say thanks and good-bye. I decide against Pike Place Market, since I don't have money, and walk across the city, my legs barely able to move as I approach the tower where our apartment was. The tower is still there. It looks older, not so well taken care of.

At the front glass entrance, I poke in the old security code. Wonder of wonders, the door opens.

I take the shuddering elevator up to the right floor, and as the door opens to let me out, I see an elderly woman with white-flecked black hair, quite plump, wearing a nicely tailored pantsuit, waiting for me.

"Welcome back, Skyrine!" she says.

At my look, she puts her hands on her ample hips and gives me a glare.

"It's Alice, First Lieutenant Alice Harper—fuckhead!" she says. "I heard you might be coming back. Joe sent me a call from Mars. He says you should look me up, and here you are! Anybody else with you?"

I tell her not yet.

The apartment's very different, but there's a spare bedroom, I meet Alice's husband, a nice enough guy, a former Air Force flight surgeon, but not a prick about it—they've been married twenty years and living here, taking care of the place—

But first, Alice goes to the refrigerator and brings me a head of celery, green and freshly washed, dripping. "I remember, Vinnie," she says. "Welcome home."

I take the celery and hold it in my hands, not quite sure what to do with something so utterly precious.

"What about Teal?" I ask.

Alice takes a deep breath. "She's in Africa, I think," she says. "She's widowed again, and Division Four buddies tell me she's been asking if she can return to Mars. Martians always want to go home, isn't that right, Stu?" she asks her husband.

He smiles. "That's what we hear. But she's pretty old now."

"What's that got to do with it?" Alice asks. Stu demurs.

They hand me a glass of apple juice that gives me a solid sugar high, and Stu loans me a pair of pajamas—real pajamas, flannel, corded—and then they take me to the guest room and insist I sleep and after that, join them for breakfast.

SAYONARA

The room is quiet.

I try to sleep, but still can't. All night I toss and turn, and then comes the panic attack—I could feel it coming—a sudden fear that Ulyanova never actually cleared my head, that it was all deception, and that the last instauration has been upon me ever since I got back, maybe even before, and my head is still filled with Guru shit waiting to bring me up short, bring me down, fill me with fear, make me *interesting* again.

I keep asking myself, and keep trying to stop these questions—

What next?

Why would the mover of moons and planets have come alive while we were watching?

I lie on the bed in a pool of rank sweat, as if I'm about to be executed, when I receive another kind of dream.

A genuine, human vision.

It's Ulyanova. She assures me I'm free—we are *all* about

to be free. Looking through her eyes, I see Litvinov and Verushka, and I see Kumar, all standing by the window of the apartment in Moscow, enjoying what seems to be a glorious Russian summer, the air balmy, birds flying, sounds of children playing. They're eating bread with thick sweet butter, and soup, and sausages.

They're waiting. Laughing. Even Litvinov.

They seem happy.

The sun is growing brighter. Much, much brighter.

It's over, Vinnie.

Their end is quick.

I wake up. The curtains have been drawn, but the morning is upon us, and I don't feel anybody or anything out there. No voices. No presences. My head is really and truly empty, except for my own memories, my own thoughts, which will take me a long while to deal with. But…

I'm still human. I'm still here.

And Gurus lie.

All except one.

PUTTING ON FLESH

I take walks around Seattle every day, building up my muscles, my strength, airing out my head and my thoughts, just watching people go on about living. For the first few weeks, I felt both deeply sad and somehow superior, for all the amazing and terrifying and deadly things I've seen and the brave and insanely dedicated people I've known and faraway places I've been. Here, people just walk, just drive, just talk, sitting in coffee shops, some staring at nothing as their implants guide them around the world...

Not every second could be their last.

These people I understand and envy and pity at the same time.

Mostly at the ends of my hikes I find a place that's new and peaceful and observe the play of light and shadow on trees, or the sheen and sparkle of rain and grayness, on buildings, on faces, on gardens and flowers and clouds and birds and squirrels, and slowly get back to realizing that the simplest pleasures are the most important, the biggest reasons we're here—if there is ever an explanation for being alive, for observing, for taking up space and eating food.

For not being a War Dog much longer.

Assuming true physical form, true emotion.

Putting on flesh.

One evening at dusk I make my way back to the condominium, where Alice and her husband are setting out dinner in front of that fabulous view of Puget Sound. They put a whiskey-and-soda in my hand—I can drink again, after a week or two when anything of the sort made me queasy, just as if I were still sweating out Cosmoline.

And Alice tells me, setting out a fourth place at the table, that she's invited a guest to join us.

"I hope you don't mind," she says, with a cat-on-mouse expression that dares me to object, to get all pissy and closed down and neurotic. I don't dare do that, so I smile and ask who it is. I know it isn't Joe or DJ. I'd feel them, somehow.

But then I *do* feel who it is.

"It's a young woman," Alice says, more cat than ever, playing with me, playing with me for what she thinks is my own good. "She's in town finishing medical treatments and she asked if we were open to a visit."

"Sure," I say.

"She says you were very sweet out there"—Alice waves her hand at the sky—"when you weren't being a complete bastard—but you were pretty sweet to her when it counted. She says don't expect anything, but she'd like to see you again. I answered for you."

Someone else putting on flesh.

Stu brings in a freshly opened bottle of wine. The deep green bottle glints in the setting sun. His golden smile is big enough to show teeth. He wants me out of here as soon as possible. "We're having pinot noir with the salmon," he says. "Special occasion."

God save me.

UPGRADES

We've been home three years, and I won't go into our life after war, except to add that Joe has sent me a package from Mars, possible now that relations are reestablished—but no doubt incredibly expensive.

Chihiro and I open the box with a sense of strong doubt. In the box is a vial of beige powder—Ice Moon Tea, I suspect—and a note scrawled with a shaky hand in pencil on rough paper.

The note reads, "Heard the good news! Don't want to upset the domestic applecart, but you've had enough peace and quiet. You and Ishida should both return to Mars. We've found Teal's daughter. She's much more than we could have expected. Major upgrade. She says big changes are coming—good changes. I can't deal with her all by myself, old friends!

"Come back and see."